THE END OF
THE WORLD

ALASTAIR WILKINS

A CIP catalogue record for this book is available from the British Library

ISBN 978-1-7396748-2-3 (paperback)

ISBN 978-1-7396748-3-0 (ebook)

Cover Design by Creative Covers

Typesetting by Book Polishers

For my parents

Incessant the falling Mind labour'd,
Organising itself, till the Vacuum
Became element, pliant to rise
Or to fall or to swim or to fly,
With ease searching the dire vacuity.

William Blake

By the same author

The Hospital

PROLOGUE

SOME YEARS AGO, one bright April day, a seemingly random event occurred that triggered widespread panic and consternation throughout the land. The event itself started as a mundane, everyday occurrence in a central English city – a meeting between two men – and developed into a less commonplace event – a murder, followed by arrest, trial and incarceration. The whole thing might, on the face of it, appear to have been driven by chance occurrences. It was, however, believed by many to be far from random and indeed predicted by ancient prophets. The two men in question had never met prior to that morning in April, in the year when the seas boiled and the rivers flowed with dead fish; the year when the augurs declared the end of the world and the fulfilment of a multitude of other prophecies to the uneasy and mutinous throngs.

1

THE MAN WHO is to be the victim of the murder rises early from restless slumbers. His morning routine has not been unusual. His wife has complained (once again) about the state of the bathroom and has threatened to leave home. But he has heard it all before and takes little notice of her words, save for: 'Today it will all end'. He thinks these words are muttered in a rather odd tone; indeed, in a voice that does not sound like the voice of his wife of twenty years, not at all. It causes him to stop for a moment and look his wife up and down. But she carries on throwing towels, and so he thinks no more of it. His son, not yet eleven years of age, is still asleep, yet the man enters his room and kisses him lightly on the forehead. It is an action that, in the light of subsequent events, might be interpreted as profound.

After a quick breakfast and a prolonged look in the mirror to check the state of his greying, bedraggled hair, he steps into the street, which feels hostile and menacing with its urban threats; the atmosphere of oppression is always more intense in April.

On his way to the train station, he is struck by the number of insects hanging around his head; an infestation of black kicking creatures swarms heavily in the dense air. After a while, one of the beasts comes to rest on the hem of his dull-grey raincoat. Immediately he stops and attempts to shoo it off his coat, but the small black thing clings on and refuses to be dislodged. Limpet-like, it resists the various manoeuvres the man makes to rid himself of the unwelcome parasite. Eventually, he abandons his attempts to flick it off his coat and studies the creature in closer detail. It is jet black and shines in the drabness of the morning, reflecting what little light the sun manages to shine through the clouds. Periodically it flicks its wing cases up and down, which causes it to make a rhythmic and, to the man's mind, menacing hum. After a time, it spreads out its lacy wings as if preparing to fly. Its head, which is square and bull-like, twists occasionally, perhaps turning towards some stimulus, and yet the man can make out no eyes or vestiges of any sensory organs. Most notably of all, the two stubby antlers that project from the featureless head remain motionless. For several moments, the man considers the creature – without doubt a type of beetle – with as much concentration as he had just devoted to trying to dislodge it from his clothing. He has never seen its like before, and the swarming of hundreds of other similar beasts in the sky leads him to the conclusion that a new infestation of some foreign parasite has reached the shores of the country, which is usually immune to this kind of entomological attack.

He starts to take off his coat. In an instant, the shiny black passenger flies off high into the sky with the other members of its swarm, which all vanish as quickly as they had appeared. If the man had possessed any religious leaning, he might have placed some biblical relevance on the incident, but he is not prone to such musings and forgets the whole scene in a trice before continuing on his way.

The sky turns greyer and the impression of rain clings on the air. He quickens his pace and reaches the train station in time to catch his regular train.

After finding a seat in his usual compartment (the daily ritual of platform jostling having been negotiated once more), he slumps down into the uncomfortable and narrow seat. Around him, the mix of regular and incidental passengers start their own rituals of disrobing, filling the luggage racks, taking out newspapers, plugging in computers, checking phones, or pretending to read. Several stand, unable to find a seat, shifting their weight uneasily from foot to foot as if performing some dirgeful dance. Opposite him, a youthful traveller plunges into his seat, yawning aggressively before instantly falling asleep. Over time, many others follow suit, lured into sleep more by the excesses of the previous night than by any soporific motion the train provides.

From his black leather suitcase, the man takes out a transparent document wallet and places it on his lap, taking out the topmost document in the wallet. He begins to read. *A reproducible and highly efficacious method of generating non-tumorigenic cellular immortality* runs the first line in large, bold font, followed by a list of authors and their affiliations. He looks up from the document, pondering the title of this latest scientific paper, the result of at least ten years of experiments within his laboratory. His senior postdoctoral scientist has revised certain aspects of the methodology and sent it to him last night. Despite his eagerness to send it off to a journal as soon as possible, he'd had no time to read it then, owing to a combination of late-running committee meetings and a particularly severe migraine. Now, with a clear head and only a dull aching behind his left eye, he wonders whether the title is too clumsy. It needs something catchier, he thinks. Science has become a marketable commodity, and his job as a scientist sometimes seems to be more about sponsorship, wealth generation and his public persona rather than discovery of previously unknown truths. Indeed, in recent months, and not without a moderate sense of unease, he has appeared in various popular newspapers, featured – in journalist-speak – as *the man who wants to live forever*. In that claim they were wrong, of course, but the words published in newspapers are far more shameful and less prone to scrutiny than those in the scientific press. He (and the university office for that matter) had considered it good for the department to appear in the newspapers, despite the gnawing thought in the back of his mind that he was selling his scientific rigour to populism.

The train passes jerkily through a tunnel and the carriage lights flicker. The man to the left of the scientist twitches awake and clutches the bag on his lap, a brown leather attaché case, pulling it up to his chest, appearing suspicious of something untoward in the motion of the train. He looks around at the other passengers and slumps down further in his seat, a furtive action which makes a man in a bowler hat sitting opposite look up from his newspaper and frown at the clandestine behaviour of his fellow traveller.

The scientist continues to read his article. *Until recently cellular immortality has relied on the introduction of oncogenes by viral transfection or other means. Whilst these have led to the generation of multiple stem cell lines which have advanced knowledge of cellular and molecular biology, such methods lead invariably to cellular tumorigenesis.* He pauses. Invariably or always? If the work is to be deemed truly novel and innovative, he is better off using the word *always*. Taking a pen from his pocket he scratches out the word *invariably* but hesitates at writing *always*. He decides that *such methods lead to cellular tumorigenesis* will suffice. Best not to be too dogmatic or vague, he reasons. People can add their own adverbs or qualifying words if they wish.

He continues reading. *The science of senescence has for many years occupied itself with understanding processes of cell death and finding methods to counter molecular signals which lead to cellular demise. Defining a method of inducing cellular immortality without induction of tumour genes may improve therapies which counter the deleterious effects of ageing. That is to say: defining a cellular mechanism which leads to non-senescence without uncontrolled replication would be a major breakthrough in the fight against diseases of the elderly. In this paper we describe such a method.*

He looks up and sucks the top of his pen, a habit he has had since his school days, too comforting to forsake. Is the text becoming too emotive? *Breakthrough* and *fight* are words more suited to the popular press than a scientific journal. *Stick to the facts*, he tells his students, *let the reader decide its importance*. He knows what the reviewers of the paper, who will judge its acceptability for publication, will say about the use of such language. He underlines the two words under debate and puts a big question mark in the margin.

The train stops at a dimly lit station. Several passengers alight, only to be replaced by new sallow-faced sleep-ridden itinerants. One man, with a grey complexion and small beads of sweat on his forehead, looks gravely unwell. His eyelids droop, his breathing is shallow, and he gives the impression of one about to swoon. He keeps himself upright, rubbing his nose and loosening his collar at intervals throughout the journey in a manner that suggests these are his only methods to prevent him falling. Others look equally world-weary. Not without reason has this early morning sojourn into the city been dubbed the ghost train. Forty years of this every morning of one's life would be enough to sap the resolve from anyone. The atmosphere is carriage-to-carriage drabness, an enforced melancholy in a crowd of dissimilar travellers who could not have looked more dispirited if they were being sent off to war. No one speaks or even smiles, and yet some faint recognition, ungestured, exists between the regular passengers, each seeing deep within the others' unease; the cost of the many years of living in such a manner.

He looks further down the train and sees a heavyset man who is standing in the train aisle and peering in his direction. He appears to be looking at him with an intensity, or an intent. Or maybe his stare is vacant. The scientist looks away, momentarily feeling uneasy. He has a feeling he has seen the man already this morning. Perhaps he was behind him when he encountered the beetles?

'Boss!' A salutation from behind his left shoulder interrupts the scientist's musing. He turns round to see John Breckenridge, a postdoctoral scientist in his laboratory, scarved, hatted and bespectacled.

'Oh, hello!' he replies in a friendly enough manner – although, in truth, he is annoyed at the interruption and the expectation that he will now be required to engage in redundant small talk. Breckenridge sits in the window seat directly behind his own, so he has to twist his neck awkwardly to see him. His face is chubby and rosy, displaying a sort of jolly radiance even within the dimly lit carriage. His disposition is always equally joyful. He is an optimist by nature, which helps greatly in the field of scientific research, strewn as it is with doubts and the harshest of critics.

'What do you think?' asks Breckenridge, nodding in the direction of the manuscript lying on the scientist's lap. He looks down at the paper, again irritated by the thought that someone, even a member of his own laboratory and a co-author on the paper, should be looking over his shoulder without his agreement.

'Yes ...' He starts, about to explain about the committee meetings and the migraine, but he has neither the inclination nor the energy, so leaves it at a cryptic *yes*. Breckenridge waits a little longer for a more expansive answer but, realising his senior is not in a talkative mood, turns back round to face the heart of the train with a noncommittal: 'Oh ... well, have a nice journey'.

The scientist looks again at his work, feeling neither unfriendly nor guilty at his unwillingness to engage the man in further conversation. It is not his way to engage in small talk. Some presume this to be arrogance; an assumption that his time is too precious for such an activity, but he never takes notice of such opinions and cares little for judgements on his sociability. Unsocial he plans to remain in perpetuity.

He looks back up the train carriage for the man who has been staring at him, but he is no longer there. A young woman holding a sleeping baby is now in his place. She rocks the baby up and down, staring into the child's face with a smile.

The other passengers are becoming restless at their impending disembarkation and, after another five minutes, during which the scientist has made little progress in considering the language of the manuscript, the train crawls to a halt. He waits until the other passengers have alighted before packing his papers away into his case then donning his coat. Breckenridge has already left, one of the first to the door. Clearly he has got the hint and has wisely chosen to put distance between himself and his curmudgeonly boss.

Being the last off the train, the scientist avoids the crush of the platform and the jostling at the ticket barriers. He is in no particular rush today. He has nothing scheduled until ten o'clock. He knows he will arrive at the office at half past eight or so after the ten-minute walk from the station. He plans to make himself some coffee, check his mail and read the contents page from the latest journals to determine whether there are any articles he should be reading. He thinks that by ten o'clock, he will be ready to face the dean and his latest theories on money generation for the university or whatever it is he wants to see him about.

But despite this carefully thought-out plan, the day will not turn out like this at all. He will, in fact, be dead before nine o'clock, the victim of a savage knife attack.

The clock ticks.

2

ON THE THIRTEENTH day after the vernal equinox, the procurator for the city of New Canterbury sits in his office thinking about matters unrelated to the law. Behind his seat, positioned on the wall in a dark, ornate frame is a detailed chart of the phases of the moon. So striking is it, by virtue of its colours and bold use of cryptic symbols, that it often distracts his clients – that motley bunch of down-at-heels who come to provide paltry attempts at justification for their petty crimes and harbour the expectation of impunity. He keeps it there since he feels it aids in the curtailment of their stories, in which he has little interest. In front of him, however, on the far wall next to some well-used filing cabinets, is a similar chart depicting the motion of the planets around the sun. This is much more sober in its aspect, less noticeable, but to the mind of the procurator, altogether more figurative. It is this one he had been studying for the past half hour, imagining the course of the celestial bodies and how they might relate to current events on Earth – a world that is a mix of conflicts, that is in need of clarification. He focusses most of his attention on Mars, which, for the next decade or so, will be the closest to Earth that it will ever be in his lifetime, and which, when in the ascendant, is associated with aggression and recklessness.

The door opens and in walks his secretary carrying coffee and a small plate of biscuits. She crosses his line of vision, breaking his train of thought, and deposits the refreshments on his desk. He will return to Mars later.

'Mr George,' says the secretary, feeling the need to address him formally.

The procurator looks at her and makes a quiet grunt, acknowledging her in a minimalist manner.

'Your ten-thirty has rung to say he can't make it.' She pauses to check he is paying attention, then reads from her notepad. 'Says the lift in his apartment block is broken, so he can't get out.'

She turns to him again, a glib expression on her face. Merely to provoke a reaction, she says, 'Don't know why he can't use the stairs.'

'He's got no legs,' retorts the procurator in a flash. Whether that is true or not is irrelevant. It serves to provide his secretary with the conversation she feels is necessary. She leaves the room, deflated and put down, but no more so than she is used to.

The procurator picks up a biscuit and considers its form; circular with an irregular edge and a series of holes dotted randomly on its surface, like pockmarks. Holding it up a certain distance from his eye and leaning back in his chair, he can cover over the sun in the solar system chart to produce a solar eclipse. Pleased with himself, he holds it there for several seconds before hunger gets the better of him and he eats it in one mouthful.

He picks up the coffee cup in one hand and a sheet of paper in the other. Sipping the drink, he reads the order of events in court for next week. He will be busy with pointless hearings and hopeless appeals, with little time for this sort of contemplation. He doesn't know how long he can continue with this job.

The phone rings. A man with a voice that is hard to understand launches into a vehement diatribe. The procurator listens not to the words but the manner in which they are spoken, a violent explosion of slurred vowels and guttural appeals. He recognises the caller from the multiple other times he has called. The gist of the call concerns (he assumes) his court appearance in a few days' time and the need to take into account his medical circumstances, which are forever changing. He is a sick man, and the stress of legal proceedings has caused his condition to relapse.

The procurator holds the phone some distance from his ear, as though phone signals might transmit disease if not heard at a distance. The words are now barely audible, a dissonance of sound punctuated by sobs. The procurator has noticed that this client can turn on the tears at a moment's notice – a talent that often goes down well in court if the jury are of a sentimental variety. Some time ago, he even suggested to the client that he might take up acting as an outlet for his talents, but this was, of course, met with indignation. The client has gone as far as to complain to the ombudsman about the way he has been treated by his lawyer. But what did the procurator care if he offended the clients? They would keep coming back. By the nature of their actions, this crowd of transgressors would always need his sort.

'Are you listening?' comes the cry through the distanced earpiece.

The procurator brings the phone closer to his face.

'Mr Talbot,' he says in a dispassionate voice, 'there is no need to shout.'

As if he is a dog chastised for entering a disallowed garden, the client is now silent. Given that they are people who break the law, the procurator is always fascinated at how easy it is to train these low-lifes in his way of doing things. One pull on the leash and they will generally come into line. He imagines that if, moments before committing their crimes, someone were to be on hand to tell them not to, then the majority of them would be unlikely to continue. It is, he reckons, predominantly their stupidity that gets them into trouble. As far as he is concerned, they are the most rule-abiding group of people he knows.

'This is how it's going to go,' begins the procurator, not allowing any interjections, reeling through a list of actions he expects his client to take.

'Is that clear?' he finishes, giving the caller little option but to agree.

He puts down the phone and scribbles a few words, barely legible and to which he is unlikely refer later, on the notepad next to the phone.

At that moment, he hears a commotion outside his window.

People are running in the street, and he hears distant sirens. He puts down his pen, resisting the urge to look out of the window, and looks back at the solar system chart opposite. There is something reassuring about the picture, or, more precisely, the objects it represents. The planets are an immutable presence, varying only in their position relative to each other, but ultimately returning to their original positions; a repeatable pattern occurring *ad infinitum*. As a boy, he had been fascinated by the fact that an event, albeit unrecorded, occurring on a distant star or planet observed (if he had a powerful enough telescope) at a precise moment, had, in the truest sense of time, happened long before he was born. Such was the length of time it took for light to travel. The concept of time occurring at an actual and an observed point was a mesmerising enigma to one who had so much to consider. And which was the true time? His juvenile self, believing alien lives to exist – sentient and bothered by the same dilemmas as his forming mind – asked: *To you who lives so far away, is my time different to your time?* His conclusions on this telescope enigma led him further to a fatalistic philosophy, dangerous in one so young: the gap between something occurring and it being observed means that everything is predetermined, immutable. Such were the thoughts of one so young, an only child alone in his world of introversion.

And now, years later, he questions the naïve thoughts of his youth, and understands that it is man's nature to rage against the passivity of existence. One can only go so far with fatalism before insanity appears. Thus, he struggles to reconcile himself fully to the uncontrollable inevitability of fate, entrenched in his grey-walled office, watching his life pass by. His occupation is to defend the perpetrators of acts which, if his youthful philosophy is to be followed, are destined to occur and whose consequences are inescapable.

His mission, however, is something altogether different.

Outside, the commotion continues and voices become louder. He takes another drink of his coffee, now cold, and picks up a further biscuit before eating it whole.

3

A FAINT MIST on Galahad Bridge curls around the ornate palisades which make up the sides the pedestrian walkway. All-pervasive, it slides along the cobbled ground, filling the gaps between the walkers' shoes, winding its yarn of haziness in an imperceptible net around the whole of the bridge. The walkers, oblivious to its power, trudge on, unaware of the force binding them to the bridge – binding them in so many ways on this morning, ways they would struggle to comprehend but which would leave a mark forever.

At a precise moment in time, foreseen, maybe, by a soothsayer or haruspex from times of old, a middle-aged man steps onto the bridge – that structure spanning a deep and rushing river. In doing so, he surrenders the safety of hard ground to a brick-built design that has carried thousands, or rather millions, over the perilous route – from horse-drawn carriages running over dung-filled roads, carving a path through the hoi polloi cowering at the edges, to military vehicles defending the most vital of trading routes. And at the very same moment, at the opposite end of the bridge, which runs precisely from north to south, another man – much younger and with an intent fomented through the clouded propaganda of rage – places his first foot forward, across the threshold of providence.

The bridge feels the weight of the approaching pair, if indeed an artificial construction is able to comprehend forces of gravity and turn them into feelings of anticipation. But let us say that history, which is constantly being absorbed and documented in its stones and lintels, understands the gravity of moments such as this. Owing to a pronounced incline in the bridge – a most unusual architectural feature relating to the differences in the elevations in the banks on the north and south sides – the younger man, the one on the bridge's north side and the one who knows that something indescribable (in the sense that he has not fully formulated the sequence of events) will occur in a matter of minutes, is immediately able to see his target and focuses on his task. Even now, his task is more of a concept rather than a fully-fledged plan. Preparation of the most miniscule details is not in his make-up. The element of surprise will be enhanced if he himself is unaware of how it will play out. At least, that is his reasoning.

He dodges around several people who have stopped on the pavement to admire the view along the river. The bridge is crowded. The early morning rush has begun, augmented by the recent weather that has drawn people out into the open to admire the beauty of spring and worship the sun gods. A woman wearing a red cap with a recognisable logo points vigorously in the direction of a steamboat making its way in a leisurely manner down the river. Her gesticulation is so enthusiastic that several people, not just those for whom it was intended, turn their heads and observe what seems a noteworthy incident to her, but is, in fact, an everyday occurrence. Boats travel on rivers. She continues to point excitedly. Perhaps she has seen someone she recognises on the bow of the boat. She then lowers her hand, as it has turned out not to be the person she expected, or perhaps desired, but rather an uninterested tour guide, who is resting on an overturned crate and smoking a soothing cigarette whilst waiting for the morning's boat tours to begin. A man in formal attire, not prone to observing novel occurrences on his mundane route to work, shuffles around her disapprovingly, making a point of looking her in the eye, his expression relaying the message that this is not how one behaves on the morning commuter's route. She takes no notice, caught up in the novelty of boats and rivers and mistaken identities.

Step by step, the two protagonists approach one another. In the terminology of storytelling, technically it is one protagonist and one antagonist. Which is which? The man on the north side of the bridge would differ from the man on the south side in ascribing their roles. Yet the man on the south side is currently unaware that there is a need for these two people, seemingly innocent walkers, to be given roles.

The older man, oblivious to his impending demise, pauses momentarily to check he has not forgotten to pick up his phone. He has nurtured this habit for years, this need to reassure himself that the world has not changed since the last time he checked. Yet, this reassurance is to be proven worthless in less than a minute. He finds his phone, looks at the screen and places it back deep within his pocket. He draws the belt on his raincoat tighter. Again, he sees a shiny black beetle flying in front of him and looks up towards the heavens to discern whether a swarm, similar to that which accompanied him on his way to the station, albeit momentarily, is present in the polluted confines of the city. He has been put on alert to parasitic invasions since the odd encounter. The sky above is clear, save for the delicate mist which deposits a film of moisture on his face with a cooling, almost chilling sensation. For the second time in as many seconds, he is reassured. It only needs a third time now, since things occurring in threes are deemed to be significant and therefore laden with the purest of truth, or so he believes. The mind looks for patterns in all things.

However, notwithstanding these self-proclaimed auspices or good omens, a menace from which there will be no prospect of comfort is fast approaching. The man on the north side's heart beats faster, preparing for what might occur. The reason for his tachycardia is the mysterious autonomic nervous system, which reacts to a stimulus whilst oblivious to its true meaning – only sensing some fear, readying the body for the fight. His foot falters on uneven ground and he feels his ankle turn inwards. Correcting himself, he stays upright with a perceptible lurch to the right. He clutches his weapon more tightly with his left hand, concealed within the deep lining of his industrial jacket. Ten metres or so away now. His intended target becomes invisible for a second, hidden behind a thick-set man, a giant towering above the throng. The bridge is busier than on the occasions he has walked its length in recent days. A bird flies overhead, calling: a raucous cry.

The scientist, the man walking from the south side of the bridge, clutches his briefcase to his chest. He has noticed that the straps are fraying and may snap at any moment, so in such close company has decided to hold it in such a manner. He too sees the bird (not one typically associated with good luck) and at the same time as looking up to the sky, once again checks for the black flying insects. *What's the matter with me?* he asks himself, *Am I becoming obsessed?* Yet his gaze remains fixed upwards.

The north side man once again sees his prey, its form having emerged from behind the giant, and notices that he is looking skywards. Unconsciously, he too looks up, following the other man's gaze. Perhaps the man has got wind of what is about to befall him and is looking for help or a camera to record his demise. It is a ridiculous thought, yet the mind is prone to irrationality at such times. He is nearly within touching distance – two, perhaps three, people are between them. A woman pushing a pushchair as if it is a battering ram causes him to veer off his course, but he steps back into line, forcing himself in front of an older woman carrying her week's shopping. He hears the mutters of protestation but is not distracted.

Still looking up, the man journeying from the south side spots a black beetle – vindication for his surveillance. Having not had a third reassurance, he is now concerned about the significance of the beasts. His newfound superstition is, as it turns out, well-founded, since his thoughts are accompanied by a deep searing pain in his right flank, followed by a hot, wet feeling down his side, then a fall to the ground, then blackness.

4

For a city accustomed to all manner of crimes, the one that was to occupy the majority of Detective Inspector Price's time for the best part of the next year was particularly shocking and would generate extreme outpourings of angst in an already fraught populace. A criminal act and the reaction to it depends not only on the perceived despicable nature of the sociopathic offender, but also on the character of the person upon whom wrong has been committed. Thus, the theft of goods from a person illegally squatting in a town house or the mugging of a homeless man may have much less significance in the minds of a public seeking reassurance that law and order is to be upheld at all times and that the rules of society, although disrupted, will return to normality despite the upheaval caused by a moment of evil. The murder of a respected scientist, therefore, upsets the balance and deviates so far from the concept of what is right and proper that it will take the city many years before a sense of evenness can return.

DI Price, living not ten minutes by bicycle from Galahad Bridge, is first alerted to the onset of this disequilibrium by the screeches of sirens and the flashes of blue lights that erupt in the streets around his house as he sets off on his morning journey to the police station. He has unlocked his bike and donned his helmet and is just about to swing his leg over the crossbar of his newly acquired hybrid bike when it seems that a tornado must have hit the leafy street he called home. Having a tendency to startle (a trait which might have precluded him from a profession strewn with alarm and surprise were it not for his resolve to counter his inner weaknesses), he flinches, causing his straddling leg to become hooked awkwardly on the bike crossbar and his whole body to lurch sideways and then topple onto the concrete surface of his drive. It is an undignified fall, but, since anyone who might be around will be distracted by the speeding vehicles, it is unwitnessed. His left hand, having taken the brunt of the force of his fall, is grazed, and, despite some inner voice telling him he will be needed urgently in the police station, he makes his way back inside the house to wash and bandage his palm. His wife, preoccupied by thoughts concerning the morning's commotion and rather accustomed to her husband's clumsiness and need minor nursing duties, helps to provide first aid. At the same time, she quizzes him about the sirens and what they might indicate and makes him promise that she will get a full report on their significance when he gets home that evening. She will, as it turns out, not need to wait until then, as within an hour, the news channels of the land will start running the story in the fullest of detail.

His hand is now bandaged and he has pocketed several painkillers for later (should the injury swell and cause discomfort). He mounts his bike, this time successfully. His journey is far from normal, since speeding police cars and ambulances have taken control of the road, allowing little flow of traffic. His normal route is blocked off, but his status as a senior police officer allows him through the barricades. His sense of duty is mixed with a degree of panic; he has not seen this manner of major incident for some time. Alert to the possibility of threat from the moment he is let through the police barrier, he hurries to the station, locks up his bike and seeks a report on the morning's activities.

Inside the building, the scene is one of an ants' nest that has recently been disrupted. The chief of police holds court in the large meeting room. He exudes a confidence that is needed in such times and is the reason he holds the highest-ranking job; even those engaged in the business of disorder are drawn towards those who profess calm. DI Price slips into the back of the room and listens to the directives being issued. He is reassured that a strategy already exists despite there not being a full understanding of what has occurred. Incident blueprints have been drawn up in advance. The chief of police states that the current events fall under SOP3, SOP standing for Standard Operating Procedure. DI Price – like many around him, he is certain – is amused, in a sardonic way, by the term. There is nothing standard about what is happening; of that they can be sure. But, by normalising disaster, they might be better equipped to cope with it. Or so the theory goes.

The chief of police continues issuing orders. DI Price's mind wanders. Having not caught the start of the meeting, he is still unaware of the nature of the calamity, and his thoughts concoct all manner of scenarios. *What can it be that has caused such alarm?*

He nudges the man standing next to him – a surly constable, some years his junior – and whispers, 'What exactly has happened?'

The constable, a solemn look on his stubbly face, turns to him and whispers back, 'Man stabbed on Galahad Bridge.'

DI Price ponders this and is perplexed. A sense of anti-climax is perhaps the inappropriate response to hearing that a man has been stabbed and has maybe lost his life, but stabbings happen all the time in a city of this size. Perhaps the victim is someone important, he muses as he listens further to the chief of police, who is wrapping up the meeting with a call to arms, or, rather, a call to defend the streets of this besieged city.

The ants disperse, each with an imposed sense of purpose, which is, in reality, a lack of direction and a chaotic dance to an arhythmical tune. The ants are good at constructing the ant nest, but they run in panic when the anteater comes and rips out the heart of their home.

DI Price returns to his desk and shuffles his papers before deciding what to do next. He takes some comfort in the documents on his desk, a physical presence and a rebellion against the digital age that has robbed him of permanence.

He looks at the calendar pinned up on the adjacent wall and remembers that it is April – the worst month for crime, in his opinion. He scratches his head, but as he does so his deputy, Detective Sergeant Belinda Hameed, appears behind his chair and informs him that she has gathered his team in the small meeting room for a debrief. He thanks her and takes the few short steps to the room.

Bemused, and with a feeling of shame that he is still unaware of the precise nature of today's dramatic events, he invites DS Hameed to commence the meeting. She, cognisant of his ongoing ignorance, starts by outlining what has occurred.

For the first time, DI Price hears that a prominent scientist has been stabbed in broad daylight on Galahad Bridge. His deputy emphasises the 'broad daylight' aspect of this crime, as though crimes committed in darkness are somehow more acceptable. Witnesses have stated, she explains, that a single white male, dressed in a black coat with hood, walked up to the victim and then appeared to make close contact. She continues to recount the scene, needing no prompt, since the details of the crime are so shocking, and, at present, so scanty that they are easy to remember. The victim fell to the ground silently and the hooded man walked on. The perpetrator is not yet in police custody. A knife, the presumed murder weapon has been found on the shore of the river at the southern end of the bridge, presumably tossed over after the event. Ambulances were called to the scene of the crime, but the victim died at the scene. In the commotion, the further flight of the criminal is unknown, but one witness claims he headed down Cleopatra Street, a road which runs parallel to the southern shore of the river.

She pauses, aware that the chronology of events described by her is a little awry, but happy to have filled her senior in on the events.

DI Price, as is expected, takes over and, now in control of the situation and fully briefed, says, 'SOP3'. He leaves it at that.

5

THE FIRST TWENTY-FOUR hours following any crime is considered by those with experience of such matters to be the most crucial in deciphering its mystery. After that, time fades the memory of those who have observed the event, and physical manifestation of evidence is contaminated or washed away. DI Price and DS Hameed work methodically yet rapidly, all too aware of the aphorism about haste drilled into them from the first day of forensic science studies. They work well as a team: one is more able to imagine the motive of the wrongdoer and sees patterns in the most mundane of places, the other fills in the gaps her colleague misses when speeding to a conclusion.

Within two hours of the killing, a man has come forward and admitted to murder. He sits in a basement cell of the police station, where he has sat on numerous previous occasions. The detectives hear his name and raise their eyebrows. 'Not him again,' they say, almost in unison. The most junior of the officers on duty draws the short straw and is sent to interview him. He has admitted to most serious crimes, at least those which have reached the media, for the past seven years. Despite multiple warnings and custodial sentences for wasting police time, he continues to turn up and claim that the latest offence is his doing. They now have a protocol for dealing with him. 'What if one day he actually is the perpetrator?' asks the junior officer as he descends the stairs with the station's booking-in clerk. He braces himself for half an hour of non sequiturs.

The remainder of the duty officers, many of whom have stayed behind in this moment of crisis, work their way through the witnesses to the crime. Those on the bridge at the time of the killing have come forward in number, whilst others call the hotline set up for gathering information. Surprisingly few report anything of note. Most agree that they witnessed a man falling to the ground and another running away at speed. Beyond that, the stories diverge. A few seconds after the event, when awareness of the atrocity had spread through the crowd, widespread panic had set in. People had started to run in all directions. The act caused the release of adrenaline in the bridge walkers, the so-called fight-or-flight hormone, and since most had no desire to fight, a stampede was set in motion, with screams and shouts further adding to the confusion. The act of killing triggered the desire of most around the dying man to get off the bridge, and, being on a linear structure, some ran one way, others the other. A few tended to the man on the floor, at first uncertain of what was happening, unclear as to the nature of the crimson, viscous substance coating the pavement, not comprehending that an event of this nature could occur in the morning rush hour. One man, who rapidly understood what had happened, dropped to his knees and felt for a wound, knowing that he needed to stem the flow of blood. He loosened the coat and then the shirt, placing his hand firmly on the expanding red patch on the striped, blue shirt. In an instant, his hand became engulfed in the blood, so he pulled out, not least because of the repulsion he felt at the uncomfortable warmth of the man's (a stranger's) blood, which drained rapidly all over his own clothes.

Now in the police station, his hands clean but dark stains evident on his cuffs, the man sits in the incident room staring forward, thinking of very little. He is brought tea with sugar, which he does not drink.

Another man tells of how he gave chase to the fleeing form of the attacker. He serves in the army and is alert to the possibility of conflict, so his own profile of hormones tend towards the fight scenario. It is his week off. He has recently return from a tour of duty – six months in a faraway desert – yet he is on guard at all times, he says. When he started the pursuit, he was unaware of what the running man had done, but the commotion generated around him indicated that he must be stopped. The fleeing man was quick, nimble on his feet as he side-stepped the throngs, most of whom got out of his way. The soldier, being more stocky and less able to circumnavigate the masses, collided with the other people on the bridge at regular intervals.

'I nearly had him,' he tells the officer who interviews him. He is unsure in which direction the man escaped, since the final collision of his pursuit caused him to fall and knock his head against the pavement.

'I've had worse,' he says to the officer, repeating the exact words he uttered to the paramedic who assessed him at the scene. He now sports a line of thin white plasters on his forehead through which blood oozes, forming a trickle down to just above his right eye. He wears this as a badge of honour.

A third man witnessed the throwing of the murder weapon down to the bank of the river below the bridge. Unaware at the time of its significance, he followed the trajectory of the object – 'like a tiny silver javelin' – from the man's hand to the shore. He corroborates the statement of a witness at the scene who stated that the man ran in the direction of Cleopatra Street.

'He was gone like a flash,' he adds, as though feeling the need to justify his own failure to apprehend the evil man. In contrast to the man who tried to staunch the flow of blood, he is animated, even excited about what has occurred. He talks rapidly. This is the first time he has been in a police station. 'It's just like on the TV,' he says to the woman sitting next to him, who smiles politely, then gets up to go to the toilet. She will sit somewhere else when she returns.

After three hours of interviews, the officers convene in the meeting room to go through the evidence and set up a timeline of events. Surprisingly little is known: a stabbing in the middle of Galahad Bridge, the discarding of the murder weapon, and an escape in the direction of Cleopatra Street. After that, the flight of the fugitive is mysterious. They have an update from the police officers who are searching the area around the bridge. They have found no trace of the man whom they seek. The bridge, Cleopatra Street and all surrounding streets remain closed. Forensics are out in force.

DI Price and DS Hameed return to the senior officer's room after the briefing.

'I'd have hoped we had more to go on,' DI Price declares, slumping down into his chair, tapping his pen on his desk.

DS Hameed nods. 'Someone must know something,' she adds.

'Looks like we are looking at a well-planned attack. The fact he was able to get away so effortlessly suggests he had accomplices.'

6

THE COMMON MAN understands that the city is under attack from those who abhor its godlessness. Reason enough, these enemies claim, to force the city into submission, to bring to its streets the order of divinity. In former times, men of a certain calling felt it their duty to take crusades to far-flung lands, to modernise and to domesticise under the banner of scriptures. Darkest jungles, a thousand miles from the churches of this industrial land, were the erstwhile targets. These caricatures of righteous men, in linen shirts and Panama hats, would brave the journey across the most uninviting continents to save the people in their mud huts and their children with beriberi. Theirs was a noble cause, unwavering in its intent, unflinching in its execution. In the end, such missions gave rise to colonies of malcontents and communities harbouring an overwhelming sense of rebellion and a bellicose unrest. These continents had nowhere to go but into civil war. Colonials were driven out for the most part, but God remained amongst the many like a shop sign above a burned-out warehouse.

In these current troubled times, however, the new mission is a reversal of this old order. No longer is a man from an overdeveloped nation taking his vision of industry to the deserts of an uncouth land. Now the uncivilised ones, the uncouth, are trying to break down the pillars of the cities which have bred such latter-day ungodliness. Those labelled uncouth demand a return to godliness. Industrialisation is their byword for decay. They will not cease until all have returned to a society of prayer and servitude. The idle hand is a godless hand. Industry is for the sake of God. The past weighs heavily upon the present.

And so, this itinerant, shaken to his core by the irreversibility of action, prowls the besieged streets of the city's outskirts. Half-dazed, half-disbelieving, he seeks clues as to how this calamitous act, forged by his own hand, has been received. It is five o'clock in the morning and a faint glow burns near the horizon. All is quiet. Only one other man is about, staggering from post to post, drunk on the fatigue of ignorance or on some other poison. The man holds out his hands as the itinerant passes but in a moment is left behind. Battle lines are drawn in blue and white tape. There are signs reading: *Closed: Incident*.

The central grassed square is empty now, its park bench wet with a light dew. The wanderer touches its dampness, a cool sensation on his feverish skin, yet sits down for a moment's rest. In front of him, the white-fronted hostel towers over the street. The shutters are closed. There is an air of repose in its clean façade, an air of invincibility about the concrete and metal construction. There is the sound of a helicopter in the distance, then the faint screech of a cat. There is never silence in this metropolis for more than a few moments. Some would take this as an attraction, a reason for visiting: a city that doesn't sleep. But the insomniac is always sick, deep down.

A truck carrying large bundles of newspapers drives by. The wanderer gets up and walks back in the direction of the hostel, a slow trudge to his bed, where he will have no rest. A bundle of newspapers has been deposited outside the door of the hostel. On the front page, he notices, is a woman, her face bloodied, her expression frightened. Below it runs the headline: *Carnage: we are under attack*. The bundle of newspapers is tightly bound, and he is unable to extricate the top copy so enters the hostel empty-handed. Behind the desk, the dark-eyed receptionist smiles and stands up.

'Good morning,' he says, as if not really awake. 'Would you like a newspaper this morning?' he enquires.

The wanderer suspects he was being watched when trying to remove a copy from the bundle outside, so he has no option but to reply in the affirmative. The receptionist, youthful and squat, smiles again and ticks a box on the sheet of paper in front of him. 'And sir …' he starts.

The wanderer turns around, having just set off towards the stairs. The youth looks at him sheepishly and continues to speak. 'Are you alright?'

This is a question that has been asked repeatedly for the past sixteen hours in streets and gathering places. The city's collective charity is harnessed to show its concern for all those others in its ranks. Those who, only yesterday, fought and spat at each other and honked their horns for the tiniest of indiscretions now hold out a hand of friendship. *Today we are united.* Life's pettiness and affrontery put aside for a moment in order to stand as one. *Our city.* The boy behind the desk, pock-marked, high-foreheaded, bespectacled, continues to gaze expectantly but sees the scowl of a man disconnected and alone amid all this mess.

Outside, the city sleeps on. It is safe, for now, since the man who has committed such an atrocious act is now in a drab hostel room, lying on his bed and thinking of oblivion. He has stayed at the scene of the crime. Capture and trial are not his concern now. The city will engulf him in time. His punishment is his fate.

In a neighbouring room, a travelling salesman, who has been caught up in the chaos of events, wakes early and switches on his television. The twenty-four-hour news channel reminds him, in an instant, of the magnitude of yesterday's peril. It tells him that the city is hurtling chaotically into the void. Previous attempts to fête an international achievement have already been consigned to the editor's cutting room. Bad news trumps good news. In the face of what has occurred, all else seems trivial and not worth recording. Half-listening with the weight of sleep still upon him, he imagines that the newsreader is telling a fairy story of a pied piper figure, leading the good and the naïve away to the door in the mountainside. He thinks of his own children and their bedtime story he has missed and then falls back into a light snooze.

The receptionist is on the prowl. He has set an early alarm to deliver breakfast to Room 27. Placing the tray – two eggs and toast, no butter – outside the room, he hears a sobbing from inside, which causes him to pause, lean his ear closer to the door and wonder if he should knock to enquire whether the occupant needs assistance. He would, in other circumstances, not have such thoughts. It is none of his business, and he does not engage with what goes on in the confines of hostel rooms. He hears a key turn in the door and recoils, scuttling away down the hallway, his footsteps muffled by the brightly patterned carpet.

Others stir. A travelling saleswoman in Room 15 does not want to be here. She has things to do, but the trains stopped running yesterday and she is marooned in this metropolis like a cat stuck in a tree. She has already complained about the lack of telephone reception, the internet, the food, and the general cleanliness of the place. This enforced exile from her life has come at a cost. She counts up the hours of lost productivity in items of kitchenware, as she has done for years, measuring out her existence in stainless steel and reinforced plastic.

She calls down to reception, glancing at the clock as she dials. Her latest demand goes unheard, since the receptionist is taking a call from the police. They have rung (returning the call from the receptionist who is certain the man is up to no good) to talk about the curious man in Room 19 who has recently arrived on these shores and who fits their description of an urban warrior, one capable of unspeakable acts. The receptionist pulls the phone closer to his ear and shrinks down in his chair. Lodging the phone between his ear and his shoulder, he pulls out the file from Slot 19 in the cabinet beneath the counter and reads the man's name and passport number to him. 'I'm sorry, officer,' he says, 'I can't tell you much more about him.' The police officer thanks him and is about to ring off when the receptionist feels the need to recount the story of man in Room 23's early morning ramble and his attempt to steal the newspaper. 'Yes,' he says, 'I believe that he was trying to commit a theft.' The man's cold expression, he recalls, was undoubtedly the look of a miscreant and a fugitive.

The policeman seems uninterested and tells the receptionist that, despite the arguments he has presented, there is no evidence to take either the man in Room 19 or the man in Room 23 in for questioning – but that if he notices any further suspicious behaviour by the men, he should call back. The officer recites his mobile phone number, half-wondering whether he should, given the fantasies the receptionist was likely to concoct.

Putting the phone down, the receptionist feels a sense of panic. He decides to call the owner of the hostel. However, in the moment between glancing up at the clock and picking up the phone to dial the number, the phone sounds once again, a muted tone for the early morning. It is the woman in Room 15. He hears her protestations and wants to tell her to get off the line: *this is a moment of emergency*. But as she drones on about the plumbing and the lack of hot water, he slips back into the mundane nature of his job and promises to get someone to look at it when the maintenance team get in at 9 o'clock. She is pacified for now.

Again, he picks up the phone to call the hostel's owner but thinks it best to avail himself of the details concerning the guest in Room 23. He pulls out the file from Slot 23 and is surprised to find the file empty.

7

SIFTING THROUGH THE evidence on a case compares to scrutinising the remains of a fallen sandcastle; deciding which grain of sand holds significance is the key to cracking a case. DI Price often muses on this point when lecturing the trainee police officers passing through his patch. Most ignore the facetiousness of a comment thought up to break the monotony of a dry subject, suspecting it to be a cliché they will encounter again. Some write it down. One or two, brought up on a diet of TV detective programmes, which in a deep-seated way has driven their desire to join the police force, smile knowingly, their belief in the glamour of a job that demands the sharpest of wit reinforced.

The evidence in the current case is, however, scant, such that the sand particles would not fill a teaspoon. It is curious, ponders DI Price, that a crime committed in a crowded street and in broad daylight, should offer so little. They have the murder weapon – the knife cast over the side of the bridge – but little else. Eyewitness reports have been minimal, and those who have had something to testify are plainly unreliable. It is as though the crime has been committed in a vacuum by an invisible force. Of course, this is not the first time that his team has been working with so little to go on, yet such cases are usually the ones involving crimes committed in the dark, on the edge of the city and intertwined with the underworld, which demands silence in its witnesses and its protectorates.

His deputy, DS Hameed, efficient as ever, has drawn up a profile of the likely perpetrator, but it is a sparse offering. To say that they are completely at a loss after a few days would be an overstatement; there is an air of despair, the like of which they have not experienced for some time. Even the most enthusiastic have all but given up, their interest wavering, their desire for a new case, something with teeth, to be assigned to them growing as each dead end in the current case is met with a moment of inevitability.

DI Price, as is his duty, makes an effort to rally the troops, suggesting to the workers that they are one piece of evidence (or one grain of sand) away from a breakthrough. He alone believes this, thinking that all is not lost, that the fatigue for the case is misguided and that they will be rewarded by persistence. He has a feeling that the answer will come from the most unorthodox of sources. That all-important motive which baffles the team is, he reasons, likely to be something they had not yet considered – but unearthing it will lead them to a resolution.

Why should an eminent scientist be stabbed while walking to work? Even DS Hameed, the wiliest of his underlings, has reached the conclusion that the attack must have been random. As soon as this thought takes hold, resolve falters. A motiveless crime is not only harder to solve but is also the most unsatisfactory. A motive leads the investigator down the most curious of paths, paths that are revelatory. No one writes books about detectives solving unpremeditated crimes.

'Let's think again,' says DI Price at the morning brief, stroking his beard and looking around for his coffee cup, now empty. He picks it up, nonetheless, and peers into its cylindrical emptiness. Not even a drop remains.

DS Hameed, eager as ever, suggests she makes another coffee. She is a dutiful deputy, perhaps more like a spouse, noticing his every nuance and anticipating his needs. DI Price, happily married, encourages such behaviour. He needs more than one wife figure in his life, of that he has no doubt. A mollycoddled childhood meant that the expectation of nurturing was ever-present. DS Hameed picks up the empty cup and visits the kitchen area, still within earshot. DI Price continues, raising the volume of his voice a touch to keep the connection with his most faithful of team members.

'Galahad Bridge,' he declares, floating out the geographical feature in the hope of triggering a connection in the thoughts of those listening. In his own mind, the words conjure an image of a late afternoon in the height of summer, the bridge in profile viewed from the fashionable north bank, the sun glinting on the rippling river that flows lugubriously, the tourists peering over the edge of the railings spying sailboats or, further downstream, a solitary fisherman who will not catch a single fish. Others in the room, including the surly George Tomaris, a constable who has recently returned to work after being assaulted on a callout to a drug deal, are not so prone to visual recollections and become impatient at the DI's call to reverie. Constable Fiona Banner, sitting next to George, picks up a pen and a pad of paper to write down something that has just occurred to her, but instead, aware of the insignificance of her thought, starts to draw a picture of the bridge, a visual memory stored deep within her brain from the day she spent sketching its form during her A-Level Art course.

DS Hameed returns with a tray of coffee cups, a pint of milk and a cafetiere of dark brown coffee, accompanied by its awakening aroma. She places the tray in the centre of the room and waits for a moment before half-plunging the filter down.

'I've had a thought that we should look further into the subject of the doctor's research,' she declares. By 'the doctor,' she means the man who was stabbed on the bridge. She uses his professional title because it sounds much better than calling him a victim. Despite all she has experienced, she still prefers to see the person on whom a crime has been committed in the context of their life prior to the event.

DI Price nods and completes the plunge of the coffee pot.

'Something to do with genetics?' he says in a half-statement, half-question.

Fiona Banner, casting aside her sketch which, she decides, is a poor effort, speaks. 'He was researching ageing. I think it was to do with turning cancer genes into …' she hesitates, 'into making cells of the body not die.' She realises the awkwardness of her statement, so qualifies it. 'My brother-in-law works in his building and told me a bit about it. Although, I'm not sure I understood exactly what he meant.'

George Tomaris, reaching for a coffee cup, sniggers. 'Yeah, I think you could say that,' he says.

DI Price ignores the comment and asks Fiona if she knows any more. She offers to quiz her brother-in-law further.

DS Hameed, always one step ahead, pulls out a copy of the latest scientific paper to come out of the scientist's lab. She holds it up and reads the title: *Cellular immortality as a method to reverse ageing processes in FVS45 cells: the role of the ratchet pathway.* She tries to sound knowledgeable but stumbles over the words, an imposter to the language of science.

DI Price contemplates this. 'Anti-ageing,' he says, letting the concept take hold in the room. Fiona Banner picks up her pad of paper and writes this down, as well as *Call David*.

'Do we think this is important?' asks DS Hameed.

DI Price raises his eyebrows. 'Who knows?'

'Anti-ageing – isn't that all about those creams on TV? You know, with the fancy vitamins and all that?' interjects George Tomaris, flipping a coin in the air and catching it with a rapid snatch. He is becoming fractious, thinks DI Price. Time for the meeting to end before it degenerates.

DS Hameed pours some coffee and hands out the cups.

'Well, let's find out all we can about his research and his colleagues. Look for any conflicts he may have had, any differences of opinion. They are often a spiky lot, these university types,' says DI Price, picking up his coffee cup. He draws the meeting to a close and heads back to his office, taking the scientific paper from DS Hameed as he leaves the room. 'Good work,' he says to her in a quiet voice, almost too quiet for her to hear. She smiles, their communication becoming more innate as their partnership develops.

Cellular immortality as a method to reverse ageing processes, DI Price reads, having settled into his black revolving chair. He recalls reading in the local papers some years back that the university had received an endowment of several million dollars from an American organisation interested in slowing down ageing. He had casually thought at the time that it was something to do with cryopreservation – deep-freezing people so they could exist in a suspended state of living before, one day, being reborn in an age of immortality: some Dorian-Gray-style fantasy. It had set off a vigorous debate about the ethics of that type of research at the time: *the old should make way for the young* versus *you can't stand in the way of medical progress*. That sort of thing. His own ideas on this were, of course, guided by fanciful movies and cheap science fiction novels in which he occasionally indulged if on a long journey or visiting his wife's mother, the dreariness of the stay needing escapist interludes. His views were born of ignorance, and he had no real concept of the subject. Furthermore, he assumed that it was the donation of some crackpot millionaire who wanted to invest in the science of his own immortality. The university wouldn't turn down millions, even though there was probably very little prospect of making the rich donor live forever. So long as they were making some efforts to research the field, they would assume the benefactor would be happy.

He reads further on in the scientist's paper, skimming the more technical sections. Perhaps there was a genuine scientific value to the research. He couldn't think of one off the top of his head. Who wants to live forever anyway? He was pretty sure that by the time he had reached his allotted length of stay on this earth, he'd be ready for the end.

He looks up and peers through the glass panels of his door to the office beyond. Police officers sit behind desks, typing on computers and answering phones. Crimes are committed, crimes are reported, crimes are solved, or not. If he were to live forever and never age, there would be no prospect of ever retiring from the police, he thinks. He sighs heavily.

8

DOWN THE STREET, a dog barks repeatedly and a car engine revs. Wishing to determine the connection, if any, between the two, the procurator walks to the window and, pulling aside the dusty blind, looks in the direction of the commotion. The noise stops and, seeing little other than a woman pushing a pram and a series of rubbish bins lined up on the opposite pavement, he sits down again. He is on edge; any disturbance could hold significance. He picks up the newspaper, which acts as both a comforter and an agitator, and sits down behind the desk once more. The paper is dishevelled, despite having been purchased only an hour ago. The front page is torn as a result of his eagerness to scan the contents as fully as possible, an action which he has repeated on innumerable occasions since he arrived at the office.

The paper is full of outrage and exaggeration. The pages show as much graphic detail of a crime as a man eating his breakfast will stomach. The font is bold and menacing. The photographs are grainy enough to bestow menace, a terrifying presence that can only be represented out of focus.

Going past the headlines, he opens up the middle pages, frantically reading any words that catch his eye. The coverage is extensive. The story will be newsworthy for days to come. He needs to understand how yesterday's events are being reported, how they will enter history. Time changes and distorts perceptions, but the original response will always shape the legacy of an action. In a world with little time for excessive platitudes, each event in the past is only allowed a single soundbite. He is not expecting sympathy, particularly in the medium of journalism, but hopes for understanding.

The door opens and his secretary walks in. He awaits coffee, yet she is empty-handed. Her brow is furrowed, and dark hollows hang below her eyes. She remains silent, expecting, even requiring him, her boss, to say something. He is not so hard-hearted, she hopes, that he will not notice her distress, on this day of all days. A city is in shock, and she is reeling from the circumstances of yesterday.

He looks at her. She annoys him, today more than other days: her acceptance of the world, her capitulation to the collective grief. She would be the first to indulge in a communal wail. *March in the streets and cry for the loss of your perceived liberty rather than bothering me*, he thinks, turning away from her and looking out of the window, his irritation having been interrupted by further noises in the street. She walks silently from the room, musing on her imagined resignation letter for the hundredth time.

The dog is barking again. Between the crack in the blinds, he spots a man walking slowly. He has the faintest of limps, a stiffness of his right leg accompanied by a hint of circumduction at the hip. He wears dark clothes and a hat with ear flaps. He walks on the opposite pavement, beyond the tiny courtyard garden and the quiet narrow lane.

The procurator feels alarm rising from his stomach. It is *him*.

He looks away for a second, a panic gripping him. His head pounds and a prickling heat rises through his body and grips his neck, constricting his breath. He looks again at where the man was walking, not able to bear looking, yet not having any choice. There is no one there. Nobody. Nothing, not even the barking dog. He presses closer to the window and peers out, up and down the lane. Not even a fleeing form. No sign of the man who walked there a second or two ago.

His heart is racing, and sweat is trickling down his forehead. Perhaps he imagined it. Did his preoccupation with the event of yesterday summon a hallucination? A physical embodiment of thoughts so dark and improper?

He sits down, breathing heavily. The looped thoughts he has had for the past twenty-four hours, uninterrupted even by sleep, play again in his mind.

The man he has seen (or imagined) on the opposite side of the street had entered the very office in which the procurator now sits exactly two weeks ago. He had come to ask for legal representation to help him slither through the cracks of the justice system that he now faced in all its might and impenetrability. Like the multitudes before him, he presented a feeble figure, armed with excuses and an unlikely appeal for pathos, along with an expectation that the lawyer, hackneyed and cynical, would believe his trumped-up version of events. The procurator had read the file in the minutes before the man had entered and was uninspired. And yet, on meeting him, he felt strangely connected to him. This was a soul who may be malleable, not least because he was utterly without any other options; an insignificant barnacle in the fierce ocean, ready to latch onto any rock that would accept him.

In the game of chess, that old and noble art, a pawn, on reaching the end of the board, the sacred kingdom of the opposition, can be exchanged for a piece of the player's choosing. Thus, a man may enter the room as one thing and leave as another. It is all a matter of directing the one who seeks direction.

And what of the man's crime? Like many that made its way to his desk, the details were almost comical. Events which, if written down and presented to a jury in their raw state, would be laughed out of court; a series of incomplete blunders conjured through whim and fancy, no doubt fuelled by intoxication: a sledgehammer crime, driving improper desires for another's wealth with as much brute force as imaginable and as little refinement. The coveting of another's property is a strong and base need. The details of the misdemeanour matter little, save to say that the comical element was imparted by a series of odd coincidences. Fate influences both the good and the bad. Looking back, the criminal thinks his capture is down to bad luck, but it is just luck. Suffice to say, the Brownian motion of the community's collective industry combined to put the crime at the heart of an ongoing police operation. He had been caught red-handed, as they say.

The procurator has read similar tales of woe before, and he has already begun to concoct some counter-narrative to influence those passing judgement in the court: a distraction aimed at throwing those baying for blood off the scent.

Meeting the man, however, fascinated him. His expression was animated, unhackneyed by the hardships of life, not yet tarnished by the act of digging a hole deeper into the ground, so common in others in his peer group. He displayed a lust for new experiences, and the procurator saw that it was only the circumstances of his environment that had sent the man down the path to his door. He could equally have been walking a tightrope or scaling a mountain. That is all to say: he was not a formed being. He had a rawness of spirit, even a wildness in his eyes. The window of opportunity is narrow in such a man. Give him a few months in prison and he would be a lost cause, forever.

After only a few moments, the lawyer moved on from the man's crime to his own idea; the one that he had been constructing for years, a mission of sorts, one needing a perpetrator. Was this the man? He saw the spark of anger born of a wandering naivety in the man, but at the same time a cruel ruthlessness – which was required for what he had in mind. He imagined that the man before him stood on the edge of a precipice, one dividing a lifetime of incarceration with an eternity of salvation. Yes, this directionless foot soldier was exactly what he had been looking for.

And so, invigorated like a hunter seeing a faltering prey, he discarded the formality of conversation and discussed what was on his mind.

And his mind was awash with thoughts – some holy, some raging against the sensibility of his position, most poorly formed. One vision recurred, an allegory, derived from a childhood story, yet one which was as vivid and relevant as ever: visible on the broad, sweeping horizon, his shadow cast long, his form highlighted in a pinkish glow, is the figure of the piper, tasselled and spindly, playing the imperfect notes of the calling tune, followed by the hoi polloi who hear whatever it is they wish to hear. The mountain with its promise of a route to salvation is menacing, and the splintered terrain causes the most terrifying of echoes to seep into the air. His music becomes more mesmerising, more enticing. They will say: *we, who have sought this leadership for so long, will follow wherever you are taking us.* Even this mountain of hard granite must contain somewhere in its sheer rock face a portal to a better life. The piper stops and reassures, changing his tune at the last minute before going out of sight.

The man opposite – to whom the procurator had, at that moment, decided to ascribe the name Peter – knew nothing of these visions, yet being prone to visions of his own, now controlled through the irregular taking of pills to dull his psychoses, he might have been open to discussing or even comparing them. Yet he sat in silence as an air of hostility rose between the two.

The procurator, distracted from his thoughts of mythical characters, broke the barrier – the lack of sound which, in the age where communication has been deemed to be our salvation, is unacceptable and leads to dispute – by smiling and saying: 'I see good things for you.'

This utterance, being such an unexpected thing to a man who has spent all his grown life and even his life before that hearing only words which denigrated him, caused Peter to lift his head and look the man in the eye for the first time in their brief encounter.

'What did you say?' he asked, thinking he must have misheard.

The lawyer sat back and restored the silence for a further period. He had recently elevated himself to the role of procurator, an archaic term for one who acts in the court of law in reference to crimes which are relevant enough to require some form of punishment, yet trivial enough to be decided outside of the crown courts with all their pomp and regalia. He practises, he thinks, in the hinterland between subservience and true evil. That was to be his lot for the rest of his working days, he imagined. Unless something came his way to change his direction, to take him towards the fulfilment of a spiritual journey.

He picked up a copy of *The Canterbury Tales*, a dark, leather-bound book which sat beside a sheaf of papers on his desk.

'Have you ever read *The Man of Law's Tale*?' he asked, knowing the answer.

Peter looked back blankly. He had become agitated, believing the strange lawyer to be wasting his time.

'Look, man,' he said, standing up, puffing out his frame, lurching his shoulders forward in order to present as much of his form as possible. 'Stop messing with me.'

He made to leave, scraping the chair across the hard laminate floor.

The procurator remained calm. 'Please sit down,' he said. 'What I have to tell you will not only get you off the charges that have been brought before you but will also be lucrative to you.'

He paused. Peter turned around, his face stony. The procurator sensed that the meaning of lucrative was unknown to his client, so clarified. 'Money. It will bring you riches.'

Peter sniggered and raised a hand as if to banish the foolish words of the man in the grey suit and striped tie. What would he know of the way to riches? If circumstances were different, he might have pulled out a knife and robbed the man. That would have taught him a lesson. No one messed with Peter. No one talked to him like that, least of all the old fool who was meant to be representing him.

Yet he stayed a while longer and he listened, and the words spoken caused an idea, a terrible idea, to take hold in the mind of the petty criminal. That event would lead to this moment in time – this moment when the procurator is peering out of the window, scarred by the turn of events, hoping that Peter will not return in any form.

9

IN WHAT WOULD turn out to be a curiously prophetic act, the murdered scientist had visited a solicitor to draw up his will two days before his death. Those believing in theories relating to the preordained nature of existence might think that an underlying premonition had taken hold of him in the run-up to his murder; one that made him feel the need to get his affairs in order. The concept of fate and predetermination requires time to skip around, time present being shaped by the past while investing in the future. Yet if the future shapes time present it must make itself apparent, forcing the act of malleability, an influence on events that have not yet happened.

Several days have passed since the awful event. The investigation is in full swing, although it is yielding little at the moment. Files are constructed and stored on computer hard drives. Papers and assorted items deemed to be significant are gathered in red crates. DI Price reads about the visit to the solicitor in the report his deputy has drawn up concerning the last few weeks of the scientist's life. He checks back on the age of the victim – just fifty – and wonders whether he himself, being only a few years short of that age, should think about making his will. He makes a mental note to discuss it later with his wife, although he suspects she will view the topic as too morbid and quickly change the subject. He reads on.

The scientist had recently been invited to speak at an international conference on ageing in Portugal. His topic was cellular immortality; his talk title seemingly similar to the paper he had been working on prior to his death. He had stayed at

The Hotel Bristol in Lisbon at the expense of the organising committee; a perk for the eminent scientist. The scientific programme had included a grand reception at the Belem Tower, an ancient fortification in the heart of Lisbon along the tram tracks, near to the bridge spanning the Tagus river and to the Monument to the Discoveries, which points the way to adventures and conquests.

DI Price had himself visited the city some years ago and had enjoyed spending time in its streets, which were bustling yet friendly. He recalls the steep hills and the corner cafes selling strong coffee and the ever-present *Pastéis de nata*. He wonders how much time the scientist would have had to enjoy the delights of the city. Presumably the reason for having the conference in such a place is to allow the participants to enjoy the local attractions. How many *Pastéis de nata* did he consume?

DI Price inspects the conference programme. He thinks it unlikely that clues regarding the murder will be gleaned from the document, but it might give him a more detailed idea about the victim's work. He, like his deputy, now thinks that his line of research may have some relevance to his death. At this moment, neither are clear about exactly how. The conference was split up into sessions: plenaries, workshops and parallel scientific sessions. At the end of each day, posters were displayed in a large hall, and scientists were invited to stand by visual representations of their research findings to discuss them with others who might be interested. The police officer imagines that this is like salesmen selling their wares in a market or a bazaar. On the programme, about three hundred posters were listed – a plethora of information, no doubt too much to be fully absorbed by the delegates, but presumably fiercely debated. The posters were split into groups. The broad headings included: *Genetic influences on ageing, Cellular senescence processes, Animal models* and *The pharmacology of ageing*. However, one catches his eye: *The ethics of altering the ageing process*. He looks down the list of titles, skim-reading but picking out key words: *religious, moral, integrity*. Elsewhere in the programme he notices that a bishop gave a plenary lecture titled: *The sanctity of death*.

DI Price pauses, putting down the reports. He leaves his office and goes to the kitchen area to make a cup of tea. Next to the kettle, waiting for it to boil, stands a uniformed officer who has recently been transferred to the unit. She smiles briefly as he enters, then returns to kettle-watching. They both wait.

'Do you mind if I use your water?' asks the senior officer. 'If there's enough.'

'Be my guest!' she replies. She feels the need to introduce herself, having not formally met him before this moment. She is aware of DI Price, the hierarchy of the police office evident from the moment she started. 'I'm Samantha – Jo's replacement.'

They shake hands, and DI Price states his name, despite being aware that she is likely to know his identity anyway. Her body language in the presence of a senior officer has made that apparent.

'What are you working on at the moment?' he enquires of Samantha, more out of the need for small talk than as a matter of genuine interest. He has too much on his plate to be concerned with the duties of others outside his team. Half the office is focused on the bridge murder and the other half, like poor relations, on the multitude of mundane, everyday crimes that have not stopped, nor will stop, because of the major investigation.

'Fellow who was found in the canal a few days ago with multiple stab wounds,' she replies.

He raises his eyebrows to acknowledge an interest. The kettle clicks off in a cloud of steam and she pours the boiling water over the tea bag in his cup, followed by her own cup, which she picks up.

'Oh, well – see you around,' she says before scuttling off with an unhidden keenness to leave the kitchen.

DI Price picks up a spoon to stir his tea. He wonders out of which canal Samantha's subject had been fished. No doubt the one next to the disused warehouses in the eastern borders of the city, where the majority of criminal activity relating to the burgeoning drug trades is committed. A feud between gangs of dealers has seen a number of their lot ending up in the polluted waterways which, in former years, were vital to the development of the wool trade but which were now little more than dumping grounds for the debris of society, including bodies.

He thinks back to the conference programme he has been reading. *The sanctity of death*? The ethics of the drug gang were a world away from that of the eminent bishop, talking or maybe preaching in Lisbon. He suspects the bishop spoke of tolerance and treating each life as equal, whereas the drug gangs from the east apply the law of the jungle: survival of the fittest. If a life gets in the way of what they are trying to achieve, then there is little hesitation to destroy it. Another man ending up at the bottom of the canal is of no moral interest.

DS Hameed enters the kitchen area carrying a sheaf of papers and an empty cup.

'Great minds!' she says, holding up the cup and taking a teabag from the counter.

DI Price smiles and removes the teabag from his own cup, reckoning it has had long enough to brew.

'Any news?' he asks, blowing the surface of his tea.

She pauses, wanting not to be seen as too eager. She knows her boss appreciates calm and collected thoughts, not speculation.

'I've been going through his work emails. There are some odd ones.' She hesitates.

Her boss looks up expectantly from his tea. 'Oh yes?'

'Emails from a while back relating to his work presented at an ethics committee.'

DI Price hears about ethics for the second time today.

'It seems there was an issue with …' she looks for the right words, '… unusual practices on a committee. It was disbanded a few years ago, but there was clearly some beef between the scientists and one of the lay members.'

The two look at each other. Maybe there is something in it.

'Who was the lay member of the committee?' asks DI Price.

She checks her notes and reads, 'Brian George. He's a lawyer. An interesting character, by all accounts. Seems that he was suspended a while back for harassing a witness but is back practising now. He was also sacked from the ethics committee and barred from standing again. I'm not certain of the reasons, but I can look into it.'

DI Price nods, then stands motionless for a few moments.

'Ethics!' he proclaims before taking his tea back to his office.

10

THE PROCURATOR CLIMBS the hills of the eastern range, from whose summit the whole city can be seen. The walk is hard going; a bogginess to the ground means that his boots pick up mud, which cakes their undersides, slowing his progress. He trudges on. In truth he is uncertain why he is making this sojourn, save for an idea that his head will have space to think, high up, free from the confines and the claustrophobia of the city streets. Heading skywards, anyway, appeals to one who is unable to flee in a conventional manner.

The air becomes thinner, and he feels a labour to his breathing, causing him to pause every hundred steps or so. He is alone, and for the first time on his walk he cannot see another soul in any direction. The clouds look more menacing over the back of the summit, so perhaps weather warnings have put off other climbers. He relishes the solitude. There has been too much of people for the past few days, too much chatter and frenzied motion in the streets and in the meeting places where people talk in panicked tones.

For the last few hundred metres of his climb, the path is bordered by a rivulet, no more than a trickle in parts, which flows downhill bathing the roots of bog plants, seeping through the black peat sods. It shimmers in the morning sun. In places a miniature waterfall forms, natural wonders in a microcosm.

He reaches the summit. Down below, the serpentine river, formed by a thousand draining rivulets, winds through the distant plain, taking the rainfall of the hills away to the sea. Each single drop of water starts its journey on the unadulterated slopes of moss and heather, then flows through the polluted city, divested of its pureness, and away to the horizon, hidden from view. It is a vast landscape of fields and woods and dwelling places – some alone, some in groups of twenty or thirty, some crowded into the city – which sprawls along the river and beyond, taking up every scrap of land on what was once a flood plain but is now a place defended against tides of water by upstream diversions, dams and barriers. The people have lived on these fertile soils for generations, initially suffering the infrequent floods, just as the tomato grower tolerates the risk of volcanic eruptions when setting up his lucrative farm on the ancient lava fields, as his father did and his ancestors in turn, back to the time when the volcano erupted for the first time in memory, causing the people to flee. They always come back.

Looking beyond the foothills of the mountain range, he sees the western part of the plain and the huge factory which harnesses the power of the river for turning ores mined from the rocks of the region into explosives. The chimneys, three dirty, grey constructions, churn out a constant plume of black smoke that blows along the course of the river towards the city. The factory is surrounded on all sides by a high fence through which few are granted entry. The alchemy going on behind its gates – turning the power of water into the potential for destruction – should be kept secret; or so say the owners. The city councillors, who rely on its wealth for the running of the sewers and the employment of road sweepers, agree, and no one questions the nature of their business.

The stretch of river between the factory and the outskirts of the city is devoid of the greenery of the wider stretch of plain. The riverbanks here are dark brown, and few trees grow. Some time back, a fire spread through the factory, scorching the ground, reducing the foliage to ash. The factory was rebuilt, bigger and shinier, but the land around did not recover. Occasionally, a bird will stop and peck at the earth, imagining this might have once been a place to make a nest before flying off with its homing instinct unsatiated.

Just upstream from this barren land, the procurator sees the river barrier – four shiny cylinders perched on stone plinths, spanning the river and preventing the floods that previously blighted the city and caused such destruction. Since their construction, the residents have not witnessed the devastation of yesteryear. They are confident they will be protected from the rising sea levels, about which they read in the morning papers. The cylinders, coated in aluminium plates, rise and fall depending on the threat of downpours that would otherwise swamp an ill-prepared city.

His eyes scan further along the river to the Galahad Bridge, and his thoughts are brought back to the subject which has preoccupied his thinking these past few days. Too far away to see the flow of people on its walkway, he imagines the scene: the conglomeration of bodies jostling for position, the jagged paths of the walkers as they dodge those intent on following a different direction. Some are on business; others seek out coffee shops and refuge from the crowds. The policemen will be there, having cordoned off a section and erected tents to shield the indelicate from the awful crime. A crime in which he is implicated and from which he will not escape.

He understands that the bridge will be forever linked to the event of a few days ago, just as buildings bear the ghosts of past sufferings. Perhaps, once the dust has settled, a plaque will be placed at the site of the killing, a commemoration of a life. The bridge has stood for centuries and will stand for many more, no doubt. But it is tarnished, and the people walking its span will feel the moment of infamy, glancing to the side at the collection of flowers, dwindling over time – at least until such a time as another misdemeanour overtakes their consciousness and they can walk over the bridge without a shudder and a sideways glance.

The river flows on beneath the bridge, carrying boats, which look like long murky torpedoes travelling at various velocities. The crews of the cargo boats will slow their vessels, ever so slightly, when passing underneath its arches in subliminal acts of reverence. Some may even bow their heads, standing on the oily decks of overburdened barges, makeshift flotillas for the dead man.

The procurator continues to gaze at the bridge. He has come this high to distance himself from the location, but his mind, resisting the desire to be purged of all that has occurred, draws him back in an instant. There will be no escape. Not unless a great tidal wave breaks through the shiny cylinders of the river barriers and drowns the city, its buildings, and its weary citizens.

Annihilate the city in a cleansing torrent and wash it all away. Leave no trace.

11

THE FUGITIVE, A status recently acquired following the dramatic events of five days ago, sits on an overturned metal crate by the canal bank. It is early and no one is around. He hears the faint cries of children making their way to school or engaging in truancy – he does not know which. An unpleasant stench emanates from the canal, the water level of which is low enough to reveal the variety of debris that has been dumped in its waters over the years. On the opposite bank, a series of obstacles connected with blue and white tape have been arranged to prevent access. Another crime scene in an area notorious for the whole spectrum of heinous activities.

The fugitive – Peter, as the procurator has called him – is hungry and fatigued. He has barely eaten since the moment he forced his life into this crisis. A single act, in all its violence, has changed his life forever. It is one from which he will never escape, to which he will be eternally bound.

A small bird lands a few steps away from his feet, wagging its tail. It displays the vigour of an uncomplicated life, a naïve curiosity. It turns its head, noticing the dark figure of the man for the first time, then flits off towards an island of junk in the middle of the canal. No boats have traversed these waterways for a generation; it is now a depository for domestic jetsam, unwanted on land. From there, the bird flies high in the sky and away, as it is free to do.

Peter, hunching forward, feels a pain in his back, a consequence of sleeping, or rather lying awake, on the rough concrete surface of the canal towpath that has been his bed for the last two nights. In the days when he was a member of a society which provided care for its citizens, he had seen a back specialist, who had pronounced the diagnosis of ankylosing spondylitis – an extravagant term, the doctor had said, for hardening of the structures in the back to produce a rigid tree trunk of a spine rather than a flexible one. He would be prone to a bad back for the rest of his days. The doctor had asked about his relatives, since the condition runs in families. He remembers his feelings on being asked about his family history: an invitation to dredge up the sadness of his past. He had baulked and told the doctor he was adopted and didn't know his parents. Both statements were untrue – he had not been adopted, and did at least know his mother; but keeping this concealed from the doctor allowed him to keep the pains of his upbringing deeply sequestered. His father had died when he was small, when Peter was at an age when memory is mostly fabricated by the stories of others. But these stories were never favourable, and the truth was in no doubt; his father had been a wastrel, who had only ever been destined to depart this earth to a chorus of opprobrium and the sentiment that it was a good riddance. His mother had fared little better in terms of life skills, being possessed of a selfishness and a lack of purpose that made child-rearing doomed from the start. Her four children had drifted away from her with minimal resistance once the council authorities had deemed her incapable. No one disputed this, least of all his mother. Her pregnancies and childbirth were merely part of some natural order: the way her life was meant to run, like all those before her and those following. Most made a good fist of raising their children. However, his mother's inadequacy was overwhelming, and she resigned herself early to failure. The children, playing pieces in a dystopian game of Happy Families, were flung to homes and houses throughout the county. Peter lost track of his two brothers and his sister without really knowing them. His bond to them had been perfunctory anyway. He was a loner by design and of necessity.

An elderly man with a mangey dog walks by. He ignores Peter, or perhaps pretends not to see him. Yet he has glimpsed Peter, and that is all it takes to form an opinion. In that second, which is enough time to make a certain judgement that he should have nothing to do with Peter, should not even make eye contact, he understands how far this vagrant has fallen, down and out on the canal path, a few feet from oblivion. He sees a human form without definition: blurred edges, an urban camouflage that indicates how assimilated into this wretched environment he has become – hair filthy, face dirty or maybe bruised, dried blood creating a tattoo from the scalp to the cheek, deep crimson and encrusted. His clothes hang around him like a pitiful shroud. His eyes look out into the distance, fixing on nothing: they are eyes that no longer see. And in that split second, the walker understands that there is nothing more to observe, nothing that will change his first impression. His pace quickens and he is gone.

Peter scratches his head and feels the laceration in his scalp that was inflicted last night as he scaled a fence, catching his leg and falling headfirst into concrete. The wound burns and oozes a yellow fluid. He reaches inside the pocket of his dirty jacket and takes out a cloth – a facecloth bearing the initials *AH* – which he stole from the hostel where he stayed for the two nights after the incident. He dabs the wound and feels lightheaded. He vomits on the stony ground and then lies down to prevent himself from passing out.

Above him, the sky is a grey-blue, covered in amorphous clouds that herald the promise of rain. A cold wind blows over his supine form, carrying with it an orange plastic bag, which swirls and leaps in the air currents before becoming entangled in a barbed-wire fence. Peter falls asleep. A deep sleep. The sleep of one who has not rested for days. The sleep of resignation.

12

IS AN EVIL act performed for selfish reasons any more monstrous that one which purports to be performed for the glory of a higher being? In Chaucer's *The Man of Law's Tale*, the Sultan's mother lays a trap for her son and his intended bride, resulting in his death and her banishment. Does she sanction such atrocities in the name of Mohammed or for her own megalomaniac tendencies? And does it matter? Some would say a crime is a crime, a murder is a murder and the reasons underlying the act matter little. Yet the law pays much attention to mitigating circumstances, to motive and to the character of the criminal. Since one man's belief and purpose may differ so much from another's, it would seem that the legal tenet that *all are equal before the law* becomes illogical.

This modern-day man of law ponders these arguments. He convinces himself more and more each day that his profession is so skewed from righteousness that it holds almost no value. Only rarely is a court case so black and white that there appears to be no argument. Faced with his own predicament, his conviction in these thoughts solidifies as he seeks justification for the act in which he is now so implicated. He has instigated an act of barbarism the nature of which shocks even him. He had never imagined it would come to this.

It is two o'clock in the morning and the procurator sits in his office. The lights are off, although both the outside streetlights and the bluish glow from his computer screen produce sufficient light to allow him to read. He hears the faint hum of electrical activity and the intermittent beeping of an unlocated alarm. On his desk, cleared of legal documents now, is a large hardback book displaying the pictures of Pieter Bruegel the Elder. It is open at a reproduction of *Landscape with Fall of Icarus*, a picture to which he often returns for confirmation, a comfort blanket for a misdirected soul. The medieval painter understood that an individual's aspiration and eventual failure is uninteresting to the majority. The ploughman is intent on his work, the horse trudges slowly and the shepherd does not hear the splash. At a time of such turmoil and rage, the procurator is faintly reassured that there are other worlds that exist in which all this carnage is unknown.

He glances at his phone and sees the multiple missed calls. He has not yet decided how he will respond to the persistence of the man. He knows that his caller is becoming more desperate, and it is only a matter of time before he is caught or hands himself in, thus revealing the true instigator of the crime. Three times in the last hour he has called. Neither of them sleeps. Insomnia drives madness. Madness will not be accepted as a line of defence in a court of law; of that he is now certain.

He considers calling the man but cannot bear to listen to the argument with which he will be faced. It will be a blackmail, a threat to expose the nature of the deed. But what will be his demand? What will be the way out for the two of them, so mired in the complexity of justification? He could deny all association with the killer, but if the man is caught, too much evidence drives him back to his door: his last few weeks of activity will be painstakingly reconstructed and the meeting the two men had in this office will be exposed and viewed with utmost suspicion. And then the procurator's past will be raked over and his link to the victim made in no time at all. Perhaps that has already been unearthed, anyway.

On an impulse, driven by fatigue and a realisation that time is running out, he dials the number. He hears the ringing tone, each one shrill, the time between the sounds long enough to raise the possibility that the call has been answered. After four rings he hears a click and then the quiet voice, no more than a mumble.

They have both been anticipating this moment for several

days. Each is anxious about the conversation; each has played out the words in their own minds a thousand times, forcing the hypothetical into reality, shaping the words of the other, as if by doing so in an imagined dialogue it will come to fruition, the situation will be diffused and a reconciliation, an escape, will be fashioned.

The procurator struggles to hear what the man at the other end of the line is saying, if he is saying anything at all. He waits for silence and then says, 'I can't hear you.'

The procurator's voice is hushed, not knowing the circumstances of the other, whether his words are being heard by others. The lawyer knows he may already be in custody. The police may have kept up the pretence of his fugitive status in order to lure the mastermind of his crime. They will have realised, no doubt, from the moment they captured the half-wit that he is being manipulated by a greater force. The procurator can almost imagine the officers standing around with their recording devices, tracking the call, silently. This will direct the police cars to his door, and in a few moments it will all be over.

All this is fantasy, of course, he tells himself. He knows that the police are clutching at straws. Peter, for all his shortcomings, has proven to be a supreme escape artist.

He listens for any sound and hears soft breathing. He can sense the angst of the man in his exhalations.

'Are you there?' he asks.

Outside the office, a car drives down the street, its headlights throwing fleeting shadows on the walls. It screeches to a halt further up the street, reinforcing the paranoia that the procurator feels concerning his imminent arrest.

'Are you there?' he says again, louder, feeling the urgency of the moment rising.

This time Peter replies, as though suddenly jolted into life by the forcefulness of his exclamation. His reply, however, is a single word. 'What?' he says. The cryptic nature of this throws the procurator into confusion.

'Where are you?' asks the procurator, hoping that asking a specific question will garner more than an ambiguous interrogative word.

There is a pause at the end of the line before Peter replies, 'Do you want to know?'

The procurator suffers the dilemma of wanting to distance himself as far from the man as possible, yet also wishing to know his every movement, like a schoolchild who has thrown a stink bomb into a classroom and wants to see its effects yet not to suffer the consequences. He now imagines himself, as he has done throughout his life, as an observer of his deeds, a fly on the wall, distant and protected. His life is not real but an observation of existence, perhaps a rehearsal that can be corrected. But these thoughts fail to hold, and he now has to contend with the reality of this moment. He has a choice to make: is being in control better than letting forces outside his command drive the situation to its conclusion? He listens further, gauging the mental state of the man at the end of the line by the silence broken only with his breathing.

'I need to see you,' the procurator says, breaking the deadlock of the anxious stillness.

'Midnight tonight. Galahad Bridge.'

13

THE FIVE ARCHES of Galahad Bridge span a distance of sixty metres; no mean feat of architectural design for the craftsmen of five hundred years ago. Its construction marked the opening up of multiple trade routes and great prosperity for the city. Yet bridges don't come cheaply, so initially a toll was levied on those using the crossing. In a few decades, the taxes generated by the expanding businesses along the riverbank more than paid for its construction, and the bridge rapidly became the focal point of the city. Over the years, it has been widened and strengthened, the sides have been made taller to prevent people falling in the river, and a tram line has been both constructed and removed. Twenty years ago, due to the construction of a much stronger bridge several hundred metres downstream, traffic was banned and the bridge became fully pedestrianised.

Half of this walkway of Galahad Bridge now remains cordoned off, and a white plastic tent covers the site of the scientist's death. It has been five days since the murder, and the forensic officers have finished their painstaking examination of the crime scene. The tent will come down tomorrow and the walkway will open up completely. The mayor has liaised with the police to bring about a return to normality as quickly as possible, hoping that the popularity of the bridge's route will quickly cause people to forget the dreadful crime. Many will seek alternative routes to cross the river, anxious of a possible repetition of the crime. Underground train lines cross under the river at multiple points. But, undoubtedly, people will be just as wary going into confined spaces underground at these times of high alert.

DI Price and DS Hameed stand on the bridge next to the plastic tent. They both look down the river, observing the cargo boats that float, even dawdle, down the sparkling waterway. It is the fourth time since the day of the crime that they have been back.

'It's so calm today,' says DS Hameed, referring to the river, which is flat and unhurried, but she could equally be referring to the contrast with the day of the murder. On that occasion, there had been no time to watch the boats go by.

DI Price nods and diverts his gaze to the southern bank of the river where the murder weapon was found, and from there down Cleopatra Street, the probable route the attacker took to escape and where two red double-decker buses are now meandering down its tree-lined route.

'You know, Belinda,' he says, still looking at the buses, 'the bridge was originally designed to take traffic across the river – horse and carts and the like, back then. But the chief architect's son was run over and killed by a postal wagon the day before the final plans were due to be submitted and he changed it into a pedestrian walkway. He got a law passed that vehicles should never be allowed to drive over the bridge. No one challenged him. His grief was so powerful that it changed the whole city.'

DS Hameed smiles. 'I think it's better as a pedestrian-only road. There are too many cars in this city, anyway,' she replies.

'The fact is, however, that his wishes were not respected, and only a year later the law was overturned and vehicles were allowed. It was only after structural reports suggested the weight of lorries and buses would cause it to collapse that the bridge once again became pedestrian-only.'

DS Hameed smiles again, amused at the story, its whimsical nature contrasting with the horrors of the crime committed. She suspects he has made up some of this story.

The two police officers enter the tent, a cramped space with barely room for the pair. On the ground there are small red arrows pointing at various stains on the concrete and larger blue and white signs with numbers referring to objects of evidence that have been removed for further analysis. A light bulb surrounded by a bright orange cage dangles from the ceiling, low enough to cause the senior police officer to collide with it on a few occasions. He crouches down, mainly to inspect the areas highlighted by the red arrows, but also to prevent further injury from the encaged bulb.

The two officers survey the stains: a large area of dried blood surrounded by smaller splatters arranged like an archipelago around a larger land mass. One arrow points to the faint dried lines of blood representing the print of a shoe that had stepped in the blood. It is not the victim's footprint, but whether it is that of the fleeing murderer is not clear. There had been a large number of people on the bridge at the time, and it could have belonged to any one of them. Appeals have gone out for anyone on the bridge at the time of the murder to report to the police (with their shoes), but the officers know that the likelihood of this line of enquiry yielding anything important to the investigation is negligible.

'Do we have anything back from the labs about the blood?' asks DI Price, looking up at his deputy.

She shakes her head. 'The blood on the knife and the blood on the ground come from the deceased. No one else's DNA was detected.'

He looks further among the patches of dark, but he knows he would most likely get just as many clues from reading tea leaves at the bottom of a cup. Blood falls to the ground after a stabbing; some is trodden in. What more can they say about it?

He stands up and scratches his head. The early morning sun has started to burn the skin on his scalp through his thinning hair. DS Hameed points to one of the large blue and white signs. It shows the number 18 written in a thick black font.

'The most curious item recovered from the scene was a coin from three hundred years ago, just there. It was lodged in the crack in the concrete, so could have been there for months or even years. It's a collector's piece, worth quite a bit of money, I'm told. So it's odd someone should be carrying it around.'

The senior detective stares at the ground and the small crevice that held the coin. DS Hameed has already taken out her laptop and has summoned up the photograph of the coin *in situ*. She shows it to her superior, who stands up and takes the computer. He scrolls through some pictures, including a close-up of the coin: first the side displaying the head and shoulders of a stern-looking man, possibly in military uniform, then the reverse side, which depicts a leaping beast, horned and lithe. A deer, perhaps. The coin is silver, and the detail is worn. A close-up of the writing reveals a year of MDCCVIII.

'It seems unlikely it would have been there long,' he says, handing back the laptop. 'Someone would have picked it up, wouldn't they?'

DS Hameed nods. Even on a bustling street rammed with people fixed on reaching their destination, there are always opportunists who seek good fortune in finding treasure.

'Fingerprints?' he asks.

'Nothing.'

They exit the tent and agree to walk to the shore and from there down Cleopatra Street, retracing the supposed steps of the man they seek. The sun goes behind the clouds and a cool wind blows across the bridge. Descending the stone steps at the end of the bridge, DI Price, in his heightened state of vigilance, notices – for the first time despite having descended and ascended these steps for years – a small brass plaque on the wall where the steps turn around on themselves. The rusted sign, no bigger than an envelope, is positioned at ankle height, as though wishing to be hidden. It refers to the civil unrest of the early sixteenth century, during which stones were removed from the bridge primarily to prevent the river being crossed, but also to form a barricade protecting the rebel forces from the law enforcers. The small sign, now barely readable, also commemorates the dead from the conflict. It seems ironic that those who had tried to destroy the bridge are now remembered and have formed part of its legacy.

The stone steps take them to a riverside path and the adjoining shore, which is covered in small pebbles. Occasional weeds grow up between the stones, and a line of moss grows at the shore edge, marking the boundary between land and water. The shore remains roped off, although the physical barrier is flimsy and recent litter and cigarette ends attest to its ineffectiveness in preventing access to the area where the knife was found. Like those on the bridge, these barriers were due to be removed soon anyway. People would once again be able to walk down to the shoreline and skim stones across the river, this time with a macabre fascination, knowing that the instrument of a murder had been disposed of right there, where they were standing.

The stones are rounded and even, hardly differing in size. Their homogeneity sums up the investigation so far. Neither police officer speaks. Neither really knows the reasons for coming back to the crime scene. It has told them little. Perhaps they have been hoping to spark a new idea, one engendered by the ghost of the criminal act.

Nonetheless they continue, climbing back up to the side of the bridge, then turning left onto Cleopatra Street.

14

IN TIMES OF upheaval, there are some who return to ancient texts, seeking inspiration and a means to manage their predicament. Whether they abstract solace from words, or a reassurance that their torment is part of a collective suffering, stories can be interpreted for comfort. Nothing is new, so the argument goes, and thus rehearsing the response to a similar calamity from eras past is worthwhile. Some take this dive into history one step further, seeking clues concerning the origin of what now occurs. Its divination, they claim, is written in the words of the old mystics, whose pronouncements on plagues and tempests and wars have been proven correct time and time again. Nothing is new.

One such scripture recounts the teachings of a man, John Corn, who walked the hallowed streets of this city in the early years after the bridge was constructed and who was, some say, responsible for the reconciliation of communities on either side of the river. Civil unrest had sparked a year before, fuelled by a desire for power in twin brothers, which had succeeded in dividing a once-peaceful populace. The brothers hailed from the ruling classes of the city, a noble blood line derived from crusading knights whose origin was linked to the mists of legend and birthright. The pretext of the dispute, which utilised the river as a physical barrier between the factions, each of which formed an encampment on one of the banks, concerned the sanctity of life itself. One brother, schooled in monastic ways from an early age, forbade the killing of any creature and lived a devout and frugal life. The other was in all ways his opposite. He saw no issue in crushing a lesser force, in killing the weak, in subjugating for the sake of power. When the brothers were children, those around them were dumbfounded as to how such a contrast could exist in those brought up together. One brother had no hesitation in pulling the legs off spiders or dashing the eggs from a bird's nest on the hard ground; the other prayed for the cows as they entered the slaughterhouse. The brothers were heirs of the city's ruler, and when their ageing and demented father could no longer command, they both sought to gain dominance, each with a conviction that his way of living was the truest form. Being twins, their right to rule was equal and, since none could recall which of the twins was born first, a dispute arose and a struggle to gain the upper hand was set in motion. The meek brother, as was his nature, gathered around him the academics and the pure of heart, who used their guile to construct a sophisticated community on the south bank. Its people were content and self-sufficient and would congratulate themselves that indeed the way of non-violence leads to happiness and fulfilment.

Those following the warrior brother, however, lived a chaotic and brutal life on the north shore. The concept of kindness to other men was alien to them, and they were spurred on by selfish thoughts and the prospect of riches, or, at the very least, release from the poverty that gripped them. There was no doubt, they thought, that they would crush the southsiders, armed only with their books and their prayers. Yet the scholar twin and his followers resisted and prospered, eventually bringing the majority of the northsiders to their way of life. A few, including the evil brother, escaped far into the hills, never understanding how they could have been exiled in such a manner, how peace could resist the sword's blade, how logic could defy the cut-throat knife.

Central to the philosophy of the southsiders was John Corn, adviser and minister to the peaceful twin. He was a man of conviction who, most say, was pivotal to the establishment of the new order. In modern terms, he would be called a shaman, a spiritual figure who used his powers to effect an unlikely victory.

Despite his success, many, even those in his immediate company, viewed him with suspicion, uncertain as to what pacts he may have made to deliver the eventual banishment of the bloodthirsty brother and his sidekicks. In the early days of the commune, he remained true to the cause, preaching a utopian existence based on peace and purity. However, in time his life became chaotic and his decisions increasingly erratic.

He wrote frantically in this period of his life, wishing to establish a legacy. *The Chronicles of John Corn* outlined the philosophy of the man and his followers. Much was thought to have been added after Corn's death; the book, published for the first time more than a century after his death, is a collection of different styles and indeed different, even conflicting, moral attitudes. The dichotomy of views is thought by some to be an attempt to blacken his legacy. Others reconcile the differences and find meaning in its incongruities. It is a prophecy for our time, they say, a time in which polarisation is a way of life.

A later section of the book is titled *The Prophecies* and contains the writings that generate the most interest, both academic and in popular culture. Within this text, which often appears unstructured and haphazard, is a further subsection titled *The Affliction of the Insane*, which is perhaps the most cryptic. It is composed in the form of a dialogue between two voices: the tormentor and the tormented. Several of his final works also take this form, and scholars and enthusiasts have debated which character represents the voice of John Corn. The parables written at the height of the struggle between the twin brothers are now seen as a guide to overcoming the vice and iniquities of the world. Or, perhaps, simply, the evils of the mutinous twin, since the wrench between two twins is clear in the words, manifesting itself (some say) as a cautionary polemic on fraternal love. Later in his writing, as he strayed further from convention and after allegations of witchcraft rose up against him, critics and judges came to view him as the tormentor, his twisted and conflicting views the voice of his modern crusade. He died a man in anguish, rejected by the utopian society he had helped to create on the south bank. In the years after his death, the existentialist intelligentsia took up his case and labelled him as the first man to lay out the fundamental paradoxes of existence. Whether John Corn was the tormentor or the tormented probably makes little difference to the whole idea of the book. However, such arguments, while they will inevitably burn in academic circles *ad infinitum*, perhaps miss the whole point of the book. *The Chronicles of John Corn* is not a book about John Corn but about the society of the time and its connection with a higher force. In his later days, his descent into isolation was undoubtedly fuelled by his inability to resolve the dilemmas about which he wrote. In simple terms, he thought too much and couldn't stop until he had made a definitive conclusion to a question lacking one. The misanthropic ending to his philosophy, outlined in *The Affliction of the Insane*, which contrasts so bleakly with the sentiment of the early books, was the result of his experience of so much of man's fundamental illogicality and its unbearable whimsicality. *To escape the hell which is inevitable, a man makes tolerable his decline by forming an early alliance with the Devil's progeny*, he wrote in his final lines under the further subsection *Armageddon*. Phrases like this, understandably in the heated atmosphere of a schizophrenic century, got him into deep water. And in hindsight it seems to have been inevitable that he should have lived out his final days as a hermit, starving to death on the edge of the city, his city.

15

THERE IS A cold breeze in the darkness. The city is quiet, its people sleeping or, perhaps, too afraid to come out. Under Galahad Bridge, the procurator waits impatiently. Half of him regrets coming out; the other half hopes the man he is due to meet will fail to show. What was he doing, coming out on a night like this, in the midst of the chaos that has unfurled itself? He would be better lying low, deep within a bunker, where he is better able to remain undetected, anonymous. The rabbit that bolts from the shelter of the hedge gets shot. He has no desire for conflict now.

He hears the flow of the water in the river accompanied by the alarm call of a blackbird, piercing then diminishing. Overhead, people walk in ones and twos upon the bridge, most of them silent. Only the occasional reveller breaks the quiet, summoning up a tuneless song or stumbling heavily with a curse.

The hour of their meeting has passed. He looks around. A feeling of relief rises in him with every second. Upstream, a light on a boat flickers. Around it a faint mist, yellowed by the light, rises up and curls around the mast. It floats, then forms a spiral before the darkness dims its form. The boat bobs gently in the black water, its rhythmic motion casting shadows by the side of the towpath. They loom eerily, fragmented by the irregularity of the wall that borders the riverbank. The calmness is, for a moment, mesmerising. He readies himself to leave, to head back home or even to his office, as he knows he will not sleep. Once again, he glances first left and then right but this time, in his peripheral vision, he notices a man walking the narrow path along the shore towards the bridge, towards him. He is heavyset and darkly silhouetted against the sheen of light cast upon the river. His gait is festinant, unsteady, poised at any moment to fall, he thinks. If the procurator didn't know any better, he might have thought the man drunk. He wears a head-covering that is tightly fitted against his scalp and that tapers to a point like a bullet. His hands are forced down into his pockets as though he is pushing his coat and the body it contains downwards, ensuring the forces of gravity will not fail him. His pace quickens a little, edging closer, stooping slightly, his centre of gravity lowering as he nears. He carries a rucksack slung over his back and in his hand a small metal blade which glints when it catches the light.

The procurator retreats further into the shadows under the bridge. Although this is the person for whom he has been waiting, a sense of panic grips him and he thinks of running. The lure of obscurity pervades his rapid thoughts. But he is too deep into the mire of the unfolding catastrophe, and he knows he will have to face the approaching man at some point. He stands his ground and braces himself. He views the river again, focusing on its gentle flow. Perhaps that is a way out; into its icy waters and out into the wide expanse of the estuary and thence the oceans? Free like a whale?

The dark figure now stands in front of him, and a clear and urgent thought comes to the procurator – that only four weeks ago they had not met and that now, in the shadows of the bridge, each depends on the other for a form of salvation; a form so different from that which he had envisaged.

'You know, I never meant for this to happen,' he says, shaking as he speaks, pausing before the word *happen*, the shame of his explanation barely hidden.

The other man remains impassive. He is, by virtue of his career in misconduct, better-placed to take the upper hand in this negotiation.

'But it did happen,' he says, with the experience of a criminal who is well-aware that actions have consequences.

'I didn't mean for you to kill him.' The procurator is becoming agitated, expressing the days of pent-up anger in a high-pitched whisper. 'You did kill him, didn't you?'

He has heard all about the crime in the newspapers and on the news channels on TV and has assumed this to be the case, but he needs it confirmed.

Peter exhales loudly. 'What did you want me to do?' he asks, looking over his shoulder.

The procurator looks in the direction of the other man's gaze but sees nothing. Peter continues to look over his shoulder at the far side of the river. The procurator sees several bin bags lined up against the wall on the opposite bank. Each one has a different shape, hiding its offensive cargo. He scans them nervously. If there were something lurking, it would likely be a rat, he thinks. The place must be infested with them.

Peter turns his head back to face the procurator, perhaps expecting an answer. The procurator is aware that every morsel of calm is being squeezed from him; he feels perilously close to his breaking point.

He looks down at Peter's left hand, remembering the shining object he was carrying. But his hands are now empty and the knife, if that is what it was, is now concealed.

'Look,' says the procurator, 'we've got to find a way to …' He is not sure what to say. The events that have occurred have been so far from what he originally conceived that he has no plan for their consequences. 'When I said we need to put an end to his work, I didn't mean by killing him.' His voice is louder now, and if anyone is passing over head, they might be able to make out the words; the harshness of the word *killing*, at the very least.

Peter pulls at his left sleeve, and the procurator takes a step back.

'Relax, man,' says Peter. 'I've slipped through their net so far.'

The procurator screws his eyes up and runs a hand through his hair. He can't fathom the psychology of the man before him. He is much calmer now than he seemed over the phone in the early hours of yesterday, almost blasé. He has the attitude of those hardened criminals who pass through the procurator's door, sure of themselves, mocking of authority. Yet the crime this man has committed goes so far beyond the transgressions of those others.

Peter steps forward. 'This is your problem now. You're up to your neck in this.' Then he says in a low, menacing voice, almost a whisper. 'If I get caught, you are going down with me.' He smiles and then slips out the knife from his sleeve, fingering it, rubbing its metal shaft, then holding it up at their eyeline, before putting it back in his pocket.

The procurator is frozen to the spot, unable to speak. He feels a coldness in his neck and shoulders and a heaviness in his chest.

Peter leans forward, a faint smile upon his lips, the smile of one who has the upper hand for the first time in days, maybe months. 'Bring me money,' he demands. 'I'll be back in two hours.' Then he turns and walks along the path away from the bridge, keeping to the shadows.

The procurator remains motionless. Then, when the man is out of sight, looks at his watch and starts running.

16

DI PRICE AND DS Hameed sit in a side room just off the main hall of the police station. They have a day of interviews ahead of them. One of them anticipates that the day will be fruitless, but the other reckons it to be their only lead in what is proving to be a challenging case. *Call it female intuition*, she implies in her attempt to summon up the even the smallest degree of enthusiasm in her senior partner.

'I really do think that his work is relevant,' she says, holding up a copy of the scientific paper on which the murdered man had been working at the time of his death. 'His wife says that he had been very distracted recently. The university had logged several incidents of possible intruders in the labs in the week prior to his death.'

She looks at DI Price, who nods, then yawns, making no effort to conceal his fatigue.

'Something funny was going on,' she continues.

'OK. Maybe you're right,' he replies, clearly unconvinced.

She hands him a piece of paper with a list of names.

'These are the laboratory team. We've got them all to come along and give statements. First up is John Breckenridge, postdoctoral scientist, and the last man to talk to the deceased, we think. They were on the train together but then walked separately to the university. He had already crossed the bridge at the time the murder was committed.'

'OK. Let's get him in,' replies DI Price, reading down the list. They will only get through a couple before the need for coffee hits.

DS Hameed steps outside the door, where a young man in a red shirt sits. She ushers him in.

'Mr Breckenridge?' says DI Price. 'Sorry, Dr Breckenridge?' he corrects himself.

The scientist nods. He is nervous, never having sat in a police station before.

'Relax,' says DS Hameed. 'These are routine parts of our enquiry. This is Detective Inspector Price, and I am Detective Sergeant Hameed. We want to know about your work, your relationship with the deceased and also the conversation you had with him on the train.'

Dr Breckenridge pushes up the glasses on his nose and then sweeps back his unruly fringe. He feels sweat on his forehead and his ears start to burn, as they have done since childhood whenever he finds himself being questioned by authority. He would have made a terrible criminal, he thinks.

DS Hameed smiles and continues. 'Tell us what you talked about on the train.'

Dr Breckenridge starts to talk, but his throat is dry, and he struggles to form his words. 'May I have some water?' he splutters out.

DS Hameed pours him a glass of water. He feels under scrutiny, despite not having done anything wrong. He notices the eyes of the DI are fixed on him, cold and suspecting. His heart starts to race and his hands tremble, so much so that as he puts the glass to his mouth, some runs down his chin and onto his shirt, immediately making a dark streak near the collar. The DI doesn't take his eyes off him, worsening his discomfort, his misfortune. He has the demeanour of one who is waiting for an error.

'Sorry,' says Dr Breckenridge, placing his hand on the damp patch, rubbing it gently. He collects himself and takes a deep breath. 'We talked about the paper we are writing in our research group. Our latest research finding which will, hopefully, be published soon.' He stops, reflecting on his words. Everything has changed now. The group leader is dead. Who knows what will become of the research group or the paper now? The whole team, emerging from the horror of the incident, is now in limbo.

'How did he seem to you?' asks DS Hameed. 'On the train,' she adds.

He thinks for a moment, not certain what she means. Is she trying to trap him into saying something he shouldn't?

'Much the same as usual, I think.'

'Did he seem nervous or anxious about anything?'

Dr Breckenridge thinks back to the morning journey. Perhaps he missed some signs that the man was in danger. The line of questioning is disturbing. He had no idea that the killing was anything other than a random event, but now the implication is that his boss was targeted.

'What would he be nervous about?' asks the scientist, feeling a drop of sweat form on his left temple and start to roll down his face.

The DI, silent until now except for the utterance of the interviewee's name, sits forward and says, 'You tell us?'

He then sits back and folds his arms, waiting for a story to be recanted. Dr Breckenridge wipes the sweat bead from his left cheek.

'I don't know what you're talking about.' He feels the eyes of the two police officers on him. He is surrounded by their suspicion, and a guilty feeling takes hold in him, born of illogicality, rising by the second as his silence buries him deeper in a hole of an outrageous fabrication.

'I don't know what you're talking about,' repeats Dr Breckenridge in a quiet, almost pathetic voice.

DS Hameed smiles.

'Look, you're not in any trouble. We just want to know what happened.'

Dr Breckenridge looks back and returns an unconvincing smile. He needs to get out of this interview, he thinks. He went in oblivious to the possibilities and now they are talking about trouble. He looks over to the senior police officer who is still sitting back, arms folded, awaiting his narrative. He feels his menacing persona, a man who has extracted the worst out of people, true or false, in the pursuit of his version of justice.

'Did you have much to do with the ethics committees relating to your work?' asks DS Hameed.

Dr Breckenridge nods and replies in the affirmative.

'What was your role?'

'I attended the ethics committee relating to the generation of immortalised cells.'

'Did the deceased attend the same committees?'

'Yes, he would have done.'

The DI uncrosses his arms and points at Dr Breckenridge: 'Would have done or did?' he asks.

The scientist looks at the pointing finger, in half a mind to tell the DI that he doesn't care for his gesticulation.

'Did,' he says meekly, reasoning that he will not win this battle of psychology, in which he is a novice.

DS Hameed shuffles some of the papers and takes out a photograph. It is a black and white image of a man's head and shoulders.

'Do you recognise this man, who was a member of one of the ethics committees?'

There is an instant recognition. 'Oh, him,' says Dr Breckenridge.

And suddenly, a connection is made in the mind of the interviewee and the two interviewers. None, at this moment, is clear regarding the precise link, but each now understands that the line of questioning is relevant. A moment of clarification has occurred. John Breckenridge feels some relief; the mysterious suspicion that was mounting upon him now seems deflected to another.

'Yes,' he says, once again feeling like the confident man who had entered the building a few minutes ago, 'the boss had trouble from him. He was eventually chucked off the ethics committee.'

'Do you know if the deceased had contact with this man after he was suspended from the committee?' asks the DI, now taking an encouraging tone.

'I don't know. He never mentioned it.'

The DI stands up. 'OK, thanks. You've been a great help.' He offers a hand and Dr Breckenridge shakes it limply.

'I'll show you out,' says DS Hameed, opening the door.

Dr Breckenridge follows the officer to the door. He is subdued, unsure whether he has been of assistance or merely a subject of castigation. He passes through a number of doors, each one opening only with the placing of a plastic card on a black sensor that beeps, then flashes, just for good measure.

Finally, they reach the outside door. Dr Breckenridge feels a sense of relief, his escape from his imagined custody complete. Then DS Hameed smiles at him, shakes his hand and thanks him once more.

17

WHY DOES AN irrational way of thinking gain such a level of prominence that it governs the lives of the masses? People seek a code of conduct, a common law to protect from the radical and the criminal. Yet a set of secular rules is often not enough. A spiritual basis for morality, based on the teachings of a cult figure and offering eternal salvation, is the most commonly followed. *I say to you, follow me and you will live forever even after the flesh has rotted.* So, it is death that drives religion. Or, more precisely, what happens after death. Death terrifies and fascinates. The prospect of a life outside of this wretched and material domain entices the world-weary. Living, or not living (the verb for such a way of *being* is not defined in earthly realms), in a paradise of God's heavenly court is worth the worship, the dedication and the doubt. Heaven, being a place of love, peace and community, is the driver for belief, without which religion cannot exist. Those admitted to heaven will be given new bodies without disease, injury, age or sin. The potential to be born again, to have a new start, is worth the suffering of the mortal life. People tolerate punishment and misery only when something better awaits them. A belief system without an afterlife cannot rely on blind faith. Death, therefore, becomes crucial to religion. Attaining a place in heaven depends most crucially on death and, so, if death were not to happen, heaven would not exist, and religion would become redundant. Hoards of the unholy would roam the earth for all eternity, festering in the crowds, damned by their iniquities.

The sun sparkles on the river. The fugitive is downstream from the city, an escapee from its oppressive bustle. Here, all is calm. Clouds float by serenely, in no hurry to pass over the unobservant walkers who stroll the riverbank. Grey wading birds scamper among the rocks of the shore, pecking in the cracks, and a heron stands tall on the opposite bank, motionless, fooling the fish into thinking it presents no threat. Swallows, the first of the year, dart in the blue sky, their path dictated by the swarming of lesser beasts.

The squat grey birds, having reached the end of the shore, turn and head, in unison, back on themselves, this time forming a line, as though they are combing the beach for evidence. The heron cranes its neck downwards to the surface of the river and then flexes its long legs, stepping forward towards a large rock, from where it can watch the passage of its prey. The sun slips behind a cloud and the river becomes dull and brown. A light foam, formed by the churning of the shallows on the rough riverbed, floats and then disperses.

The fugitive watches the natural world, devoid of complexity, with a sense of bitterness. He envies the bird that flies as part of a flock, governed by an innate sense of duty to others in the group. He remembers being told that a flock of geese flying in a V-formation will change positions periodically, so that they all share the burden of being the leader: the one at the point of the V, the position of the greatest air resistance. One for all.

He lies back against a bank of earth and takes a book from his coat pocket, flicking through its well-fingered pages. It is the copy of *The Chronicles of John Corn* given to him by the strange lawyer at their first meeting. Amongst the back pages is distributed the two hundred pounds in notes given to him last night by the same man, a generous offering and more than he had expected. He knows this munificence has been made to keep him quiet, to allow him to live incognito for as long as it takes for things to die down, a hopeful bribe. Some has been spent already. He has feasted for the first time since the event on the bridge and now his belly feels too full. For reasons of which he is not certain, he feels a shame in his satiety. The last few days have been devoid of much emotion. Mere survival has filled his thoughts overwhelmingly, so to now experience this sentiment, generated within his gut, is curious. He slumps further down in his makeshift seat. The book falls from his hand. He feels total fatigue, as if the effort of picking up the book would be too much for him. His feelings flood back to him, having been repressed for too long. He is experiencing what it is to live again. Perhaps to exist in a repressed state would be better, he reasons, but he knows he has no control over this.

A large black crow lands on the ground a few metres from his feet. It eyes him, weighing up the likelihood of a few morsels of food, then pecks at the ground before flying off.

He picks up the book and again looks through his pages. Despite not even having heard of the book four weeks ago, he has now read it twice in its entirety and certain sections over and over again. He is looking for a particular passage. He stops at a few lines that have been underlined with a soft grey pencil mark:

… the dialogue of the tormented. Take from me my arm, infest my skin with the pox, let the leech suck my fetid bile. But take not the essence of my mind. Though I may sing to God in open congregation amongst a throng of Godly men, I act by my own self to take this step of salvation. Only a higher force can take away this precious gift of mortality …

He reads again, this time aloud, repeating the final few words.

A dog whose lead trails behind him runs along the opposite bank followed by an irate owner who, upon catching his charge admonishes the beast. The dog stops, bracing itself for punishment. The owner picks up the lead and pulls it violently, lifting the dog by the neck. Then, as though making sure that his act of brutality on the dumb animal has not been witnessed, he looks across the river at the form of the man propped up against the earth bank. At first, the impression formed is of unconsciousness, or worse, but as the man stares the form on the far bank moves and then rises to his feet. Man and dog move on.

The fugitive replaces the book in his coat pocket and climbs the earth bank back onto the main footpath. *This precious gift of mortality*, he repeats to himself, looking along the path first to the left and then to the right. He takes the route to the left, heading back towards the city.

He feels the draw of the city. For centuries, thousands have sought to make a living in the narrow streets and closely packed buildings, attracted by the industry of the collected masses. Communities, albeit separated by the river for many years, have thrived in the feeling of a common neighbourhood. Wealth has been created and, with it, crimes and injustices. The city moves on, dragging its people in whichever direction it sees fit. The environment of the city provides a place of refuge and a place to hide: the anonymity of crowds.

And so, walking slowly and checking over his shoulder every few steps, the fugitive feels the need to re-enter the city. In a manner that seems anomalous, he feels it is the best place to remain undetected. He still has an innate conviction that he will be able to escape the punishment of his crime. He knows that most crimes are solved early on if they are solved at all. It has been over five days since he stabbed the man on Galahad Bridge. Those seeking vengeance for the act appear clueless to his whereabouts. His apprehension is not imminent. The closest he has come to generating suspicion was on the night of the incident, when all were on high alert. The receptionist at the hostel where he stayed that night had suspected some impropriety in his behaviour – of that he had little doubt. And yet, he was able to hide behind the general air of crisis in which every action was interpreted with alarm.

He walks along the riverbank, following the gentle bend in its course, and views the bridge, the site of the murder. People are walking across it, and there is no indication now of the carnage that unfolded a few days ago. The sun shines and reflects intensely off the white stone of the bridge. He passes several houseboats tethered tightly to the capstans that are placed at short intervals along the path. Many are bedecked with pots full of flowers in bloom, and a bicycle hangs precariously off the back of a brightly painted boat. A rowing boat bobs gently behind one of the houseboats.

A man runs by. Approaching from behind, the fugitive hears him only at the last moment and is startled by his presence. He flinches and stumbles to the side, losing his footing for an instant. The runner puffs on by, but looks back and raises a hand in apology. He has alarmed the walker, but he will never know the reason why the man who is now rejoining the path is so on edge. The runner heads up a small track leading away from the river and is gone.

The fugitive looks around once more before continuing towards the bridge. He is less than a hundred metres from the structure now. The scene is like a picture postcard, pleasant sunshine glinting off water that portrays a hazy reflection of the bridge, suggestive of an idyll of English life. This is the England of the movies and the old-style books that describe a social hierarchy and a sense of duty. This is the city that offers up its citizens to uphold the order of the old world, to fight progress and change. This is the river that has flowed quietly since the city's early settlement and has seen it all.

The fugitive stops and sits at a bench. He needs to find some way of breaking the deadlock of his escape, he thinks, or else he will be wandering forever. He has sought guidance from the man who put him up to the mission from which he is now fleeing, but the man has changed his tune and no longer wishes to be part of the revolution he craved. Only the day before the fateful event, the two had met and discussed the philosophy that drove their brief acquaintance. He had thought the man – that strange lawyer – committed to a cause, but now the lawyer's cowardice is all that remains and he, this wretched fugitive from the law, has nowhere to turn. He is caught between turning on the man and continuing to hide, seeking out more elaborate ways to stay undetected.

He notices two police cars parked at the end of the bridge on the far side. He wonders if this is a sign, being prone, of late, to seeking significance in everyday events. His fatigue and his hunger have intensified these feelings. A man who is broken capitulates to ideas of conspiracy with alacrity. Several police officers leave their cars and walk to the central part of the bridge. One is dressed all in white, head covered, face masked. He carries a large suitcase, silver, that reflects rays of sunlight, causing episodic flashes. Another policeman, dressed in a short-sleeved shirt, is looking over the edge of the bridge. He feels the brickwork and then leans over as though inspecting the underside of the bridge. A colleague joins him. Clearly, they have seen something that warrants the attention of two officers. After a minute, they both stand up and look down the river in the direction of the fugitive. The taller man, who has put down his walkie-talkie and taken out a notebook, appears to be instructing his colleague, who nods and takes out his own notebook. The two of them stand still, almost to attention. Then the taller man raises his arm and points directly at the fugitive.

18

IN THE DAYS preceding the brutal murder of the scientist, the newspapers had carried reports of huge numbers of dead fish washing up on the banks of a river in the north-western region of the county, where the confluence of smaller tributaries occurs, in the foothills of the mountains that protect the city from the chilling effects of the sea winds. Scientific sources had investigated this phenomenon and decided their deaths were due either to a pollutant (although none was specifically identified) or the warming of the waters to levels incompatible with piscine life. Thousands of fish of all sizes lay dead on the banks of the river for a stretch of over two miles. Council officials contracted pest controllers to shovel the carcasses into lorries to be taken for incineration. The smell of fish lingered on the banks of the river and in the air of the whole county for days.

Many read these reports with concern and even sought out proof its occurrence, going down to the riverbanks to inspect the scene of devastation. They couldn't help but be shocked by such a sight and, faced with such a spectacle, some even sought an explanation in terms of fate and destiny. Thus, these modern-day augurs placed particular significance on the event. Those who seek messages from a higher force based on the behaviour of animals are not going to be unimpressed by such a display of nature. This was precisely what they had been waiting for; a sign that their God was not pleased. The unleashing of further natural calamities was divined.

And so, the murder of a prominent scientist who had been researching immortality is linked to piles of dead fish. Soon, numerous other phenomena – deemed unholy and against the natural order – are linked, and a pattern of earthly disasters is taken as proof of the scorn of God: a man wins the lottery twice in the space of a month, at odds of a billion to one; a goat gives birth to a two-headed kid; offal sold by a provincial butcher's shop contains a silver coin from the reign of King George, deep within the stomach of the slaughtered beast; a triple rainbow is sighted off the coast, forming its three arcs over the Bear's Head lighthouse. All these events have occurred contemporaneously to the murder and are now seen as evidence. Believers brace themselves for what is to come. Stories and prophecies now spread like wildfire through the great medium of unchecked speculation.

The procurator, reading these reports in a tabloid newspaper, lays down his glasses and contemplates his role in these events. He has thought of little else in the past few days. He is obsessed and oppressed by these thoughts.

A knock at the door disturbs his thinking and his secretary enters. She is dour faced, and clearly something has upset her.

'Your 2:30 is here. In the meeting room,' she says, placing a folder of notes on his desk and shuffling out. He looks at the name on the folder and makes his way to the meeting.

The man he finds in the room is the epitome of ill health The procurator has met him before a few years back and formed the opinion then that his decrepitude was as a result of a series of unremitting poor decisions. Beside the man is his walking frame, built of reinforced steel to resist the tensile forces that his bulk places upon it. His belly bulges over his elasticated trousers, and he is unashamed of the exposure of flesh between the bottom of his tight-fitting t-shirt and the ill-defined region of his waistline. Around his neck, he keeps a pendant, dull-grey with a large red button in the centre, used for calling others should he find himself in distress; a necessity for one who cannot control the descent of his life.

The procurator glances at the man and then at the notes

concerning his case, which he holds in his hand at arm's length. He calculates the man's age from the date of birth written on the front sheet. Only three years older in chronology than himself but aged beyond these years. Then again, three years is a long time, and, given his current predicament, the procurator has no inkling what the next three years may look like.

The client starts coughing; a rattling, unexpurgated emission, causing revulsion in the already judgemental mind of the procurator. The man won't see out the next three years. *No big loss*, the procurator thinks.

After his expectorations have ceased, the man starts to reel off the number of hardships he has experienced since their last meeting. His staccatoed words are interspersed with a harsh expiratory wheeze. Even the simple act of speaking makes him breathless and turns his lips a shade of purple. At regular intervals, he stops talking, breathing heavily, almost panting. He is hopeful that his counsel, his defender in the court of law, will take the points he makes and use them to reduce the likelihood of conviction, but instead he sees a glazed look in the lawyer's eyes, a blankness born of fatigue and anxiety. He continues anyway, and the procurator continues not to listen. The mind of the lawyer is elsewhere. Despite the ongoing narrative from the obese man, he checks his phone for the latest text message, which has been heralded by a single *ping*. It is from the fugitive.

Suddenly, the procurator is on edge. He looks up and glances at the door expecting an imminent threat. His pulse quickens and he feels an odd sensation in the middle of his abdomen, as though some peritoneal implements were churning up his insides. Some compare this feeling to internal butterflies, but the beast inside is far-removed from the beauty and delicate nature of this winged creature. At any moment, he feels, a diabolic animal will emerge from his abdomen, baring sharp teeth, thirsting for revenge. The fat man continues to talk, but his words continue to fall unheard. The procurator looks down at the screen of the phone in dread. He reads the message and at the same time feels a hot prickling in his neck rising to his cheeks. It says: *TONIGHT MIDNIGHT SAME PLACE.*

He touches his forehead, wet with sweat, and then rubs his fingers across the left eyebrow, channelling the moisture away from his eye. The man sitting in front of him gabbles on and the procurator hears the word *custody*, which seems so out of place, such a bizarre word. The talker repeats his last sentence, then watches for a reaction. He gets none. He stops and leans forward, his centre of gravity shifting, making his chair creak.

'Mr George,' he says, 'are you listening to me?'

The procurator, on hearing his name, looks at the man and replies simply: 'No.'

Stunned by the bluntness of his lawyer's response, the fat man merely stares, unable to form a coherent retort.

Outside the window, the view from which is obscured by partially closed venetian blinds, a car pulls up and rapid, decisive footsteps are heard: two people, by the sound of it, one likely a man in clumpy boots, the other a woman in shoes which give a higher pitch when colliding with the dull tarmac. The procurator, being one who is convinced that the vicissitudes of life are indeed driven by fate, comprehends that these people who are now knocking on the door of his office are wanting to talk to him about the event of a few days ago.

With a second moment of panic striking him, this time relating to a different threat, he leaves the room abruptly, leaving the client still sitting, mouth agape, like a stranded cetacean waiting to be rescued by firemen with buckets of water. The procurator has no idea where he should go, save for the notion that leaving the room, which is entered via a door emblazoned with his name, post-nominals and job title, is a good move. He enters the kitchen area and lurks behind a cabinet positioned at head height. From here he can just about view the reception area, where two people stand, their backs to him – unmistakably a man and a woman, confirming his auditory suspicions from seconds before. The receptionist is stonewalling, he thinks (or rather hopes), but after a short period of resistance he sees her stand up and point in the direction of his office.

From this moment he knows he is trapped. He remains in the kitchen, since he is unable to enact the instinct to flee because of a fear that has rendered him rooted to the spot. He capitulates. Before long, DI Price and DS Hameed discover him, pale and shaking, holding a mug of cold water in his hand.

19

HE IS PALE, and a dull, grey tone hangs on the areas of his face on which the bright light shines. Deep recesses have formed beneath his eyes, reflecting his mode of living in recent times, his sleepless days and nights.

His head throbs. Sitting at the table, alone, he tries to focus on his breathing, regulating its intake and exhalation, so as to appear calm. Breathing too rapidly will cloud his thoughts and lead to panic. He was prone to hyperventilation in his youth and used to carry a paper bag around with him – for all the good it did. His hands are clammy, and he waves them below the desk to dry off lest he needs to shake the hands of his accusers. Dampness would send a message of guilt, he figures. He knows how lie detectors circumvent the cunning mind to betray the unconscious admission of culpability.

He notices for the first time that a large clock on the wall, numbered with black Roman numerals, has stopped at a time of five past eleven. Either broken or out of battery, it has displayed this time since he was escorted to the room twenty minutes or so ago – although he is not sure how long he has been seated in this austere room. He is aware that the perception of time is altered at times of such anxiety. Perhaps the broken clock is a ploy to upset the points of reference for the accused as they sit in the interrogation room. It is saying that time is irrelevant; time will not save you from your fate; we have all the time in the world. We have the time.

The police officers enter the room, one placing a laptop computer on the desk, the other a sheaf of papers in a brown card folder. The male policeman immediately glances at the clock, and then looks at his own watch.

'I think the clock is broken,' he says in a low, almost whispering voice. This seems to upset him, since the chronology of events is of such importance to those in the profession of solving crimes. The other police officer, a young, neatly dressed woman, repeats the action of her colleague by studying two timepieces in the same fashion and then nods in agreement.

'It is 3 pm exactly,' she says.

The two exchange confirmatory glances, then look at the man in front of them.

'Mr George,' begins the junior colleague, 'we would like to talk to you in connection with the killing on Galahad Bridge that occurred three days ago.'

The procurator feels the pounding in his head increase.

'You are not under arrest, nor are you suspected of any crime, but we feel you may have important information which may be of relevance to our enquiries,' she continues.

Her expression is impassive, and the procurator is unsure whether she is trying to threaten or is genuinely being encouraging to him. He nods.

'Detective Inspector Price will ask some questions. You are free to leave at any point, and you are also entitled to take up our offer of legal representation, should you wish.'

She stops and looks at her colleague, inviting him to speak. The senior police officer clears his throat then looks again at the clock.

'Mr George, what were your connections to the murdered man?'

Brian George, self-proclaimed procurator of the city of New Canterbury, has known from the moment that he heard of the crime – in all its shocking glory – that he would need to answer this very question. From the moment he first heard commotion in the streets, saw the running people and heard the utterances of his secretary, confused and terrified, who told of a brutal stabbing on Galahad Bridge, a stone's throw from where she stood; that moment when the whole spectrum of his life's potential became focused into one point, there had been only one question in his mind.

'Mr George, what were your connections to the murdered man?'

The words, spoken a second time, surprise him. They seem a baffling utterance – his name articulated in the same sentence as the word *murdered*. It seems the words should not be placed together; it feels to him like an accusation. He stares back at the two officers, wide-eyed, summoning an explanation from the chaos of his reasoning.

What was his connection to the man? The truth (if indeed it exists) and his frenzied conjectures have become so jumbled that there is no answer to the surly officer's question. His rehearsed response has, in the heat of interrogation, vanished into a muddle of absurdity and non sequiturs. He is completely unprepared.

'I don't … I'm not,' he starts, now entirely unsure what line to take: deny any involvement, or at least any recollection of his previous interactions with the man, or openly discuss the ethics committee confrontation, which is, he presumes, the reason they are questioning him. To obfuscate or to lay all the cards on the table? This is the dilemma of everyone accused who has something to hide; one which each one will ponder every hour, if not every minute, long before any apprehension or accusation, and one which is accompanied by sleepless nights spent going over the ramifications of each line of defence. And yet, when faced with the question, the procurator's mind is blank.

The DI looks at him intently, waiting for a formulated response, and is surprised by the initial spluttered output. The man is a lawyer, after all. He must have prepared some defence.

'I met him a few times,' says the procurator, deciding that any other tack would be too incriminating. He settles on the strategy of downplaying his connection.

'Yes?' the DI raises his eyebrows.

'Only once or twice,' continues the procurator. He is marginally more composed now, conjuring up the persona of himself defending another, an act he has performed on countless previous occasions. *Imagine you are in the courtroom*, he tells himself. He glances at the police inspector. *I've met your type before*, his mind tells him: *all swagger and no substance. Put up the weakest of contradiction and you'll capitulate.*

DI Price is impatient. 'What were the circumstances of your meeting?' he asks tersely, looking down at the pile of papers before him.

The procurator is quiet, eyes lowered, his mind calculating, yet coming to incompatible conclusions: *You've got nothing on me. I've done nothing wrong. I didn't kill the man.* His momentary feeling of confidence has now departed. By nature a fatalist concerning the direction of his life, he can see no route through the current predicament other than one which will end badly.

DI Price taps his fingers against the desk. 'What were the circumstances of your meeting?' he repeats, now a few decibels louder.

The procurator looks up at his interrogators.

'Look,' he says, 'maybe I should have a lawyer present. I don't like the line of questioning you're taking.'

DI Price, visibly angry, turns over a piece of paper in front of him and then slams his hand down.

'Fine,' he says, nodding at his partner before stomping out of the room, muttering inaudible terms.

20

It is midnight. The night is cold, and few stars sparkle in the sky. A cat, scrawny and lame, lies on the towpath, moonlight reflecting off its smooth black coat. A blackbird looks on, screeching its displeasure at the presence of the predator, warning of the imminent threat, albeit one so supine, so inactive. Another alarm, this time manmade, sounds in the distance, a high-pitched whine indicating some infringement of lawful order. Even with the half-awake consciousness of one who has not slept for days, the fugitive is aware that something is wrong. The place is not safe, he tells himself; something is wrong, something is rotten. A part of him no longer cares and will concede to his fate and the prospect of a night's sleep. That part is ready to walk to the nearest police station and hand himself in, declaring his culpability concerning the matter that has consumed the days and nights of so many. Would he really give up his freedom for a night's sleep? The spark of survival tells him that the rendezvous with the lawyer is not going to happen and that he should get as far away from their proposed meeting place as possible.

He hears a rustling in the bushes to his left, followed by the scurrying of a small creature – a rat, no doubt – which runs along the path before dropping down into the canal. He looks in the direction of the city, from where sparkling lights, some blue, some red, mesmerise him. They are both alluring and terrifying, an urban contradiction generated by the complex lives of those within the boundaries of the city. The longer he stands here, by the shimmering canal, the more he feels the presence of others. More than just the rats and the cats, he is certain that he is being observed by people, each one with a purpose: his subjugation.

His resolve to stay, to see this through, finally snaps. He runs. He runs away from the sparkling lights and the noise of the alarm, along the towpath, under the old railway bridge and, from there, up into the old wood that borders Briar Bank and through which runs the gentle River Cal, a tributary of the mighty river running through the city.

At the same moment that the fugitive enters this woodland, sheltered for now by its dense overhead foliage, the police officers appear at the canal bank. Difficulties with the fleet of patrol cars, two of which had flat tyres (an almost unheard-of occurrence: a co-incidence, or maybe an attempt at coercion by forces linked to this unusual investigation) meant that they were late on the scene. DI Price, the officer in charge of the intended apprehension, curses when they arrive at an empty scene. They have scrutinised calls and messages and worked out that this was to be the rendezvous point between two suspects in the case, one of whom was undoubtedly scared off the meeting by their earlier intrusion into his workplace. The other suspect, whose identity is unknown to the police, however, is unlikely to have realised that the pieces of the case are falling into place, so has no reason not to turn up. There have been no messages to or from Brian George since the one which read TONIGHT MIDNIGHT SAME PLACE. And yet there is no one here.

DI Price curses for a second time, hearing from a subordinate that he has just questioned another in the vicinity, who reports a man running off in the direction of the woods. He radios the command for all units to carry out a search of the woods, but he suspects that the man for whom they are searching has already departed the area and is now in hiding somewhere else. They can but try. This is their only lead, and they can't afford to lose the man, whoever he may be.

After radioing this command, his short, barked words making his mood apparent to all those subordinate to him, he issues a further order: the apprehension of the lawyer, the procurator as he calls himself, suspect number one. 'Bring him in for further questioning,' he tells an officer back at the station. His manner does not disguise his frustration at a failed operation.

'Shall I charge him, sir?' comes back the response, crackling down the radio waves.

'Just hold him for now and I'll speak to him when I get back.'

The radio line goes silent, but the message has been received. Any moment now, the lawyer will be woken from his sleep – if indeed he is asleep, which seems doubtful, given the thoughts that must be racing around his mind – and escorted to the police station. It is now gone midnight, yet the night has just begun for those scouring the unwholesome environment of the riverbank, a likely site for a crime or the hiding place of a criminal.

From the undergrowth bordering the canal towpath, a police officer emerges holding a rectangular object, which he gives to DI Price. It is a book, the lower corner of its front cover battered and torn.

'*The Chronicles of John Corn*,' reads DI Price, turning the face of the book in the direction of the towpath's dim lighting. 'Where did you find this?'

The officer points in the direction of a bush, an indeterminate form in the darkness.

'There's also a blanket and a bag full of rubbish,' he adds, placing little significance on the finding, such is the nature of the area: a dumping ground for all manner of human debris. The book, however, is an unusual finding. DI Price leafs through the pages to determine whether anything, a bus ticket or a shop receipt, for instance, is hidden within the pages. Finding nothing extraneous within the pages, he is about to toss it back into the bushes, but stops to read a few lines from a randomly selected page. At this moment, he fails to see the significance of the words on the pages, and closes the book.

'Could be anyone's,' he says to the other officer. Feeling a sense of duty and a dislike of littering, born of a childhood filled with obedience and order, he does not throw the book away, but puts it in the pocket of his long grey overcoat.

A radio message comes through, telling him that the other members of his team have reached the woods and are searching the site. He doesn't hold much hope of them finding anything of significance. The man they seek seems as elusive as the wind, a force unable to be captured. He pulls the coat collar up around his neck, feeling the chill of the late night, and then heads back to the road and a waiting police car that will take him to the station. He yawns and rubs his eyes. A night of interrogation awaits.

21

THE PROCURATOR IS not asleep when the police turn up to his house, an austere brick-faced abode on the outskirts of the city, a short walk from the law offices where he practises. He has lived there for ten years but he feels no sense of home. The walls remain drab and there is little ornament. The furniture is functional. He lives alone and has considered getting a cat or maybe a dog but has remained in unsettled solitude. He observes those around him – his neighbours with whom he has no more interaction than an occasional greeting – and feels an oppressive expectation of conformity: the well-mowed lawn, the clipped hedge. Until a few weeks ago, he envisaged this future precisely. He was slipping into suburban anonymity. But all that changed with the events on the bridge, when a man died and panic gripped the land.

He is looking out of the front window into the streetlamp-lit street when the police car pulls up. It arrives without fanfare, almost surreptitiously, sneaking up, wanting no trouble. He has expected this for several hours, has indeed rehearsed this instant in the recesses of his mind. He has considered on multiple occasions what he might do at this moment. Initially, thinking his home a sanctuary, he imagines a barricade in the manner of the olden-day's oppressed, who would flee to the crypts of the local church and rely on the godliness of their pursuers not to break the code of conduct relating to ecclesiastical safe havens. But his house holds no such sanctity, and the police will not hesitate to break in should they need to, brandishing their tools of subjugation, like the reivers in the border lands who would think nothing of destroying anything in their sight, capturing for the sake of capturing.

Then he considers fleeing, getting as far from here as possible. But he thinks again, understanding that the anxiety of ceding all control would be too much for him. At least he can control the flow of information when he is in the thick of it. He thrives on conflict – at least, that is what he used to think. His choice of career had been a recognition of this: the combative nature of courtrooms, the act of arguing in a form of academic gladiatorial contest was highly suitable. When he was making life and career choices as a youngster, those close to him had agreed. He rarely stopped to think of the lives of those he defended or prosecuted. Some had advised him when he had started that this was the best way: *don't get involved in their sob stories, just do your job.* Yet it is very different on the other side. Now he is the accused the art of law loses its sheen. The egotist in him is now marooned in a world he cannot recognise. He has often observed that the self-important navigate the courtrooms with the utmost of difficulty, failing to comprehend that the law is not built around them. Now he is that man.

In the end, he settles for capitulation. He waits for the police officers to walk up the gravel path to his front door, just after midnight while all around him sleep. In the moments between the car pulling up and the sound of approaching footsteps, he even considers tidying up for his guests. Perhaps he should offer them some tea?

The absurdity of these thoughts is broken by a knock on the door. He presumes they do not ring the doorbell because of the hour, wanting to keep a sense of decorum and a calmness to aid the swift completion of their project. No point rattling the cage of a frightened animal.

He gets up and approaches the door, stopping momentarily by the mirror in the hallway to assess his appearance. He is unsure of the reason for this. Perhaps an ingrained mantra inherited from his mother to look presentable at all times. He opens the door.

Outside, two men stand, clad in the black of their office. One wears a constable's helmet and the other carries a torch, which shines an ellipsoid shape on the ground.

The other steps forward. 'Mr George,' he says, 'would you come with us?'

The lawyer nods, steps outside and pulls the door shut behind him.

The two policemen exchange a confused glance. They are not expecting this. An exclamation of surprise, the demand for an explanation, some form of resistance, or at least a word or two of assent is the norm. But not this man, who is taciturn and unemotional. They hesitate on the doorstep as though in a stand-off, yet one where both parties are in agreement.

The constable with the torch breaks the deadlock by shining it on the path as an indication of the route the lawyer needs to take down to the car. Not that any other route is possible, but it has the desired effect. The policemen realise they are not going to get any trouble and are happy to remain silent. They imagine the man doesn't want to wake the neighbours. This is a nice neighbourhood. Few lights are on. For law-abiding citizens, this is a time to sleep.

The lawyer reaches the car and waits for one of the policemen to open the door, in a manner suggesting to the officers of law that their man has already taken on the mantle of the vanquished. One obliges, and the lawyer slips silently into the back seat, buckling his own seat belt. The constable, who has now removed his helmet in order to sit comfortably in the car, notices this act of locking up and smiles at his colleague. The car drives off with its three passengers and the quiet street sleeps on.

Only one other man in the street is awake and has observed the incident. The pastry chef in the house directly opposite is prone to insomnia and has recently had a lot on his plate (a pun he often utters in his role as a man who puts things on the plates of others), such that he only sleeps in short bursts. There being nothing on the television, he happened to be staring out of the window at the time the policemen arrived. He has observed a fox in the front garden of his house for the past few nights and has been hoping to glimpse it again, but has found himself even more interested by the sight of his neighbour – a lawyer, no less – being driven off.

For a second or two, he connects the arrival of the officers with the recent event on the bridge. These are strange times, and the police are everywhere, it seems, rooting out the evil in society, which has reached extreme levels. However, he quickly reasons that they have taken him to defend a client, since he is unable to think beyond the occupation of the man. It doesn't even cross his mind that neighbour might be the criminal. He regards the seriousness of his neighbour as being good enough to mark him down forever as a man of law. He will ask him next time he sees him, he decides, although they have barely said a word to each other in the years they have both lived their own versions of suburban solitude. He goes back to looking out for the fox for a few minutes before returning to bed and forgetting about the whole incident.

As the pastry chef dozes off, contented that the order of the world, or at least the order of the street, seems appropriate, the lawyer and his captors arrive at the police station. The lights burn brightly throughout the building, which is still a hive of activity despite the hour. The officer on the reception desk presses the button to allow them admittance to the inner sanctum of the station. He looks very young to the lawyer, who often thinks about such things these days, being at the plateau of his middle age. He wonders if it is a sign of his own decrepitude, or an indication that he is slipping into judging on the basis of gerontocracy.

He is directed into a small room with no windows. The policemen do not follow and close the door after he has entered. A simple table and white plastic chairs are the only furniture. A large clock ticks on the bare wall. On the table, a single blank sheet of paper has been placed at an angle to the edge of the table in a manner that appears haphazard. A black pen rests upon the sheet. The lawyer is on edge and notices the asymmetry of the objects. He looks for clues in everything, of late, seeking some kind of reassurance, he assumes, that the laws of mathematics, which never lie, are upheld. To think otherwise would be proof that the deeds of an unholy being are being wrought upon the world. The mystics have always observed shapes and patterns. They believed that order would negate the ambiguities of a demonic force and perhaps make sense of the inherent irregularity of the world, which is built on chance and random events.

He waits. The clock ticks ever more loudly. He feels a wave of tiredness. It is pushing down on the top of his head, heavy and all-consuming. In the corridor beyond the door, he hears footsteps, some sharp and shrill, others trudging. Occasionally he hears words spoken, soft mumblings of indiscernible, likely indiscrete phrases concerning the nature of maleficence. This is the verbal currency of those tasked with upholding order in all its muffled inexactitude; this is the vocabulary of those who have so much to conceal.

The door opens and a man, whom the lawyer recognises immediately as one of the police officers who had questioned him earlier in the day, enters. He looks haggard, heavy skin folds languishing beneath his eye sockets. A pale waxiness, exaggerated by the strong light, shines off his face. If this man had instead been on his side of the desk – had been one of the clients he defended – the lawyer would not have been surprised.

The police officer yawns, doing nothing to conceal the act, not even placing a hand over his mouth out of politeness. The yawn is deep-rooted, born of the fatigue of a job that necessitates irregular hours and countless shifts of unremunerated overtime. This is a man who has given up trying to mitigate the effect it is having on his body. He has the look of a beaten man.

'So, we meet again,' says the police officer with little enthusiasm, sitting down at the same time. He places his mobile phone on the table. Then, noticing the piece of paper, he picks it up and inspects its blank form. He frowns, then replaces the paper.

'Mr George,' he says. 'I'm struggling to understand your place in all this mess.'

The lawyer smiles courteously before placing his hands on the table and leaning forward.

'Am I under arrest?' he asks, before adding, 'officer.'

'Would you like to be?'

This confuses the lawyer. The question is an odd one and, presumably, designed to wrong-foot him. He has ascertained that the policeman is an unconventional type, one not bothered by the odd rule bend, even an occasional breaking of the law. In his experience, these are often the easiest to deal with. By focusing on the investigation and the deviations from protocol, rather than the misdemeanour itself, he has had many cases thrown out. They hardly ever learn. A man of law who thinks the end justifies the means is misguided.

'I don't think that's a relevant question,' he replies.

'What is a relevant question?'

The lawyer is becoming irritated.

'Look, officer. I don't know what you are talking about. You know, as well as I do, that you need to arrest me in order to keep me here, and at the very least you need to allow me access to legal advice.'

The police officer picks up the paper once again and inspects it, before folding it in half and placing it back in its original position.

'Mr George, I am arresting you on suspicion of being an accessory to the murder on Galahad Bridge.'

22

HE SITS IN the cell, his whitewashed cavern, windowless and illuminated by a single light bulb, which is constant and yet gives the illusion of a flicker. *How have I arrived at this point*, he wonders, noticing a crack in the far wall, the tiniest of imperfections in a room whose purpose was uniformity. An obtuse thought comes into his head – a hackneyed joke, the punchline of which runs: *I wouldn't start from here if I were you.* But he had started, blind and unknowing, all those years ago, just as everyone does – and everyone ends up somewhere. He knows this is no time for jokes, though; it is a time for reflection. There is little else to do.

His early life had been *comfortable*. Even now, he imagines that will be the adjective applied to his upbringing by the newspapers reporting his connection with the dreadful crime that has gripped the nation. His parents had both been dentists, his father working as a lecturer and researcher for a large, red-bricked university. When he was of an age to take an interest in his parent's careers, albeit only as a subject for a quaint school project, he had been confused at this job description, thinking that all there was to know about teeth must surely have been figured out by now, thus rendering a researcher in dentistry redundant. Clean your teeth, fill them, remove them. That was about it, as far as he could tell. His father had attempted to educate him in his line of work, but he had never understood the precise nature of it, both due to a lack of interest but also a deeper inherent rebellion against the occupation towards which he felt he was being pushed for his own eventual career.

Naturally dental hygiene had been a large part of his life – at least until his early teens, when the grip of his parents had been relaxed because of his discovery of autonomy and angst-ridden attitudes. His parents had regularly sat him in the big blue reclining chair for as long as he could remember, masked and talking in riddles about the emerging molars and canines, pouncing on any imperfection and correcting whatever needed correcting before the problem became too large. He had started to feel like an experiment in acquiring perfection in dentistry, keeping his teeth pristine for the whole of his long life. Yet people live happily without teeth, he began to think, and then say, when the monthly checks were becoming an obsession. As he grew older, he thought, but didn't say, that it was his mind and his happiness they should be looking after rather than his ridiculous smile. He kept this to himself, since he initially had no desire to hurt his parents and had taken to suffering in silence. He knew they wouldn't understand anyway, being fixated on only one aspect of his pubertal development.

This fixation, of course, led to rebellion, and he stopped all aspect of dental hygiene. His parents couldn't force him to clean his teeth, he knew that, and it was his way of exerting some influence over his own destiny. A life so regimented was bound to fall apart, and he had worked out pretty early on that having dirty, caries-ridden teeth was the optimal way to repay his parents for the years of unhappiness they had inflicted on him. He watched as they despaired and failed to comprehend his actions, yet, at the same time, he never felt any sense of remorse, not even the slightest. He had become hard, uncompromising and imbued with an obsession to be different. Punishment of others delighted him like nothing else ever had. On his fifteenth birthday, he ran away from home and ended up miles away, in a small seaside town which was as bleak as the place from which he had fled, if not bleaker. Within hours, he had been retrieved by his mother who cried all the way back in the car, her eyes red by the time they arrived home, her pleading at a fever pitch. He had been promised the earth on that journey, even the autonomy to decide his own degree of oral hygiene, provided he wouldn't run away again. They had patched up their relationship, at least for the time being, and he returned to suburban conformity, even cleaning his teeth twice a day, which he had craved anyway since the moment he had stopped, abhorring the feeling (and smell) of his unclean mouth. Oral hygiene was, however, never mentioned again; both sides backing off the subject for fear of some form of relapse. Brushes and toothpaste were deposited surreptitiously in his bathroom, this family's own version of the tooth fairy (which had never featured in the infant's life). It was a ritual of lives skirting around each other for fear of fragmentation.

The peep hole in the door slides open, and a disembodied eye peers through, scanning left and right. Then the door opens with a rattle of keys and the sliding of a metal rod.

A policeman, hatless and open-collared, enters with a plate of food, which he deposits on the floor of the cell. The cutlery is wooden, blunt and unbreakable.

'Do you need anything?' asks the policeman uninterestedly.

'Anything?' replies the imprisoned man, half-mocking the absurdity of the question, despite knowing exactly to what he was referring.

'The toilet?'

He shakes his head then turns away. The policeman exits, and the ritualistic noises of incarceration are repeated.

He has been well-trained for these sorts of stand-offs. This could have been any night from his late teenage years when he refused to eat at the family table and his mother would carry a tray of food up to his room, lest he should starve to death. He did, however, continue to work hard at school, seeing that as a way out of the domestic perdition, as he saw it. Thus, his parents tolerated his anti-social behaviour, again figuring that rocking the boat might lead to his school attendance falling off. They lived in a form of communal stalemate until the day he left for university: the bright lights and freedom. Initially he felt a sense of release and did all the things from which he had been barred (at least in his own mind). Hedonism on a student budget was his aim, and he achieved this to such an extent that he received an official warning from the university – a badge of honour to his compatriots, and a further worry for the besieged parents who received notice of his misdemeanours on formal notepaper, signed by the dean. Worse followed, and he was one drunken incident away from expulsion when his life changed dramatically and instantly.

He entered the hall in the far reaches of that awful town that housed his broken academic dreams. The building was dark and foreboding, and the shutters rattled in their broken frames. Strange words were spoken as he entered, a soothing lilt which captivated by their tone alone. They were words with meaning to one flailing so violently in a sea of broken abstraction.

Even now, those words still drum a gentle beat within his head. *My sweet evangelist*, they say, making no excuse for sentimentality or faith or the myriad of inconsistencies.

23

DI Price curses under his breath, as he has done repeatedly for the past few hours. This is the worst time of day for him: the early hours of the morning when his cortisol and tolerance levels are at their lowest. He feels ready to snap. He has considered mindfulness and deep breathing at such moments, but the idea annoys him and, anyway, policing is built on conflict and suspicion. He thrives on roughing people up – at least, he thinks he does.

'What more do we know about this joker?' he asks DS Hameed tersely. She doesn't like the use of flippant terminology in relation to such a serious crime and gives a momentary stare which her senior understands. He will refine the use of his language.

She hands him a file with a few scanty pages.

'The focus has been on the ethics committee,' she says, leafing through her own copies.

'The ethics committee,' he repeats, then sighs. He has read the reports – an academic tiff, to his mind – but a credible link to the crime in question, and the only link they have unearthed so far.

DS Hameed checks her watch. It is half past midnight. She sips her coffee, having given in to her desire for caffeine, breaking her rule of none after teatime and knowing she will sleep little tonight or tomorrow. The drink is thick and black, made for her by her superior, who does not measure out the ground coffee with any accuracy, leading to the strongest and blackest of offerings. She always accepts with gratitude and without comment.

'Any word on the man by the canal?' she asks.

He shakes his head.

'Who do you think he is?'

Again, he shakes his head: 'Don't know,' he says, scratching his ear with the pencil that he has been using to write occasional observations in his notepad. He inspects the end of the pencil and then writes the word *canal* on a fresh page.

'Shall we continue the interview, then?' DS Hameed enquires. The night is dragging on, and the prospect of any sleep is diminishing.

He nods slowly, almost solemnly, suggesting a lack of enthusiasm, but, in reality, recognising the gravity of the next few hours and how they will shape the whole investigation.

DS Hameed makes to leave the office, but he stops her.

'Do you think he's our man?' he asks in a quiet voice, as though committing to the concept of the man's guilt is something that should not be voiced too loudly.

DS Hameed lingers at the door. It is the first time she has been asked for her gut feeling on a case before the interviews have been finished.

She shrugs. 'We'll see, I guess.'

He is aware that she has given the answer he would give. How the student takes on the attributes of the tutor.

'We need to find the man he was going to meet down by the canal. Otherwise we haven't got a case,' says the older colleague, looking up at the clock.

DS Hameed nods in agreement. 'We're going through the list of his clients over the past few months, seeing if any of them might fit the bill,' she adds. 'A right crowd!'

DI Price smiles. 'Good work.'

They leave the room and walk down the short corridor to the interview room where Mr George, self-appointed procurator of the city of New Canterbury sits, wringing his hands, contemplating the range of possibilities which he now faces. He has a story in his head but will be malleable in his explanations depending on the direction of questioning. He looks up as they enter, sheepishly, or perhaps his expression is merely one of fatigue. His eyes lock with DS Hameed's for a second, the two eyeing each other up – the foreplay to the main event.

DI Price sits down without a word. He has taken a dislike to the man since their first meeting. He views him with an intolerance born of what he perceives to be an arrogance, a self-assurance. He has the air of someone versed in courtroom games; one of those lawyers who imagines the policeman to be the lower class of profession. Perhaps one that thinks his aim is to disprove the findings of the police whatever the circumstances or the venality of the accused. He has met hundreds like him.

DS Hameed clears her throat, which makes DI Price sit up sharply, aroused from a moment of distraction. The procurator notices this and sees the heaviness of the officer's face, the redness around the eyes, fatigue slumped on his brows.

Detective Sergeant Hameed starts the interrogation.

'Mr George,' she starts courteously, even genially, 'we need to ascertain your relationship to the man who was recently murdered on Galahad Bridge.'

The procurator remains unmoved by the question. He has prepared a response for this opening gambit.

'I knew him from the university's ethics committee,' he says, knowing that they would have already unearthed this fact; indeed, that is the reason he has been dragged here in the middle of the night, his sole connection to the case in hand. 'He and I had a ...' he pauses giving the impression that he is contemplating these words carefully, '... a difference of opinion, let us say.'

DI Price nods.

'What was the nature of your difference of opinion?' asks the younger officer, writing in her notepad as she speaks.

'We were on different sides of the ethical debate, as simple as that.'

'What was the ethical dilemma?'

The procurator pauses, gathering his thoughts once more, remembering his prepared script. 'The scientist was engaged in research on the subject of ageing and methods to reverse and even stop the process. His work, or at least the work under consideration at the ethics committee, proposed creating transgenic creatures engineered not to age. In essence to manufacture immortal animals.'

'What exactly was your concern with this line of research?' asks DI Price, speaking for the first time.

'It was, and is, against the natural order of the world. To tamper with such a process is highly unethical,' he says before adding, 'in my opinion.'

DI Price leans forward. 'Are these objections from a religious standpoint?'

'They are from a principled standpoint.'

The junior officer pulls out a piece of paper from the file in front of her.

'We have been looking at your phone records for the past few days,' she says, showing the paper to the procurator.

He scans the page, but retains the persona of one uninterested in their findings.

'You have been in phone conversation and text message exchange with someone at these times.' She points to a series of highlighted numbers indicating dates and hours.

'Who were you calling at these times?' she asks.

The procurator swallows the little saliva in his dried-up mouth, a reflex action of one wrong-footed, of one being confronted with an undesirable version of his past actions.

'I don't recall.'

DI Price, sensing blood, leans even further forward, placing his elbows on the table and interlacing his fingers.

'Really,' he says, not revealing whether this is a question or a statement.

There is silence in the room for a period of several seconds, which seem like minutes. Time moves differently at such moments, the oppressive nature of guilty thoughts and concocted alibis expanding and contracting in that fourth dimension (if indeed time can be considered in such a way) to produce the infinite permutations of what might have happened, as well as the infinite permutations of what is about to happen.

'Mr George,' says DS Hameed, breaking the silence in a soft, even enticing, voice. 'One of the messages pertains to a meeting down by the canal …' She stops, looking up at the clock, '… only a few hours ago. Can you tell us who you were meant to be meeting?'

At this moment, the procurator himself looks up at the clock, seemingly checking the validity of the last statement. It is just gone three o'clock, and he has been in the police station for less than two hours. His resolve is crumbling, and he has a mind to tell the two people in front of him the truth of the issue. He has been backed into a corner, one which promises no respite, only further hours of interview and accusation. These people are cunning, and they are closing in on the truth of the incident on the bridge, which now seems like a different lifetime, so much has he fretted, so little has he slept. How he longs for sleep, a long and peaceful sleep, and to be a million miles from here. He ponders the prospect of coming clean. *None of this was meant to happen*, he will say. *It has all been a terrible series of events which have come to pass due to the mental fragility of one man.* He suspects they have not found the man he was meeting at the canal (the man he calls Peter) and reasons, therefore, that they are still very much in the dark. However, it is only a matter of time before they find Peter, and then what? He cannot trust the deranged mind of his unintentional accomplice. He needs to keep as much distance from the man and his crime as possible.

He stops talking.

24

LIGHT SEEPS THROUGH the branches, faint and pink, heralding dawn. The fugitive lies in a ditch, covered for the most part by dense fallen branches, spiky and angular, haphazardly pulled over himself in the darkness of the previous night. He is soaked, and his clothes stick heavily to his aching body. He has a pain in his right ankle which shoots up his leg when he tries to move. The discomfort of enforced stillness weighs heavily on his broken body. He listens and hears a soft rustling in the bushes forming the boundary of the woods: a noise of nature of which he has no fear, unlike the thrashing of men last night, with their torchlights and sticks.

He gazes out from his hiding place, lifting his head enough to see the hedge with its late spring blossom and its dense leaves. Beyond it, through a gap in the foliage, he sees a farmer's field, freshly ploughed and being picked over by ominous-looking black birds. They hop in and out of the furrows, stopping occasionally to emit raucous cries; each warning the others to leave their patch alone. The rustling sound in the bushes becomes louder, and a young deer jumps from the matted cover of the hedge, skipping erratically along its line before darting through and into the field. A few crows fly up into the sky, disturbed by the beast, before returning to their rich pickings.

The fugitive attempts to stand, but his arm is caught in the entanglement of brambles and other spiky suckers that seem to have multiplied in the night, entwining his limbs, pulling him into the earth. He contemplates the prospect of becoming one with the soil, an interment bringing him closer to an eternity he has imagined for the past few days – one which was promised, in a way, when he took on the challenge of stopping the ungodly. The thorn of a bramble sticks into his hand, causing a shock of pain, deep and searing. It wakes his senses and he pulls his hand away, a reflex withdrawal. With an effort, he pulls the rest of his frame to sitting and then standing. A bead of blood has formed on his hand, which he observes with a detached curiosity. It is a tiny speck within the expanse of mud caking his skin, but it displays a crimson sheen, slowly expanding, forming little more than a pin head. And yet it is proof of his life, his living form not ready to cede its presence at this moment. The flame of survival still burns, however dully.

The woods look different now. In the night, the darkness gave the trees a homogeneity: black shapes against a black sky. Now each one bears a different leaf, a different fruit, a different shade of green. In front of him, a thick-trunked, nearly leafless tree stands. Despite the stillness of the morning, its branches move rhythmically, giving the appearance that it is marching. It is a man, thinks the fugitive. Indeed, as he continues to stare, the tree takes on more human features, fingers, arms and, most surprisingly, a face. Now it sprouts two legs, and the marching becomes a reality.

'Stop!' says the fugitive in a voice as loud as he dares. But the marching form comes nearer. He blinks, and the clearing of his vision reveals to him new forms. The face has taken the appearance of a child, a cherubic façade, comforting and appealing. The day brightens in an instant, and sunlight seeps through the canopy of trees, illuminating the face, radiant and proud. The fugitive feels a heat in his abdomen, accompanied by a feeling of familiarity, a strong sense that everything he now experiences is a repeat of episodes that have recurred in his life. He feels the need to speak to the forest form but fears the breaking of the spell that has led to this moment. He watches this forest spectacle, real and unreal at the same time. Light glints off the waxy leaves of an adjacent tree, directing their glow to the new being the forest has created. The form shifts further into an older child. A youth, no less comforting, but one imbued with a more mature purpose. In his hand, now clearly bearing five fingers, he holds a bow, ready for the loading of arrows. The boy has bellicose intent. Perhaps a knife or sword will appear, thinks the fugitive, but his imagination settles on the bow and arrow. A deer, perhaps the same beast he saw a few moments ago, reappears, and the tree creature lifts his weapon. In an instant, the prey is gone. The moment has passed.

The fugitive sits down on a nearby log. He is reassured by the presence of this tree beast. It is a friend among the multitude who would do him harm; who would chase him to the ends of the earth; who would not think twice about keeping him captive for eternity. He hears a voice coming from behind him; a soft, soothing sound which makes him think of his mother. *Where is she now*, he wonders: *In some park, begging for money or in the company of thieves, prospering from ill-gotten fortunes?* He shivers, despite the sun.

The voice now comes from the tree, its quality more piercing, its rhythm erratic, its words indiscernible. An image of his mother appears, projected onto the rough bark of the tree. She is young, perhaps a schoolgirl, and she is reading a book, quiet and diligent. She appears carefree, almost angelic, one untouched with by horrors of what is to come. She sits on the steps outside a large white house, the sun glinting off a plastic hairband she wears to pull her hair back into a tight black mat. The fugitive now understands that the voice is that of the man sent by demons to do evil to his mother. This is not the first time he has heard him. He clutches his head, covering his ears and trying to drown out the words, which rise and fall in pitch and echo in discord. Like a radio going in and out of tune, some words become recognisable, and his attention becomes sharpened to the possibility of their significance; the meaning of other words remains obscure.

He stands and approaches the tree beast. The form looms high above him, consuming the space of the sky, forming a dark canopy, obliterating the light of a protective sun. He sees greys and pinks, shimmering and then dissolving into an amorphous plane. The breeze, the call of the birds and the scurrying of insects in the hedge have taken on their own colours, some dull, some vivid, which swirl around his head and enter his body, where they are converted back into sounds: words, messages, instructions that must be heeded.

If he had an axe he would cut down the tree beast: cut off its life form, dig up its roots. But he only has his bare hands, so he throws himself at the form and rips at the bark, the branches and the leaves until his fingers bleed. Then, doglike, he paws at the ground, making digging attempts at the solid earth, succeeding only in scratching the surface of the soil, which becomes darkened by his crimson blood.

For a time immeasurable, he continues his assault on the stately life form until he falls down at its foot, too tired to continue. The sensation in his hands now becomes one of pain, and the tree is no longer his aggressor.

He curls up and sobs.

25

A LONE WALKER finds the fugitive, still curled up under a great oak tree, which has grown thick-trunked and gnarled over three hundred years. Blood is smeared copiously over his face and hands to such an extent that the walker thinks the person must have been a victim of assault. The walker recoils, initially considering the potential danger of the situation, looking around for an attacker. Not seeing a single soul, nor having heard any commotion since he entered the woods, he suspects the crime must have been committed some hours ago. Reassured, he approaches the bloodied form, not knowing whether it lives or has already succumbed to its injuries. The walker's heart beats faster, and his respiration becomes shallow, as though he is too scared to breathe. The fear of finding a dead body is always greater than the hope of discovering a pulse or a breath in these circumstances.

He shouts and then prods the man and is somewhat relieved to find a reaction: a movement of his upper torso and a flexion of his neck, like the retraction of a snail into its shell when pecked at by a bird.

'What's happened?' asks the walker, coming closer, showing genuine concern despite the repulsion he feels at the mass of blood and soil that shrouds the dreadful shape.

The injured man's face remains hidden. His long hair is matted with the detritus of the past week of hard living and has obscured his profile against the mud-spattered earth. His long beard has spread out, giving it the appearance of moss on the forest floor.

The walker peers at him more closely and makes out the shape of a nose and then lips. He prods again, fearing that the reaction he elicited a few moments ago may have been an aberration. This time the man on the floor moves more obviously and then turns his head skyward, revealing the white sclerae of his eyes in sharp contrast to his darkened face. He opens his lips as though about to speak, but instead extends his tongue, which he then curls up to meet his top lip.

'Are you hurt?'

The fugitive turns his gaze to the direction of speech and then makes to sit up. This sudden movement makes the walker step back, a defence mechanism, no doubt, against this strange man whom he has discovered battered and bruised while out on his morning walk. He has never experienced such a thing before. He feels the need to get away. He doesn't want to get involved in whatever sort of maleficence has rendered this man into such a state. His mind conjures up reports of drug gangs, human trafficking and worse. He has stumbled into the wrong place at the wrong time.

The man is now standing. The walker now feels sheer terror and his vulnerability causes panic. *Run*, he tells himself, yet he doesn't want to alarm or provoke, and, anyway, he is not sure that his legs would obey the command of his brain, which is now imagining, even preparing for, the worst. He feels a sense of paralysis, standing his ground because of the inertia of fear. He feels that this broken man is now wanting revenge for his own injuries.

The walker feels for his phone in his pocket and then takes it out, brandishing it like a weapon of the modern age. It is a threat which implies that the whole world will know of their encounter with the push of a few buttons, that we are never really alone and that all our experiences are digitally connected, encrypted and logged on the super computer of modern society. Despite the importance the walker has placed on the potential of the mobile phone, the other man doesn't seem to notice, and is looking in a different direction.

'I'll phone for ...' the walker considers this and settles for 'an ambulance.'

Surprisingly, the bloodied man turns his back and starts to walk away.

The walker takes a few steps back, adding distance between him and his discovery. Out of earshot, he starts to dial for the emergency services. They will ask him which one he requires: police, ambulance or fire? Not fire, for sure, but which of the other two? Has any crime been committed? Or is this a vagrant who has had too much to drink? Are his injuries merely a reflection of this? He glances up at the man who continues to trudge away, heavy-footed, limping.

He dials and in an instant is asking for the police.

'I've found a man in the woods. A confused man, in the woods,' he adds. In reality, he has no idea whether he is confused, but it enhances the validity of his call. Just saying he has found a man in the woods sounds odd, unconvincing.

He goes on to describe his location and is assured that someone will be down shortly. He tells them to be quick, but expects this may be a low priority, given the recent events that have stretched the police force of the city.

He feels a responsibility, having found and reported the presence of the man, so he follows the erratic steps through the woods, at a distance, not wishing to be noticed, not wishing to agitate.

The pace quickens for a while, then slows as the man reaches the edge of the trees. A wooden fence, topped with barbed wire, stretches far without offering a way through. It is new and reinforced, making the statement that the farmer does not wish anyone to enter the field. At first, the injured man attempts to climb the fence before giving up and walking along its inner border. The walker, like a hunter stalking a prey he does not wish to catch, follows at a distance but, after a while, realises that the man he stalks doesn't feel his presence. He could be walking next to him, and he would still be anonymous.

His phone sounds and it is the police, asking him for his precise location. They have arrived at the entrance to the woods near the layby on the main road. Knowing the woods well, the man directs them. It is not more than a five-minute walk, he says.

He relaxes a little and waits, seeing that the injured man has come to a stop and is now resting on a tree trunk. He seems to be inspecting his hands, which are stretched out before him, splayed and immobile. Even from a distance, the walker understands the severe pain the shredded skin on the man's hands is causing him. He has an anguished look, like an animal, thinks the walker, like one who has lived in the forest amongst the birds and the beasts for years.

He hears a soft rumble. The man is making noises, maybe praying a soft incantation. The sounds become louder, disturbing a forest bird which ascends with a clatter. The sound is more like a wail now, more like a primitive call of one in pain.

It will lead the police to the man, thinks the walker. Still needing vindication for his call to the emergency services, he tells himself that they will see that the man is clearly in need of help. They will understand this from the moment they locate the origin of the bizarre ululations.

Indeed, within a few minutes the police appear. Two men, dressed in black tunics with a faint checkerboard design, come into view behind the dense foliage. The walker watches as they tread warily, instantly aware of the dangers in the situation. One appears to be whispering into a walkie-talkie. The other has his hand on his holster, ready to pull out some sort of restraining or immobilising device, or, perhaps, a gun.

The walker takes a step back, feeling the level of risk rising by the second. He hides behind a silver-barked tree from where he peeps, holding his breath.

The taller of the two policemen walks slowly towards the injured man, who has now fallen silent. The quietness of the woods is striking. Even the birds are silent, as if the whole of the natural world is aware of the stand-off which is developing.

A twig cracks under the foot of the policeman, causing the injured man to raise his head. He stares at the policeman, who stops and raises his hands.

'I'm here to help you,' he says.

The fugitive appears to consider this before raising his own hands, blood dripping across his palms and down his arms. It is not clear whether he is surrendering or simply displaying his injuries.

26

How does a far-fetched idea – a concept so at odds with all evidence to the contrary – gain traction amongst a disparate band of believers? Those flat-earth subscribers will defend their position to their dying day, despite boats and planes circumnavigating the globe without ever falling off the edge. And yet, the flat earth, on the face of it, in the absence of scientific fact, seems highly likely. Why would primitive man think otherwise, other than the presence of a circular moon in the night sky? Perhaps the moon and the earth are both plates. The concept of gravity is hard to reckon with, and it might seem logical that people at the bottom of a sphere suspended in space would fall off. Furthermore, the idea that the earth is spinning at such a high speed as to facilitate the functionality of gravity seems highly improbable. A thousand miles per hour, no less. *If I were in a car going so fast, I'd know about it,* says the sceptic. *Ah yes,* replies the scientist, *but you only feel motion if the speed – or rather velocity, to give the more correct terminology – changes.* The sceptic shakes his head and walks away muttering, while the scientist retreats to a place where rules and law, rather than gut feelings, govern. Both are more resolute in the strength of their own opinion. There will be no meeting of minds, not now, not ever.

And so, as with other differences in opinion – explanations for natural phenomena, novel medical breakthroughs, the geological history of the world, to give a few examples – one side is labelled fact, the other a conspiracy.

When a glacial river on a remote Scandinavian island starts spewing boiling red water, the colour of blood, which destroys ancient ecosystems, some predict that the end of the world is imminent. The rational and the geographically minded, on the other hand, suggest that a volcanic chamber under the earth has broken through cracks in the earth's crust and come into contact with the underground lake that feeds the river. That chamber is, they hypothesise, so rich in iron oxides that the water has formed a concentrated solution of these red chemicals, thus producing this alarming spectacle. Most believe this version of the narrative, or at least want to believe it, the alternative being too hard to stomach. It is odd, nonetheless, that such a phenomenon has occurred, there being no precedent for such an incident. Even the scientists have their doubts.

Now, a volcano on the southern shores of the island starts spewing out a vast ash cloud which halts plane flights in the vicinity and, after the winds have picked up and blown the thick dust in all directions, has stopped all air traffic in much of the northern hemisphere. The focus of the world is therefore on the strange events in this small island. People watch in wonder at the majestic forces of nature that are threatening the very existence of the icy landmass. There are, of course, many other incidents of bizarre goings-on, both natural and unnatural, and even the most mundane of meteorological happenings are now analysed to an extreme degree. The multitude of events reported on news channels throughout the world are seized upon by climate activists, who warn of their ominous portent. Their argument has been building for a long time and is now more or less irrefutable. What is happening on a small yet dramatic scale in that remote Scandinavian island is being replicated everywhere else. The end of the world is indeed in fast-forward – not so much a whimper, but a deliberate exhalation. On the subject of dire predictions, the scientists and the conspirators are being brought together in a bizarre way, yet in a manner that each resents.

The followers of John Corn, although few and far between these days, understand the significance of this new turmoil. Revisiting the tribulations of their leader from centuries ago, they look for parallels with descriptions of erstwhile plagues, witchcraft and cruel servitude. Given the nature of the latest turn of events, there is a newfound energy. A scientist who is dabbling in the subject of immortality has now been killed. The murderer has not been found and his identity is shrouded in mystery, just as the most beguiling of prophecies are ambiguous. There is a parallel, they point out to anyone willing to listen, to occurrences of centuries ago, in the very same location as the current crisis, involving similar forces of good and evil.

One man, a disciple of the ancient prophet, now ostracised from these followers because of his militant inclinations, knows the identity of the killer (and is now trying to distance himself as far as possible from his acquaintance with him). He is, of course, the procurator of the city of New Canterbury, who rests in the city's police cells, captive and under suspicion. He had come late to *The Chronicles of John Corn*, not reading them until his early twenties, when he was desperate for some form of direction. On first reading, the words had struck him as too cryptic, almost unfathomable. Yet they had a certain draw, and he came back to them time and time again, even in his dreams, phantasmagoria of grotesque creations haunting his night-time thoughts. At the same time as his dalliance with John Corn's words, he developed an enchantment with William Blake, poet, painter and visionary. Blake's evocative images, coming from a tormented mind, were something fascinating, almost mesmerising. They made the procurator take notice of his own spirituality. He read the words, studied the elaborate drawings, and was inspired to take up a cause. A sceptic might have said that any cause would have done. A wayward soul follows the nearest crusade offering inclusion and the prospect of something better, like a river seeks the easiest path to its ocean.

And now, staring at the blank plaster, he is reminded of a picture on the wall of his student digs: Blake's *Nebuchadnezzar*, tattered at the edges and slightly faded, a dark rectangular form on a grey-painted wall, mould dotted around its edges, seeping into the crumbling bricks of the old tenement. Only the face of the berated king shone out from the gloom in all its shame and pathos. He would spend hours studying the mystical form, entranced in a manner which Blake would have desired, even required, of those gazing upon his interpretation of the Old Testament fable. King Nebuchadnezzar looks out, on all fours, in the form of one of the animals amongst which he lives. His muscles are displayed as if on a carcass. His beard drapes down to the floor, perhaps often being snagged by his newly purposed front paws when he walks, or rather prowls, across the plains of his novel habitat. His hair has been changed into the feathers of an eagle and his nails have become the claws of a bird. For seven years he has roamed since that fateful dream, an allegory interpreted by Daniel, his most wise of men. The dream imagined a giant tree that stretched far into the sky, even the heavens, such that it was visible to everyone on Earth. He is instructed to cut down the tree – a most curious request given the importance of the life force to the creatures nesting in its branches and taking shelter under its wide canopy. The tree was him, the king, so said Daniel, and it represented his power that was a rival to celestial forces. To cut it down was necessary to prove that no one is above the Almighty. No mortal being has the power to touch the heavens or to infiltrate His metaphysical omnipotence. This was the king's penance. And so, for seven years he has taken on the form of a lowly ungulate, eating the grass of the pasture and lying with the beasts of burden. The book of Daniel says that after his allotted time in the wilderness his sanity is restored, implying that in Blake's image he is insane, or at least has the mind of an animal. Yet he retains a human quality – that hard-earned humility before God and the abhorrence of conceit.

Did Nebuchadnezzar's sanity return because he confessed the error of his former ways, or did his confession follow the restoration of his human thoughts? Or was it predetermined, anyway? Seven years, so the dream says, was his sentence for the crime of arrogance. In Blake's picture, Nebuchadnezzar appears fated to crawl the earth for an eternity, not just those seven years. The tree stump, which was permitted regenerative powers, is not depicted. Perhaps Blake felt he didn't deserve a second chance. No man has the right to build that much power for himself. Indeed, the artist, viewing all life as sacrosanct, gives the exiled king a look of shame, having cut down the tree (in a metaphorical sense), leaving the creatures of the kingdom without a home.

The idea of eternal damnation is a common one among the scholars of that time. Existence in the fiery hell is a recurring depiction in Blake's prints: man heading facedown into a fiery pit while flames lick the edge of the manuscript's pages, telling the reader they are never too far from their miserable fate. Whatever happens on earth is nothing compared to what awaits the ungodly in the afterlife.

The peep hole to the cell opens and the procurator senses the gaze of his guard. He remains motionless, his gaze steady on the blank wall. The peep hole closes.

He stands up. Continuing his musings on *Nebuchadnezzar*, he considers whether the fugitive, the man he calls Peter, is in fact the incarnation of the fallen king. When they first met, on that inauspicious day in the lawyer's office, there was something about him that the procurator couldn't put his finger on: an attraction, a draw. He now contemplates whether his long beard and his claw-like fingernails were signifying that he was the modern-day repenter, a man who understood his immorality. Had he accepted his sin and come to the procurator for redemption? Even his simian walk and his tendency to snort like a pig suggested that an exile to the fields, among the livestock, was his calling.

Peter is no king in secular terms, of that there is little doubt, but perhaps he is a man who is willing to go on a moral journey.

Is it the lawyer's fate to facilitate the fulfilment of a modern-day parable?

27

THE MAN WHO has been named Peter also lies in a cell staring at a wall. He sees brightly coloured geometric shapes swirling across its luminous surface, fading at the edges into a blur of whites and blacks, zig-zags and broken lines. Focusing on the epicentre of one multi-coloured whirlpool, he experiences the feeling of motion, travelling through time and away from the confines of his newfound prison into a newer place, a place where he feels a sense of joy and a feeling of familiarity rising through him from his belly up towards the top of his head, where it explodes into a thousand notions of his own grandiosity. High up, a barred window lets in a diffused yellow artificial light, reflecting off the irregular surface of the wall, adding sparkling fractals upon the crazy patterns, fireworks for his retina, which projects the image in a retrograde manner, deep into the convolutions of his occipital cortex, where a billion associations are made within his hyperactive mind.

Time and space being so distorted in this wild visual display, he is unaware of how long he has been in the cell or indeed the location of where he now sits. In fact, he is aware of very little, other than the man who sits in the corner typing on a laptop, rhythmic clicks emanating from his fingertips. He has an inkling that the man is his father but at the same time knows that his father is dead, his body burned some time ago and his ashes scattered on the placid waters of the harbour, at the site where, in his lifetime, he had fished and spent his happy hours.

Peter is unable to see the face of the man, which is obscured by a large hat, but feels a sense of the familiar. He shows the man (who is not his father) his hands, now heavily bandaged with pristine white cotton and a plenitude of surgical tape. At the same time he thinks, *these are not my hands*, and pulls them back into his chest, trying to bury them deep within himself.

The man in the corner appears to grow larger, and a red light glows around his darkening form.

'Kill that man,' he says in an echoing voice which rises in pitch and ends in a wail.

'Which man?' asks the one called Peter.

'The man on the bridge.'

Peter, as he is called, turns his back on the man (the paternal imposter) in the corner and steps towards the door of the cell. He pulls at the handle, which creaks, but it is rigid, unyielding. The door rattles as he attempts to open it. He hears footsteps and a dull clatter outside the door. Stepping back, he waits for the door to open, but the steps become quieter and the noise stops.

He turns around, but the corner where the man was sitting is now empty.

Again, he lunges at the door, clutching its handle in two hands.

'Let me out!' he roars as though conjuring the might of all the beasts in heaven and hell.

28

THE EVENTS OF the past recur in memory like the swirling sands of a desert during storms. The components, which comprise a series of interconnected yet specific recollections, are churned up, never to return to their original location, then put together into a patchwork resembling, but by no means replicating, the original. Memory of a distant occurrence is thus made up of both the incident itself and, as time passes, the distortion of its reminiscence.

And so, the procurator recalls (for a time repeated yet uncountable) his meeting with the man he calls Peter. The central question to be recalled is this: what exactly were his instructions to Peter? He has conjured up and rehearsed the moment in his mind to such a degree that fact and fiction are intertwined in an amalgam of fabrication and what might have been. He had spoken to Peter of a threat, of a religion and of a scientist with whom he had crossed swords sometime back, of that he is certain. He had discussed the need to stop the work of that scientist: the one engaged in the unnatural and the immoral; the one who was entangled in a line of research set starkly against the instinctive order of the world – work devoid of ethical sense, despite the decision of the committee on which he was an erstwhile panel member. Was it a discussion? The man he calls Peter was taciturn, as he recalls, not offering much verbally save for the odd single word, a *yes* or a *no*. What he lacked in verbiage, he made up for in his demeanour, becoming alive, exuding an impression of enlightenment. He had listened, no doubt about it, and had seemed to be taking it in, growing in facial animation, pursing his lips at times, twisting his head in the manner of a dog awaiting instruction while looking deeply into the eyes of the procurator.

At one point, his gaze had faltered and his eyes had deviated sharply to the right while his head was pulled in the opposite direction, the action of tensed neck muscles, the veins of which throbbed with a strained intensity. Holding this pose for several seconds, he had begun to lick his lips and then, as though bothered by a fly or a beetle, had plucked at the dirty fabric of his threadbare shirt, his fingers failing to latch onto anything of substance.

He remembers feeling uncomfortable at that moment. Was the man before him still conscious? Had he entered a different realm of sensibility? Was he ill?

There was a silence for seconds, maybe minutes, but in an instant Peter once more had looked him in the eye, nodded and asked, 'What are we to do?'

He was confused by this, but at the same time encouraged that Peter had come around to his way of thinking. His deep-seated desire to stop the scientist in his unholy ways might materialise yet into definitive action.

'We must stop him,' he said, and, at that, the man had nodded, then got up and left the room.

That was all he said. *We must stop him.*

29

THE ART OF ornithomancy – the determination of the future by the behaviour of birds – has been practised for generations. Even now, in this age when it might seem that biological knowledge has explained natural phenomena well enough, vast murmurations of starlings are considered a spectacle and a gift from heaven. He who worships the natural world will come from miles away to witness the shifting black patterns in the sky as they prepare for roost. It is as it always was.

And when a bird of prey flies overhead, encircling then passing three times in the direction of the sun, carrying in its talons the carcass of a unadulterated passerine, not meant for consumption; and when the sky darkens and thunder rumbles over the black hills; and when rain falls with a heavy urgency on the bone dry land, then he will come again. So it was written. And that person, the man of the second coming, may be anyone, even the heathen or the unholy. The prophecies have confirmed that he will not be lauded in his time, but a divine sense will be imparted on whomever is willing to take up the mantle.

In his cell, Peter falls in and out of sleep, his dreams punctuated by delirium wrought by his circumstance and by a fever he has contracted from the nights in the open and the squalor of his surroundings. He feels a moisture on his forehead and a throbbing around his temples. His ears ring, a high-pitched tone, which he listens to for any sort of explanation concerning his current predicament. He has been alone in this room for a period of time, a long time, he thinks, although he has no way of knowing its exact length.

He gazes forward. A magpie lands on the lawn outside the barred windows. *One for sorrow, two for joy.* And indeed, as though the nursery rhyme is always fated to be confirmed, the magpie is joined by its mate, hopping about, wagging its tail, occasionally pecking at the ground. The two encircle each other, a ritual observed for generations, before they both hop up on the far fence and from there move out of sight. *Three for a girl and four for a boy.* A small brown bird takes their place, boldly entering the middle of the lawn, pecking at the place where the magpies had stood. The air is still, with a threat of rain. In a flash the silhouette of a silent hawk appears, shrouding the smaller bird, giving it no hope of escape. Within a second or two, all that is left of the bird is a mass of feathers, spread like autumn leaves over the patchy grass. The fugitive scans the distant horizon for the hawk, but it is gone. The sky is now quiet, grey, featureless, a solemn accompaniment to the death that it has just witnessed.

A key turns in the lock, and the door opens. A man clad in blue enters, pushing a white trolley which rattles gently. He is well-built, like a bouncer in a night club ready to extract some miscreant partygoer, or, in this case, suppress a violent inmate. After him comes a short woman, also in blue, holding a file of papers and a clear plastic tray. She looks weary and tentative, and glances repeatedly at her colleague, as though seeking the reassurance of his mere presence. He is the one who will protect her from whatever defilement comes her way.

She places the plastic tray on the window ledge, rummages around in its contents, then picks up a syringe. Its content – a bright yellow liquid – catches the sun, casting a streak of light on the far wall, a shimmering aquatic mirage.

A further man, as burly as the other, then enters the room. He harbours an intensity, a pretence of hostility. His hands are formed into fists, and he approaches the fugitive.

'Please sit down,' he says, addressing the fugitive, who is standing at the window, still hoping for a glimpse of the bird of prey. He turns around and looks at the man who has spoken, then at his partner and then at the woman, who is tapping the syringe with the nail of her index finger, holding it up and inspecting the yellow chamber.

The fugitive is uncertain of what is about to happen but sits anyway. In his short life, he has become well-practised in the observance of obedience at moments like this. The three people converge on him, the two men from the side and the woman from the front. She is hiding the syringe, not wanting to reveal that which she has already displayed to him.

'It's OK,' says the larger of the two men, placing a hand on the fugitive's shoulder and then applying a downward pressure. The other man follows suit, and the fugitive feels the conflicting forces of the hands and the upward force of the chair seat on his backside, an uncomfortable proof of the laws of physics.

The woman inches closer while the man at his left shoulder pulls up the sleeve of the fugitive's flimsy gown to reveal his bare shoulder. His muscle, puny as it is, tenses, but his shoulder is kept in place by an ever-increasing downward pressure. The fugitive looks at the woman, whom he now understands is a nurse who has the intention of injecting him with the yellow liquid. She does not look at him put focuses on the syringe. She unsheathes the needle and gently pushes up the plunger of the syringe, allowing a small bead of liquid to form at its tip.

'Wait,' says the entrapped man, feeling, at the moment of his utterance, the pressure increasing on his feeble shoulders.

The nurse looks up at him, freezing momentarily. She wears a mask over her mouth and nose, and her eyes betray little emotion.

'Do it!' says the left-hand man, who grabs the fugitive's forearm and twists it, a pronating movement which further immobilises his arm.

'What is it?' shouts the fugitive, trying to break free with the knowledge that such an effort will be futile.

The nurse moves forward and, seizing her moment, plunges the needle into the muscle of her victim's left shoulder, missing her intended target, but, nevertheless, finding something fleshy.

'Keep still!' she barks, pressing on the plunger making the yellow liquid disappear, perhaps more quickly than the ideal rate at which she has been trained to inject- *the conditions are far from ideal*, she will tell herself later.

The fugitive continues to struggle, and the two men at his side are finding it increasingly difficult to hold him down, despite his size compared to the two of them. The nurse is finding some resistance to the injection of the final few millilitres of fluid, so pushes harder, which causes the syringe to become separated from the needle, making the yellow liquid squirt onto the floor and the arm of one of the restraining men.

'He's had most of it,' says the nurse, reassuring no one but herself. She removes the needle from the man's shoulder and nods to the two men who slowly release some of the pressure on the man. They stay in position as the nurse clears up the small pool of fluid on the floor, just as one might remove evidence from the scene of a crime.

The fugitive offers no further resistance. He slumps back into his chair as a strange sensation of imposed motion, like being on the deck of a ship in a storm, overcomes him.

'Like a dog!' he says in a voice so insignificant that no one hears him.

30

THE CITY OF New Canterbury's procurator in the time of John Corn was a man by the name of Hammond Scar. When appointed, in keeping with previous holders of the office, his powers related to the management of the city's coffers, ensuring taxes were collected by employing a band of debt-collectors, who ruled over the impoverished and the unlucky. As time went by, he usurped the power of other government officials and increased his influence in judicial matters. His fiscal responsibilities became a lesser part of the job to him, and he focused on defining an almost dictatorial grip on the city. His main ammunition in this quest was his control of the coal mines which lay to the east of the city and which generated the lion's share of the income for the city's reserves. Any disruption in the flow of coal from the ground to the city's expanding industry would have been catastrophic. Hammond Scar knew this, as did the officials, who meekly gave into his advances in government for fear of the consequences. He defined the role of the city's procurator in his own way, and, in time, his remit encompassed matters of jurisdiction. He released the city magistrates and imposed his own band of law enforcers, mostly relocated from the debt-collecting business. This band of henchmen viewed a plaintiff's argument and mitigating circumstances as irrelevant, and their interpretation of the law was based not on scholarly learning of jurisprudence but the whims of their leader. Scar had become untouchable in the space of a few years.

Of note, however, was his allegiance to John Corn. Despite the increasing marginalisation of the latter-day prophet,

Hammond Scar remained sympathetic to him and his group of men and women on the southside of the river. Many of Scar's followers had become suspicious of what was viewed more and more as a cult, but Scar espoused a newfound tolerance, even encouragement. He was a religious man himself, but also a schemer who realised the power John Corn had over large sections of the city's populace. He had already been a major role in the banishment of the warrior brother and his followers from the northside of the river. Allowing his teaching, or at the very least not suppressing it, was a step towards pacifying the community. It gave them one less thing to be angry about. Religion, particularly that expounded by the curious preacher on the far bank, nullified rebellion. In time, Corn's followers grew within the city, and meetings in which his teachings were discussed happened frequently. For the first time in memory, laws were passed allowing people freedom to worship whomever and whatever they chose.

Little by little, Hammond Scar was able to take power from the ruling brother, who was side-lined into a purely ceremonial role. His ineffective colleagues in government were relieved of their duties. The exiled twin brother had long since died in the forests of the city's hinterlands, never having set foot in the city since the day of his flight, making Scar the de facto leader. It was a bloodless coup in a time when peaceful transitions of power were unheard-of. The people of the city were thankful of that, having an ingrained understanding of the city's bloody history. Curiously, the popular conception was that John Corn had been the architect of both of the twin brothers' downfall all along, effected through who knew what acts of sorcery. Scar did little to quash these rumours, happy for Corn to take on the mantle of mystery and be the subject of scepticism.

John Corn himself retreated from public life, wary of the newly anointed ruler in the high stone castle, a man who immediately toughened his stance, knowing that the retention of power was a perilous predicament and that any ruler was only a hair's breadth away from overthrow. The people, who thought they had achieved one thing, now faced the reality of the conclusion of these power struggles. Almost immediately after Scar's peaceful coup, a famine hit the city. Severe flooding damaged growing crops and established stores. The city descended into desperation and lawlessness. The army were brought into line in an act of self-preservation and Scar restored the iron-fisted rule of yesteryear, suppressing the freedoms enjoyed by the citizens in the previous few years. The city was back where it had been a decade before: an oppressed populace with no voice and no sustenance.

Despite this, the citizens endured and sought shreds of hope wherever they might be found. Indeed, John Corn's words remained as an undercurrent to the psyche of the city's population. In time, a renaissance in his philosophy grew among the frightened people, who clung to their religion with one hand and their meagre possessions with the other.

The modern-day self-styled procurator, now pacing the short distance of a dingy police cell, knows all about his predecessor several times removed. The title fell into disuse several decades after Hammond Scar's death. His offspring – three sons who lacked the intelligence and the guile to perpetuate their father's grip on the city – had successively assumed the title after his death, but all three had met their end in mutinous uprisings. The title was a byword for disgrace for the generations after, until ignorance generated by the passing of time buried it into obscurity. It remained a legal term in other parts of the country, but one solely relating to financial matters. This was more in keeping with the original Roman Empire definition. Even there, however, the role specification often slipped, as greed and opportunity reared its head in the far-flung frontiers of the failing regime.

Newly employed in law practice within the city, the modern procurator had felt a pull towards the olden times and a fascination with the title. He was, he reasoned, predominantly a financial lawyer, and there was no restriction on the title being used. It was obsolete and, just as a management consultant can call himself a management consultant without recourse to the authorities, there was no barrier to the use of this title. He used it in his business cards, although most had no idea what it meant or its relationship to the ruthless man who held the title in different times. It annoyed his fellow lawyers, no doubt, but his separation from them was almost complete, so it bothered him little. The gulf between those practitioners upholding regulations in those unquiet times and his own version of legality grew greatly in those early years, so the use of the obtuse title suited his purpose.

In particular, he found it hard to reconcile the secular lawfulness of certain acts and his own beliefs. Ethics had shifted dramatically, and what was considered punishable by prison, even death, in former times now seemed to be acceptable, even encouraged. He found himself practising with a set of codes derived from a broken rule book. At the time when he had taken up law studies, he had not considered the impact of his work on his spiritual life. He had needed something to study in order to gain a profession. Drawn to arguments which bubbled in his head, he saw law studies as a means to clarify his own ethical views and of upholding the moral code that was taking its hold on him. But over time, he saw his profession less as a calling and more of a challenge. Many of the laws, built on changing ethics, were flawed, and the idea of defending them became unpalatable. He would argue with his teachers and present an alternative to various legal tenets. His tutors, growing increasingly tired of his remonstrations, would point to the leather-bound volumes on the shelves. The law is the law, they pointed out. There was no place for their radical refashioning in the courtroom.

And so, he became disturbed at the range of immoral acts which were deemed legal. He thought of leaving, but the need for financial independence made him stay. He resolved to change things from the inside.

He joined the ethics committee of the local university, who

were only too pleased to have someone with a law background in their group. There, he witnessed rubber-stamping of multiple egregious transgressions of moral codes. The chair of the committee was merely a puppet put in place to a permit the scientists to perform whatever they pleased under the unchallenged banner of medical progress. A scientist merely had to mention the prevention of little children dying in their justification and that was enough to let through the latest attempt to distort the natural order through their own version of modern witchcraft.

He had first come across the works of the scientist who was later to be murdered on Galahad Bridge at a time when he was running out of allies on the ethics committee. The chair had made it known that he was skating on thin ice. His antagonistic behaviour, as the chair had put it, was jeopardising the good work of the committee. He had made a promise to try harder, but when the latest offering – inserting genes into animals to make them live forever – had come to the committee, he saw no option but to rebel. The meeting had been fractious and dissolved into squabbling, with the scientist leaving and refusing to have any further part in the meeting. The procurator was sacked from the committee and banned from further interaction with the university or other ethics committees. He had complained about this but knew that the powers who ran education and research governance would not listen. He took his disgruntlement to a different plane, where it seethed and swirled, bubbling up and reaching a climax in the most alarming of ways.

31

DI Price and DS Hameed return to the scene of the crime. On the face of it, it is an unintentional return; however, subliminal instructions force our psyche in so many ways. They are on their way to the coffee shop they often frequent, typically after a night of investigation. Passing over the bridge, DI Price pauses and looks down the river. A lone boat spewing out black fumes passes below, a black tarpaulin on its deck hiding its cargo.

'I just can't see the link,' he says, tracking the boat as it disappears underneath the bridge, sending up a plume of toxic gases.

DS Hameed nods. For the past hour, they have been raking over the evidence against the city lawyer. He gave away little at the latest interview, closing himself up, replying in monosyllables, if at all. The only motive for the crime they have is the disagreement at the ethics committee. Both agreed that this is flimsy, unlikely to stand up in any cross-examination. They need more. The identity of the person with whom the lawyer has been in contact is still uncertain, although word has come in that someone has reported a man acting strangely in the woods, the location where the man on the tow path had fled the night before.

'He was clearly passionate about the ethical debate,' says DS Hameed.

'Passionate enough to get someone killed?' replies DI Price, not expecting an answer.

DS Hameed notices a bunch of flowers tied to the railings next to the bridge. This is the modern form of memorial to those who have died in accidents; victims of speeding traffic or human error. Both officers approach and read the inscription. *In our thoughts* it reads in blue ink which has run because of the overnight rain. The flowers, blue and orange with a sprig of white, look rather ragged, and the presence of only one bunch gives the tribute a sense of pathos.

They continue on towards the café. Both are tired, their steps heavy against the cobbled ground. It is early and the streets remain quiet, so much so that several sea gulls walk down the centre of the bridge, stepping quickly, seeking food. A cyclist rushes past, dispersing the birds, which settle on the overhanging ledges of a disused building.

They reach the café and sit at an outside table which borders the road. Car pass up and down, stopping to let each other pass on the narrow street. A large lorry drives up and stops in front of the police officers, causing a blockage in the flow of traffic, making the car drivers irate. The lorry's driver jumps down from the cabin and asks a pedestrian something. No doubt he is lost. A waitress with a green apron comes out and takes their order, ignoring the spectacle of the lorry blockade. She disappears back into the café.

DI Price and DS Hameed observe the scene before them in silence. A car driver stuck behind the lorry attempts to pass by, mounting the pavement, but on realising the gap is too narrow, starts to reverse back to his original position, which has now been taken by the car behind. The increasing number of vehicles coming up from behind has compressed the cars into a tight queue, and now all are stuck.

The lorry driver waves the irate, pavement-mounted car driver back, indicating that he needs to reverse. This causes the car driver to get out of his car and approach the lorry driver, shouting and gesticulating in the few small steps between them.

DI Price and DS Hameed look at each other, considering whether they should, as officers of the law, intervene.

'How things escalate!' remarks DS Hameed, remaining seated. Neither has the inclination to arbitrate in such a matter.

The vehicles behind the car on the pavement start to reverse and disperse and the enraged driver is persuaded to return to his car and do the same. By the time the coffee appears, the road is unblocked and the lorry is gone. The city sees this form of conflict all the time.

DI Price sips his coffee, which is strong and black, its purpose to awaken him for the day ahead. They will need to file their reports and speak to the officers who have attended the man in the wood. They recognise the importance of this moment in their investigation, which has so far stumbled, failed to gain any momentum. There will be no sleep, at least for now.

DS Hameed's phone sounds, and she answers it after only one ring.

'Hello – Belinda here,' she says, suddenly appearing animated.

She listens, nods a few times then thanks the speaker at the other end of the line.

She hangs up, takes a deep breath and says to her senior partner, 'I think they've got our man.'

32

HE LIES IN the room, curled on his bed, holding his hands over his ears. From the door's peephole he has been observed every thirty minutes for the past few hours, each person seeing the same thing. Every two hours, someone enters (with chaperone, large, intimidating) to take a set of observations regarding his physiology and metabolism: heart rate, respiratory rate, blood pressure, temperature (although they have not been able to record this measurement as yet, given his unwillingness to receive the thermometer). It is enough for the nurse on duty to know that he is still alive. All objects which could conceivably be fashioned into a weapon or a tool of self-destruction have been removed. There can be no repeat of the bed sheet hanging that occurred in the unit several months ago. Anyway, he has been calm since the injection, most likely sleeping. It has had its desired effect.

DI Price and DS Hameed are the latest to look through the peephole, each in turn and in order of seniority. They see a pile of immobile clothes and hair, back turned to the door. The nurse has told them that he is sleeping: 'the sleep of the dead,' as she puts it.

'When can we speak to him?' asks DS Hameed.

'I suspect he'll wake up in an hour or two,' replies the nurse, who has a tattoo on her neck – an inscription of elaborate letters from an alphabet that neither police officer recognises.

'Has he said much to you?' asks DI Price.

The nurse shakes her head then walks away, a set of keys at her belt jangling as she goes.

The police officers sit on a white plastic bench below a

noticeboard. Opposite them sits another police officer, who has been assigned to guard the man. They nod at the officer who nods back, a stern look on his face. Fatigue is catching up with them, and they both consider whether it would be better to go home and return tomorrow to interview the man. The alternative is to wait.

DI Price yawns, making no attempt to hide it. 'Listen,' he says, 'why don't you head home, and I'll wait here? I'll call you if anything happens.'

DS Hameed is too tired to argue. 'OK. Let me know.'

She tramps off, and the two remaining police officers watch her as she goes. DI Price closes his eyes and feels himself drifting off into sleep.

He wakes to the sound of banging. The police officer guarding the cell is standing at the door, looking through the keyhole. He calls for the nurse, who appears with the sound of jangling, more urgent in its rhythm now. She looks through the peephole, calls for back-up, then unlocks the door.

Inside, the fugitive stands, face to the far wall, banging his forehead against the smooth white plaster. If made by a machine, the noise would not be unsettling, but the thought of flesh and skull pounding give it a sickening resonance.

'Stop!' says the nurse, who approaches but then gives way to the burly man who accompanies her.

The fugitive continues, unheeding, but does not resist restraint by the larger man, who pulls him away from the wall and from there to his bed, where he gently lays him down. Both the nurse and her accomplice are surprised regarding the ease of the operation. They had expected more of a fight.

Seeing that all is well, the police officer, who has observed from the door, resumes his position in the chair next to the door. DI Price has remained sitting throughout, reasoning that his presence would only lead to further agitation in the inmate.

'Is he OK?' he asks of the policeman, who nods to confirm that the current situation has been contained.

'Crazy lunatic!' adds the policeman, shaking his head.

DI Price is surprised by this comment, but lets it pass, too tired to point out the insensitive nature of the comment. He desires no argument.

The nurse and her henchman leave the fugitive's room, locking the door behind them. They return within a minute, the nurse carrying a tray on which sits a syringe of yellow liquid.

There will be no prospect of interview for a while.

33

A DAY HAS passed, and DI Price and DS Hameed arrive early at the police station, sleep being the nourishment of enthusiasm. Both are ready to resume their investigation into the murder of a scientist on Galahad Bridge. Such is the nature of time and memory that it seems like weeks since the murder, although it is in fact only a few days. In captivity are two men linked to the crime. One is a local lawyer, a self-titled procurator, who is in a cell in the basement of the police station; the other is in a psychiatric unit, under lock and key and large doses of sedative. Word has been received from the hospital that he is still in no position to answer questions, his behaviour being such that further doses of a drug both anxiety-reducing and soporific have been administered through the night. They will have to glean as much as they can from the lawyer. At least they now know the whereabouts of the man with whom he has been communicating – an unlikely association if ever there was one. They still have no idea regarding the identity of the man in the psychiatric unit, as he was without documents when he was captured and does not appear on any register of missing people; little wonder, as he has the look of one who would not be missed. The doctors have said he is in the middle of a psychotic episode – one which appears to be responding to treatment – but the prognosis is not clear. *They always say that*, thinks DI Price; *they will always cover their backs against the vicissitudes of pathology.*

'Does that mean he is schizophrenic?' asks DS Hameed.

'I guess he may be,' replies DI Price, 'or it could be a one-off psychosis. Who knows?'

They will need to consider how mental illness of such a nature affects the case they will build. Its impact on the legal proceedings will be wide-ranging. The subtle shades between psychology and malice are not easy to navigate. Mad or bad? Fully cognizant or diminished responsibility? Apportioning blame to those who have an altered sense of person is fraught with challenge. What is the difference between a criminal with an innate ignorance of morality versus one who has acquired a disaffected view of the world by experience? A pauper may steal from the rich man because he knows the man from whom he steals will get by without the pilfered goods. That would appear rational. And yet a man who steals with no knowledge of its consequences – in the throes of neurosis, say – commits an irrational act. Perhaps the law is willing to be lenient in that circumstance but comes down heavily on the poor man. That, in itself, would appear illogical. But the law is founded on objectivity, argue the lawmakers, and fairness is not always rational.

'We need to be patient,' says DI Price after a brief pause.

The two police officers head to a small meeting room where they meet Samantha, the newest sergeant in the station, a replacement for a colleague who was injured during a car chase and has no plans to return.

She stands and shakes the hands of the two officers.

'Detective Inspector Price,' she says, 'we met in the coffee room the other day.'

'Yes, I remember,' he says, 'and this is Belinda – Detective Sergeant Hameed.'

Formalities over, they sit down. Samantha had been present in the woods during the apprehension of the man who is now sedated in the psychiatric hospital. She recounts the details, describing the phantasmagorical form of the fugitive. Even for an experienced police officer, she is upset at the recollection of the morning.

'He was in such a state,' she says. 'Blood dripping down his face and hands.'

She pauses and takes a sip of water. 'He didn't seem to know we were there but was staring a tree with a look of panic on his face. He was like that for several minutes before we could coax him away. We didn't know if he was armed or what threat he posed to us or the man who had found him. The officers attending handled the situation professionally and were able to lead him away without much fuss.'

'Did he say anything?' asks DS Hameed.

Samantha opens her notepad and flicks the pages.

'Not much,' she replies, 'it was only after we had got him into the police car that he appeared to acknowledge our presence. He was like a ghost up to that point. Far away. It was as though the confines of the car had jolted him back to some form of reality and he suddenly seemed to come back to the real world. But, he only said one thing and then went back into his trance.'

'What did he say?'

Samantha looks back at her notepad and reads: *'this precious gift of mortality'*.

34

A PANIC ARISES in the streets of the city. Less than a week after the incident that has thrown its citizens into an unforeseen torment, a further threat emerges. The airways carry signals of impending outrage. Just as smoke signals were sent between neighbouring villages in former times, the modern devices of information exchange send a billion messages that are read, half-digested and passed on, a whispering chain letter of the confused and the terrified.

They tell of a man dressed in a long gown and hood who walks the street armed with a malevolent intent and the tools to destroy: a rucksack full of explosives that could blow the city hall apart, reduce it to rubble in a blink of an eye. Wires protrude from the bag: a dead giveaway. Reports say he has headed for the towpath and lurks in the dark recesses beneath a bridge to the east of the city, plotting his return, waiting for the right time to detonate his load, to unleash chaos on a bruised city. In time, electronic rumours claim that it is not one man but two; then it becomes a band of marauders clawing at the bonds of peaceful life.

The streets become quiet, and one might imagine the occupants of the city's houses hiding in back rooms, occasionally drawing back the curtains a fraction to peek out and look for the man or men whom they fear. Their eyes remain trained on their communication devices, ready for the latest updates. Already the national new channels have seized upon the story, urging a collective sympathy from the nation for this beleaguered city. Journalists have been dispatched and are making their way to the epicentre of impending terror. Those in studios a hundred miles away are already postulating theories, pontificating, drawing parallels with the vicious murder of a scientist in broad daylight on these very streets. A murder as yet unsolved, they emphasise, making a subliminal connection (or maybe it is more blatant than that) which will increase the event's salaciousness as well as the viewing figures. *Reports have suggested multiple armed men roaming the streets. A major incident has been declared. The advice is to stay inside and lock your doors.*

In their back rooms, the people listen to these reports. Each has one eye on their mobile phones and the other on the door, expecting at any moment the knock of the police to tell them the situation has been averted, or, heaven forbid, to order them to evacuate. Some switch on televisions, volume turned low, and see images of their streets, no more than a few metres away – streets they have walked down this very morning to exercise the dog or buy a newspaper. *How can this be happening*, they think, *in our town?* A reporter has arrived and is being filmed standing in front of the city hall. His jacket is emblazoned with the word PRESS, as though this makes his presence justified, and he talks softly into a blue microphone, choosing his words carefully.

The sound of a helicopter is heard on the television screen and, more softly, in the sky above the people watching in their houses. *This is serious*, they think in unison, becoming as one in their collective trepidation. More noises from outside herald the arrival of rapidly assembled forces: sirens and motorbike engines. The city is under siege from many angles, good and bad, it seems. 'What are we to do?' asks the young woman nursing a sickly infant, speaking on the phone with her mother, who lives in a foreign country.

The woman on the television screen updates the citizens of the city, and of the world. Her words falter as it becomes apparent that she is being fed information at an alarming rate via her hidden microphone. She stops. 'We've just had word that a man has been apprehended,' she says. A man barricaded in his back room hears this and breathes out slowly in relief. The nursing mother lets out a whimper.

In the police station, a sense of disorder abounds. Most are now patrolling the streets, seeking out the source of panic. Those few officers who have remained to co-ordinate the operation are either on telephones or being briefed by special forces. They sift through the multiple sightings of the man supposed to be a terror threat. The descriptions are muddled and don't back each other up. Makeshift incident boards are constructed to make sense of the myriad of reports and fables.

The officer who handles press communications has been in constant phone communication with news outlets across the country. She has briefed them in a way that gives little away, yet also does not admit to the police's ignorance. The newspaper reporters have told her as much as she has told them, anyway, and she scans the news channels for any update. She, like those locked in houses, watches the woman in the floral dress, who has a slight ptosis of her left eye, and hears those words: *We've just had word that a man has been apprehended.*

The officer looks up and surveys the actions of her colleagues. It's news to her and certainly her fellow police officers haven't revealed an arrest to her, nor are they behaving in a manner suggestive of success in the case. She lifts her hand and then declares in a loud voice: 'News 24 says we have arrested someone.'

The others in the office turn to her and the room becomes silent.

'Have we?' she asks.

35

'It's BEEN A bad day,' says DS Hameed in banal understatement. She drinks a cup of coffee from a chipped blue mug, one which she has been meaning to throw out for some time. She has lost count how many cups of coffee she has drunk today but knows she has had more caffeine than is good for her.

She has returned to the station with her superior officer after a day on the streets, searching for a menace that failed to materialise. DI Price, who has been with her all day, eats a sandwich and gulps down water, a hopeful antidote to the headache which has been building throughout the day.

After reports of an armed terrorist had reached the police early that morning, they had been co-ordinating patrols in the area of Galahad Bridge, lest the criminal or criminals were intent on recreating the crime of the last week; a copycat, as it is called, although the term conjures up images of playgrounds rather than ruthless murder. All day they had waited and searched, but it had come to nothing, and, in the end, the conclusion was reached that it had been a false alarm. The winds of rumour had blown up a storm and the sheltered masses had braced themselves, only to find no such inclemency. A case of misinformation, to use the modern parlance, whipped up by the collective anxiety of a city which imagines itself under siege.

They had stood on the old stone structure all day, half-anticipating a recapitulation of the crime they had been investigating for the past few days. They were on high alert as they searched the empty street and the towpath beneath the bridge. But as the panic resolved and they thought more rationally, neither believed the current alarm to be linked to the death of the scientist. They had their suspects, who were now locked up in their respective holding cells. They were convinced of the involvement of these men, although were yet to prove it or indeed establish an established motive. Nothing had suggested to them that the murder was part of a larger terrorist activity. The day had ended in anti-climax, and by the time they had left the bridge, boats had started to pass below again, and people had begun to emerge into the streets, vigilant and subdued. The two police officers had traipsed the familiar route back to the police station, frustrated by what both saw as a waste of their time.

Finishing his sandwich, DI Price stands up and throws the wrapper in the bin. He looks at his watch and considers going home. The investigation is dragging on, he thinks. The events of the day and the continued use of sedative drugs to suppress the altered thoughts of the suspect have hindered progress.

DS Hameed has opened the lid of her laptop and is typing at the keys.

'By the way,' she says, looking up from the screen. 'I found out where those words come from.'

'Which words?'

'The words the suspect used in the woods.'

'Oh yes,' says DI Price, 'what was it he said again?'

'This precious gift of mortality.'

She types some more, then brings up an image on her screen, which she turns in the direction of the DI.

'They come from *The Chronicles of John Corn*, a religious text from the Middle Ages.'

The image displays the cover of a recent imprint, a distinctive design, which the DI instantly recognises.

'That's the book we found down by the river on the night he got away from us,' he says, pointing at the screen.

'I guess he was reading it and remembered that line,' he adds, trying to recall what he had done with the book.

'It was his copy, then?' asks DS Hameed.

The DI nods. 'Probably,' he says. 'There can't be too many people going around with the book in their pocket.'

DS Hameed types some more and reads from the screen: '*Take from me my arm, infest my skin with the pox, let the leech suck my fetid bile. But take not the essence of my mind.*'

She looks up. DI Price is deep in thought. She continues: '*Though I may sing to God in open congregation amongst a throng of Godly men, I act by my own self to take this step of salvation. Only a higher force can take away this precious gift of mortality.*'

She pauses and shrugs her shoulders.

'Is it relevant?' she asks.

'*Take not the essence of my mind*,' repeats the DI. 'He's had his mind taken away from him. Hasn't he?'

DS Hameed shrugs again. She displays the façade of one too fatigued to consider ancient texts.

'I'll read up some more about it,' she replies, closing the lid of her laptop.

Taking the hint, DI Price tells her to go home. He returns to his office, where he locates the copy of *The Chronicles of John Corn* that was found on the towpath on the night the suspect evaded their capture. He flicks through the pages. There are multiple pencil marks: under-linings and scrawls in the margin. After a short time, he finds the passage they had been discussing. He notices that the phrase '*this precious gift of mortality*' has been underlined twice.

There is a knock on the door, and DS Hameed appears in her bright red coat, bag slung over her shoulder.

'I thought you were going home,' says the DI.

'I'm on my way,' she replies. 'I just wanted to remind you I'm in late tomorrow. Training session.'

DI Price nods. 'OK,' he says, 'have fun!'

She lingers on the threshold, directing her gaze at the copy of *The Chronicles of John Corn* in his hand. Perhaps she expects him to have solved the conundrum of the message by now.

'I've been thinking,' he says in response to her obvious

expectancy. 'It's something to do with mortality and immortality.'

He places down the book and picks up from his desk a copy of the paper that the scientist had been working on at the time of his murder.

He reads the title aloud: '*A reproducible and highly efficacious method of generating non-tumorigenic cellular immortality*.'

He places the paper next to the book. 'One is talking about mortality, the other about immortality.'

DS Hameed comes into the room and closes the door. 'The murderer makes the man seeking immortality mortal. He gives him the precious gift of mortality,' she says slowly, as though discerning whether such an idea is possible. The incongruities of the case dictate the answer.

'Life and death,' says the DI, 'that's what it's all about.'

There is a finality to the comment. 'Goodnight,' says DS Hameed, closing the door as she leaves.

DI Price picks up *The Chronicles of John Corn* again and starts to read from the beginning. He wonders whether its contents will hold further clues to the case of the murdered scientist. The writing is thick with imagery and reflects the mores and the conflicting doctrines of the time. There is an assumption of faith, endemic at the time, just as the social order was non-debatable; the hierarchy of civilisation entrenched, every man and woman in their place.

He reads the words with the mind of a sceptic, having never been a believer in a religious code, his rational mind finding their texts too abstract to place any confidence in them. Coupled to this, he has a longstanding inability to derive meaning from parables in all their conceptual concealment; he didn't listen to Bible readings when he was exposed to them in school and on rare visits to church. What he had seen after that had done little to push him towards an unconditional belief. During his early police career, spent walking the streets of the country's capital city, he had seen such violence arising from lives of inescapable hardship; this was so far-removed from the messages of a compassionate God that he didn't even think about it. He was grateful for the hostels run by the various religious groups who took itinerants and petty criminals off his hands but saw them as little more than an extension of social services. His brother had been a believer in his youth and had even considered a life dedicated to the service of his God. He had gone so far as joining a monastery for a time but left, telling his family that he was disheartened by what he saw as the selfishness of such a life. He wasn't sure whether his brother still considered himself a man of God. They rarely talked about that time in his life, and DI Price suspected that he felt a sense of failure at not being able to follow through with his commitment to the most extreme form of faith. Although DI Price never vocalised the sentiment, he was relieved when his brother renounced the vows of the monastery. He had viewed the lifestyle as unsuitable. His brother was a free spirit and couldn't be caged for too long. And anyway, he was concerned that the regimes of such an existence were breeding a unnatural fanaticism into which his brother was falling and from which he might not emerge – at least not in a recognisable form.

From the moment of his brother's decision to become a monk, DI Price had built up a hostility towards all forms of zealotry. The monastery was gentle and tolerant, so this reaction was thought unmerited by those closest to the DI, not least his brother. However, he had been hardened by the experience of living among criminals, where he saw political extremism driving much of the hatred with which he had to contend. Many of the sectarian principles in the capital were determined by an observance of a particular faction of religion, which made little sense to the impressionable young man. The foundations of an atheistic life had been put firmly in place.

36

THE PROCURATOR BRACES himself for further questioning. He has been told that he will attend the interview room in five minutes. Once there, he is likely to be kept waiting a further ten or even twenty minutes.

He is anxious and uncertain. He does not know whether they have captured the man who killed the scientist, nor whether they have discovered the connection between them. The police officers gave away little when they questioned him, but he sensed they were ignorant of the identity of the perpetrator of the crime. He has little doubt, however, that once they know the perpetrator's identity, they will work out his own connection, how he fits into the picture. He did nothing to cover up his association with the man for the simple reason that he did not anticipate the crime. Perhaps he should come clean? That would put an end to this current anxiety (to be replaced by another). Yet, a glimmer of hope remains that the fugitive is uncaptured, perhaps far away from the city. Perhaps even dead, which the procurator thinks would be the best result, having no problem wishing a dreadful fate on the man who has caused so much distress to so many people.

If he were to admit to his part in all this, to reveal his connection and the seed of an idea he discussed with the man who went on to kill – that barely perceptible notion of a call to arms – then it may be helpful in promoting his message. As a youth, he had been puzzled by news reports stating that a certain organisation had claimed responsibility for planting a bomb and killing people. Why would a criminal admit to a crime? Yet there is no point in committing a crime which, on the face of it, appears pointless unless there is a message behind it. If he had had time to plan the event, he might have been able to ring through in the style of the old-time paramilitary groups that had dominated the teatime news.

His rational mind promptly dismisses this thought as nonsense. He curses under his breath, wishing to scream, but only mustering this hushed expletive. The walls of his cell close in upon him. It is an unholy game being played out by his captors and in which he is an unwilling participant. There is no way out, not now and not for the foreseeable future.

Footsteps approach from the corridor and the door opens. An officer enters and tells him that he will escort him to the interview room on the floor above. His new life is one of being ushered in and out of rooms.

He enters room number two and is surprised to see the officers are already seated, awaiting his entrance. There will be no time for him to sit and collect his thoughts. Or time to get lost in the miasma of his contradictions.

DS Hameed stands up as soon as he enters. She smiles briefly, acknowledging his presence, then walks over to a large recording device on the wooden shelves. She presses a button and announces the interview to the whirring machine. There will be no foreplay today.

'Detective Sergeant Hameed and Detective Inspector Price interviewing Mr Brian George,' she starts, giving a time and a date. *'The Chronicles of John Corn.'*

The opening gambit from the DI alarms the procurator, causing an involuntary stiffening in his back muscles, pulling his neck and head back a fraction, making him sit to attention. He stares at the DI, unable to form a word.

'Well?' asks the police officer, impatience displayed by his tone and by the soft tapping of his fingers on the desk before him.

The procurator starts to reply, but is impaired by the dryness of his mouth, which makes his opening word undiscernible.

'Is … is,' he tries again, rubbing his throat, swallowing hard.

'Is that a question?' he manages to say, aware of the pitiful nature of the response, which is magnified by its delivery.

The DI continues to stare, observing the faltering motion of the man's laryngeal prominence as it attempts to summon up enough saliva to swallow.

'Perhaps you'd like some water,' asks DS Hameed, standing and walking over to a jug of water and glasses that are positioned next to the recording device. She places a glass in front of him and he accepts. His hand shakes as he brings the glass close to his mouth.

'Well, Mr George?' repeats the DI once he has had time to take a few sips. This time he holds up the book that was found on the towpath.

'*The Chronicles of John Corn*,' he repeats.

The procurator glimpses the book for a fraction of a second, then averts his gaze, looking at the glass of water on the desk.

'Do you recognise this book, Mr George?' asks DS Hameed.

The procurator continues to fix his gaze on the glass, his face expressionless. The two police officers carry on firing questions at him, but he cannot focus on more than the iridescent sparkle of light that has formed in the tiniest of the droplets of water at the top of the glass.

'Mr George,' he hears, the voice of the DI becoming more forceful.

He focuses harder on light and water, shutting out whatever can be shut out. *We are all just made up of water, the simplest of molecules, a life-giver ... Water with the memory of its existence in different life forms ... A recycled existence which will continue for as long as there is an earth to house it ... We are all just water.*

'Mr George,' he hears again, almost a shout. The DI is now standing, coming round to his side of the table, and he has no choice but to look at him.

'Mr George, is this your book?'

The procurator looks at the battered book then up at the DI.

'Yes,' he says, feeling the tension in his back and neck muscles dissipate as he slumps down in his chair.

37

Constable Fiona Banner is halfway through the list of Brian George's clients. She has a pile of photographs obtained from a vast database of wrongdoers, which she checks against the image of the man who lies drugged and anonymous in the psychiatric unit. If there is even a passing resemblance, she searches for contact details and then verifies their whereabouts. It is enough to know that the person she contacts is not in a psychiatric hospital on the edge of the city.

She ticks off the latest, a man who now resides in the Caribbean, a world away from his money-laundering operation run from an office a few hundred metres from the police station. No doubt he is involved in something similar but in a sunnier climate. She has heard the law enforcers are more malleable in that part of the world, or perhaps this is an unfounded tale.

She puts down her pen. 'He can't have been a very good lawyer,' she says to Constable George Tomaris, who sits at the adjacent desk staring into space. He has a black eye and a broken finger, acquired, he says, in the apprehension of a criminal. The details remain sketchy, and no one thinks to probe too deeply into the account.

'Most of his clients are in prison!' Constable Banner continues. She sniggers, but the observation does not raise an emotion in Constable Tomaris, who picks up a pen and crosses off a name from his own list.

'Where are you up to?' he asks.

Two hours ago, they started with the list of clients. One started at the top, the other at the bottom, aiming to meet in the middle.

'Kenneth Goldsmith,' she replies.

'We are done, then.' Constable Tomaris holds up the list of scored-through names. 'He was my next one.'

'How many have you been unable to contact?' she asks.

'Just one. A fellow called Reuben Christian, petty criminal, who managed to get himself trapped in a place he was robbing. Spent the night there, only to be arrested the next morning. Hardly an inspiring story.'

'Well, all mine are accounted for,' replies Constable Banner.

They are both surprised that the rounding-up of the miscreants of the city has been so easy. The age of surveillance and computer records means that it is hard to hide. And anyway, they have been searching a list of mostly unsophisticated crimes committed by men with little inclination to conceal their identities.

Constable Tomaris taps at his computer and brings up an image of the man – Reuben Christian – taken by police photographers at the time of his arrest.

They both look back and forth between the printed image of the man found in the woods and the computer image.

'Could be him,' says Constable Banner. The eyes look darker and deeper-set in the newer image, she thinks, but perhaps his week on the run has given him this more haunted look.

They take their list, the two images of the man whose identity they might have unearthed, freshly printed, and the report of his failed robbery attempt to the DI. The gentle sound of Vivaldi floats from his computer as they enter his office.

'We are down to one, Sir,' says Constable Tomaris, handing over the documents and the photographs.

DI Price turns off the music and asks the two constables to sit. He reads the name highlighted by a red circle. He takes his time studying the two images, his eyes flicking between the two like a slow pendulum.

'Low-level crook, arrested last month in a bungled jewellery robbery,' continues the constable after he has given the DI time to assimilate the two images.

'Was he armed?'

'No. And no previous history of violence.'

DI Price nods, then rubs his chin reflectively. The investigation is working on the theory that the lawyer employed someone to carry out the murder on the bridge – a hitman in vernacular terminology. They know that Brian George has had a longstanding grudge against the murdered scientist. They also know he has been making calls and sending messages to a phone that was in the possession of a man who escaped from the police and later turned up in a fugue state in the woods. That man, whose identity has now possibly been revealed, is their only suspect for the murder. If a lawyer wants to get a man killed, the argument runs, then he has ample access to willing candidates.

The DI glances over the report of Reuben Christian's previous transgression of the law.

'Doesn't seem the type,' he says. Everyone on the case had imagined they would unearth a man with a string of violent episodes in his past. It is rare for a man to go from petty criminal to elusive murderer. How could a man described in police reports as 'bumbling' turn into one able to commit such an act and then go undetected for days?

Again, he studies the two photographs. The angle of the jaw, covered in a light stubble in one photograph and clean shaven in the other, is a distinguishing feature; as is the nose, which is crooked at the top and straightens out, beak-like, towards its tip. He notices the eyes too. The orbital recesses are hollower in the picture taken in the psychiatric unit, yet possess the same dark irises, nearly black.

'Looks like him, though,' says the senior officer.

The three police officers nod in unison.

They will confirm their suspicion with genetic analysis, by studying the unique nucleic acids possessed by every human, laboriously churning out a one-in-a-billion series, derived from just one droplet of distilled life. Samples derived from the failed jewel thief's DNA stored within the central police laboratories will be sequenced for a match to the man in the psychiatric unit: two identities melded through a unique combination using just four letters – cryptic clues to the true nature of criminality. Perhaps if the whole library of deoxyribose nucleic acid specimens is analysed, the police will crack the code of immorality and deviancy.

The police officers disperse to inform the laboratories and to delve further into the past of the man in the psychiatric unit, whom they now believe to be Reuben Christian, one-time failed jewel thief. They are getting somewhere, each one thinks, renewed and reinvigorated.

38

THE FUGITIVE, THE wretched man whom the police now suspect is Reuben Christian, emerges from his altered consciousness. He is the same man who is called Peter by the procurator, his multiple identities now becoming unified. He sits on the edge of his hospital bed. His has been the sleep of the tormented. Fragmented dreams have been those of monsters, begat not by reason but by the unholy concoction of chemical signals in his mind and the drugs that have been administered to disrupt them. Visions have floated from his conscience into the room, appearing as phantoms: dark shadows and flying beasts. Fantasy and reality have been merged into one by the profane potions injected into his body, sometimes into the muscle of his shoulder, or onto the skin of his abdomen, or, if resistance is not considered likely, into his veins, a direct portal to the inner being.

He feels a coldness creeping under his skin, like an army of ants processing from their nest to a food source and back again. A million tiny arthropods with no means of escape from the hellish confines of his skin scurry beneath the cutaneous boundary limiting his organs within his wretched body. His limbs feel hollow, as though they are not scaffolded on bones but merely on channels of icy water flowing soundlessly in his extremities, now bound in cotton bandages, tinged with yellow stains, becoming darker. He cannot scratch, as he wishes, but paws at his arms, legs and torso, impeded by the lack of exposed fingernails. If he could, he would tear his skin right off.

Pain is everywhere. The pain in his head is constant yet hard to pinpoint. It cycles from dull aching to the unbearable: firstly, a sensation of tapping, then a deep pounding giving rise to a crescendo of searing and ripping, before he feels that his head is collapsing in on itself. The muscles in his neck tense, awaiting the fate of his malady, bracing for its resolution, which will not come.

At moments, he is aware that people come in and out of his room – that space which is illuminated constantly by varying degrees of artificial and natural light. The shape of those people is becoming more solid, more tangible, less of an after-image. Some hand him clothes, others give him pills which he swallows because there is nothing else to be done with them. He is adapting to the life of subjugation, augmented by the blue and yellow ellipsoids that lodge in his throat only to be taken away by the motion of peristalsis as they fall down his parched gullet.

These itinerants have not heard him speak yet. Words have formed in his head but remain unspoken. A barrier still exists between the unconscious and the real. They ask him how he feels, and he does not know. They keep asking, nonetheless, inferring that an answer will come in due course.

Some bring food: a collection of boiled and mashed nourishment of undefined origin, served in a blue plastic tray with blunt cutlery. His hunger has returned, and he now eats these offerings, washed down with water that tastes of disinfectant.

Others want to talk to him.

Most regularly comes a woman around whose neck is a badge bearing the name Clinical Psychologist. In fact, she has attended his room only twice, but he imagines her presence repeatedly, having the feeling that the moment of her entering the room – the jangle of keys, the creak of the door and her blue-dressed figure – has occurred many times before. She asks questions in the manner of one who would not be inclined to believe the answer, whatever is offered. Her hair is short, and her glasses sparkle in the artificial light. She has a manner that is intended to put her clients at ease, but, in fact, is grating and reveals an urgency indicating that she wishes to finish the conversation as soon as possible. She is not put off by Reuben Christian's lack of dialogue, filling up their allotted half hour with repeated questions, hoping to cajole him into answering by attrition. At least today, she has had some eye contact.

She talks of illusions and hallucinations as though they were commonplace events: happenings that are perfectly normal to talk about, even to experience. She watches for any glimpse of recognition as she explains the meaning of these terms, which she is happy to do despite not understanding what it is to feel such phenomena. When she asks whether he has seen people from his past, she believes there to be a flicker of understanding – a constriction of the pupil and a twitch around the eyes.

'Do you see someone who isn't really there?' she asks, although she has never been comfortable with this explanation. It is a phrase she has been taught to say: a therapist's method of asking a patient, entering through the doors of psychosis in language that is not up to the purpose. Surely, someone is there if they are perceived to be there, at least in the eyes of one under the thrall of this degree of awareness. How can someone be there and not there? Even so, some of those she has previously interviewed relate to this concept. They are aware of a person but know that in reality – that world from which they are temporarily absent – that person is not there. The dichotomy of this experience doesn't upset them, which she finds unsettling, given its implications: life is so fragile, so if we can't trust our mind, what can we trust?

She is not getting any verbal response from Reuben Christian, so it is not clear to her if he is seeing people who are there or are not there, or not seeing anyone at all. She will write a report that will be brief but open-ended. She will write *aphasic*, and, since communication is the bedrock of psychological analysis, means that she cannot be sure what is wrong with him. People don't talk for all manner of reasons. She suspects abulia, a lack of motivation, is driving his silence, but it could be anything, she thinks, resigning herself to ignorance. *Diagnosis uncertain.*

39

WHAT IS IN a title? Mister, Doctor, Reverend. The police force is a prime example of enforcing hierarchy by prefixing designations in the chain of command. Some even get three. So why is Detective Inspector (only two) Price so vexed by the self-awarded title of Procurator used by the suspect? It annoys him with such an intensity that he refuses to refer to the man by the name.

'Don't call him that,' he advises his faithful deputy, DS Hameed, when discussing the man. 'He's no more a procurator than I am the pope,' he continues, his anger ensuring she will not address Mr George as Procurator George again, despite the hypocrisy of institutional hierarchy, which he accepts with alacrity. If there is enough history behind a title it will stick. Some titles require qualifications and exams to be sat. Last year a man was convicted of using the title Doctor, despite not having any qualifications. He had been practising as a holistic therapist – inspecting bodily fluids and correcting their texture and hue by means of crystals or something of the sort. The judge presiding over his court case – himself titled and robed as a result of centuries of legal pageantry – had been enraged that such a thing could happen. The man had received the maximum possible sentence, despite a lack of previous law-breaking. The idea that someone could self-appoint themselves to that role was an abomination.

They explore the usage of his self-appointed nomenclature in his next interview. In this most unusual of cases, all the man's idiosyncrasies may be relevant. Perhaps it will reveal a motive in a case that lacks one, other than a spat over ethics, which neither police officer thinks enough of a basis for murder.

'Mr George,' starts the DI, 'what is the title of your office?'

The procurator, having slept so badly in his cell over the past two nights and having built up a wariness for the line of questioning which is, he feels, designed to trap him, asks: 'What do you mean?'

'The title – the prenominal, I believe it is called – that is on your nameplate outside your offices and that you print on your business cards?'

The procurator is uncertain how to reply.

'Procurator,' says DS Hameed. 'You call yourself procurator.' She glances at the DI, going along with his fixation on something that might be considered of minor significance, given the nature of the alleged crime.

The procurator nods.

'And what does that mean?' asks the DI.

'It is a legal office, used in the past for one who offers legal advice in financial terms. In the Middle Ages it was also used for lawyers who provided counsel to, and even judgement over, those in trouble with any aspect of the law.'

The DI frowns, then shakes his head.

'I don't understand why you use the term?'

The procurator shrugs. 'It's not illegal to use the terminology.'

'I'm just interested to understand why you refer to yourself in such terms.'

There is silence, reflecting an unwillingness on the part of the suspect to divulge any more information.

After a moment, DS Hameed, enforcing the line of questioning determined by her superior officer, as is the custom in the police force or any organisation built on structures of rank and obedience, asks: 'Why precisely do you call yourself procurator, when no other lawyer in the country calls themselves by that term?'

She is met with the same silence.

'It's a delusion,' exclaims the DI, banging his hand against the table.

The two officers take a break, leaving the procurator, as he calls himself, in the interview room alone. The tape is still running, making a low-pitched rumble. A light flashes from the black box that houses the tape machine.

The procurator looks up at the ceiling and then at each of the four walls of the room – his space until that time comes when he is shuffled into another room, each one with a clock positioned high on the wall facing the interviewee's chair.

He thinks about the line of questioning, the DI's interest in his title. He knows the drill. They are looking for anything that might be a clue into the inner workings of a criminal mind. He has done the same, countless times. It is like finding the chink in the armour through which the blade can pass, exposing and then delving into the soft, fleshy part. Once the knife is in, don't take it out. Keep pushing, widening the entry point, loosening the plates of armour until they all fall off.

The current attack on his title erodes his personality, even dehumanises him. *You are no different to anyone else*, they imply. Why do you think you are so special? Perhaps it has been foolish to take on that title. Now that there is a need to explain himself, the reasons seem ridiculous. Articulating his inner convictions have always been difficult. His head spins with titles and things said or not said. He has arrived at this point – an interrogation room of blank walls and ticking clocks – and he has no idea how the pieces fell to orchestrate it. He is expected to give an explanation where no explanation exists. It was an unintended outcome. He wishes to scream from the depths of his being: *it is not what I meant to happen*. It comes down to faith, conviction, a sense of what is right, perhaps. But how does one explain that? That which has been challenged beyond all recognition during the past few days. A man is dead.

DI Price and DS Hameed return from their break. The DS trails behind, holding a single sheet of paper which she places, face down, on the table. The other police officer has a flake of pastry on his lower chin, which he flicks off after sitting down.

170

'Mr George,' he says, getting straight back into questioning, 'let me read you something.'

DS Hameed eyes the tape machine and notices, with some annoyance, that she has left it on during their break. She then hands the sheet of paper to her colleague, who starts to read:

'*In line with governance procedures of the Local and Regional Ethics Committee, and having been ratified by the National Ethics Committee Governing Body, I formally discharge you of your duties as a member of the university's ethics committee. Your behaviour has breached the code of conduct to which you agreed when becoming a member. Furthermore, after reporting this behaviour and subsequent interactions with members of the university's ethics committee to the National Ethics Committee Governing Body, a decision has been made to bar you from any future interaction with all ethics committees throughout the country. This decision has been made at an Extraordinary General Meeting of the National Ethics Committee Governing Body, in keeping with its own governance procedures. This decision cannot be appealed.*'

DI Price pauses for reaction. The procurator stares forward. His eyes are heavy, and he is no mood to discuss this. He sighs deeply, then says: 'That was a while ago. It was all dealt with, and I accepted the decision.'

DI Price drums his fingers on the table, creating a soft, irregular beat.

'Really,' he says. 'Tell us what behaviour was so heinous that it caused you to be thrown off the ethics committee? And not just the university one – all of them!'

He raises his voice at the end of the sentence, emphasising the seriousness of the point.

'It's been well documented,' replies the procurator, curtly.

The DI stands up and walks over to the window, which is high and glazed in frosted glass, allowing no one to see in or out. He stands with his back to the suspect.

DS Hameed, who remains seated, picks up the questioning. 'Will you tell us what happened? From your point of view,' she adds, as though she is doing him a favour.

'As I say, it was a long time ago,' replies the procurator. He lowers his eyes. Of course, they have all the details of his time on the committee. Perhaps he should explain his point of view, since the documents available to the police were written by an organisation which had little to do with ethics and more to do with the craven inventions of immoral scientists. Soon after joining, he had become aware that it was an organisation for the rubber-stamping of dubious morality, rather than one upholding any form of ethical code. He had read their side of the story in the reams of papers that were generated following the incidents. However, none contained the central reason for his disagreement with the membership of the committee. The documents, on the face of it, were damning, but neglected one fundamental issue: ethics.

'Let me tell you, then,' continued DS Hameed after a period of silence during which the accused's explanation was not forthcoming. 'After the ethics committee, at which the scientist's work was assessed, you sent threatening and abusive messages to said scientist imploring him to desist from his work. These messages continued despite warnings from the committee chair. Furthermore, you went around to his house – his private residence – and confronted the man on one occasion. You were then suspended from the committee and subsequently barred from serving on similar committees, as we have heard.'

DI Price turns around after she finishes and looks at the lawyer.

'Is that correct?' he asks.

The procurator remains silent. He has no reason to think they are interested in his side of the story.

'Mr George,' says the younger officer, 'we are investigating a murder. The murder of a man you threatened. Do you not understand why we are asking you these questions?'

He understands, of course, but cannot see a way out of the mire into which he is sinking. He is reminded of an aphorism he tells his most hopeless of clients: whatever you say, say nothing. And yet something compels him to talk.

'I was, and remain, interested in upholding ethical codes,' he says, quietly at first, building volume as he speaks. 'The way the committee ran was, in my opinion, contrary to all laws of decency and morality. I did what I felt was the right thing to do, to speak up against the culture of the committee.'

'So, intimidating a respected scientist was the right thing to do?' asks DI Price.

'Respected,' repeats the procurator, making clear his displeasure at the use of the word. 'Respected by whom, exactly? By the general populace, who turn a blind eye to underhand activities if they are done in the name of academia and a distorted vision of progress? Or just by virtue of an academic qualification?'

'So you didn't respect him?'

The procurator immediately regrets challenging the DI's use of the word which has led to this obvious riposte. He doubts whether anything he says will not be twisted and used to portray him in a bad light.

'I had no opinion on the man. I was objecting to the work he was performing which was, in my opinion, unethical. I had assumed, incorrectly as it turned out, that the function of the ethics committee was to make judgements on the ethical acceptability of scientific studies. The committee failed to do that, in this case. That is why I acted as I did.'

He takes a sip of water, his hands faintly trembling.

'You are a man with a strong sense of right and wrong, Mr George. Do you accept it was wrong to harass the man?'

'I accepted the recommendations of the ethics committee.'

'You haven't answered the question.'

'I accepted the recommendations of the ethics committee,' he repeats.

'You see, Mr George,' says the DI, becoming more animated, 'I think you continued to hold a grudge against the man. It festered and grew in your mind. He was the cause of your humiliation at the hands of the ethics committee. You never forgave him for that and so you hatched a scheme to get him killed.'

The procurator shakes his head. 'That is not it,' he says, his voice feeble, his mouth dry. Although implicit from the moment he was taken in for questioning, this is the first time he has heard direct accusation of his involvement in the crime. 'That is not it,' he repeats. His mind is awash with the limitless combinations of words that could provide an explanation of his role in the man's death, yet none forms well enough to come out. None are believable, none will exonerate him. He is left with half-truths and excuses that no one will stomach.

The DI is becoming impatient. He starts tapping on the table again.

'What is it, then?' he asks.

They continue to spar in a stuttering manner. Sometimes the procurator is silent, sometimes he responds. The response to the DI's theory of events is met with denial, yet no alternative is proffered by the suspect, who clams up further, retreating into his confused reasoning.

'Tell me about your moral code,' says DS Hameed, breaking the deadlocked cycle of the interview.

Up to this moment, the procurator has been looking down at his hands, which writhe and interlock at jagged angles. Now he looks up at the DS.

'You have a strong moral code, don't you, Mr George?' she says, paraphrasing her words in an attempt to break the impasse.

He remains silent, staring forward. The DS picks up the copy of *The Chronicles of John Corn* from a pile of documents. It is now encased in a transparent plastic bag, an item for a future court date, its significance to the case now made official by its clear labelling as evidence.

'You admitted in our last interview that this belongs to you.'

Light glints, fragmented, off the plastic surface of the evidence bag, distorting the picture on the front of the book: an etching in brown ink. It is of an old man, stooped forward, lantern in hand. His beard hangs down from his aged face and his brow is deeply furrowed. He stands before a door upon which has been pinned a wreath. We understand that the man is seeking entrance. The door is heavy, hinged in iron, uninviting. The sky is dark. Stars twinkle.

The procurator nods. It is his book.

'Tell me about the book.'

40

NEWS OF THE deadly action of the fugitive and the procurator reaches far and wide. Reporting the events of the world to the world is necessary; everything must be known. The predilection for scandal and bloodlust coupled with its overt assault on decency makes the story run and run. News agencies from the remotest parts of the globe descend on the city, described as quintessential in many reports, making the contrast with the circumstances of the murder all the more shocking. The city is known for its scholastic and ecclesiastical endeavours, they say, emphasising that it is possible for such an event to occur even here, where the pursuits are true and days are peaceful. Nowhere is safe, no one is safe – not even the pure at heart.

One woman, herself blessed with a kind spirit, reads yesterday's papers in a café in a remote fishing village on the Atlantic coast, overlooking rocks and diving seabirds. She has never heard of the city before, let alone been there, but she looks upon the grainy photograph of Galahad Bridge, an idyllic scene, and feels an instant fear. She shows her friend, who crosses herself in the manner of religious people wishing for protection. It looks like such a nice place, they both agree, looking once more at the photograph to ensure the image has not changed to one of the slums of their own country, where killing and blood-letting is all too commonplace. They look around the café and resolve to be more careful, to look over their shoulder once in a while, particularly when crossing their own town's bridge, which connects the market square to the outskirts of the favela.

Similarly, the folk of a quaint German town in the foothills of snow-peaked mountains have taken note. Not two years ago, a businessman was gunned down in the street, an unsolved crime to this day; no murderer, no motive. The people have walked the streets in trepidation since that day. 'Someone must know who did it,' is a repeated mantra. Looking at the newspapers, the people sitting in the bars of Starnbergerstrasse are overcome by a sense of unsolicited revisitation, followed by an emotion of empathy for the people of this other city, with whom they now share a bond. The town council passes a resolution to send a message of solidarity. Some send flowers, others knit cardigans for the children of their newly twinned conurbation. The mayor will visit in due course to offer a hand of friendship and, perhaps, his own observations on overcoming tragedy. *We are all in this together*, he will say, proposing a visit to the cenotaph (constructed to commemorate a deadly war between the mayor's country and the country he visits – a fact which will be glossed over) and the laying of a wreath for the murdered men.

One journalist, writing in a neighbouring county's local paper, links the bridge murder (as he calls it) to another killing several years ago: a postman stabbed violently to death on his rounds not too far from Galahad Bridge. It had been speculated at the time that the victim had stumbled upon on a satanic ritual in a remote farmhouse high on the moors above a former mining community now gone to seed. The perpetrator had been caught, and his past history of dealings with the occult had been exposed during his court case. The papers had gone to town. This was a story that would sell, one which titillated and terrified in equal measure. The journalist saw similar patterns in the current murder and expounded his theories – half-baked and tenuous – to an audience keen to believe anything in an apparently motiveless case, for the reason that everyone desires an explanation (even the most contrived) in order to reassure themselves that similar acts would not befall them. In fact, the journalist whips up more panic by indicating that the date of the next attack – in his supposed sequence of murders – would be only a few weeks away, a date based on obscure predictions of Victorian occultists, on whose teachings the murderer of the postman had been fixated.

Stories of this kind spring up all over the news reporting outlets of the world, filling the void made by the lack of justification for the crime. In an age when finding the solution to any question is usually no more than a few taps on a screen away, ignorance is intolerable. The journalists write and the people read.

41

JOHN CORN WAS born in 1603 in this grand metropolis, which already extended far beyond the banks of the river and out towards the sea. The city numbered over ten thousand in its population, young and old crammed together within its walls. In that year, New Canterbury was reeling from the outbreak of a mysterious plague that would eventually kill more than a third of its inhabitants. A civil war that had raged for over twenty years had finished a decade before, and the people of the city had every reason to look forward to peace and a time of prosperity. New trade routes had opened, and the valley's plains seemed more fertile than ever. A huge cathedral was built to herald a new age, destined, all imagined, to become the golden age. The people gave thanks and sang new songs of a forthcoming celestial harvest. But the plague threatened to ruin all this. The illness and reports of its devastating effects had affected vital trading routes. The city was in danger of collapse and ruin. Merchants took their ships further downstream and navigated around the coast, up beyond the Cape of Dogs to the more sedate yet expanding towns that lined the shore: not as much commerce, not such great prices, but at least they were safe. Even the cathedral closed its doors for the winter months, ostensibly to preserve fuel and food but in reality as a result of the overwhelming fear that gripped the bishop and his clergy, who withdrew from their duties. Baptisms, funerals, weddings ceased to take place. Cobwebs multiplied in the pews.

It was known, even then, that the plague was spread by close human contact. The living conditions in the city – close-packed families with little sanitation – meant that it was inescapable to many. Some fled to the country, but the paucity of food drove them back to the lesser of two evils. At least in the city there was a slim chance they might recover; there was no recovery from starvation. Conflicts arose between the hungry and the terrified. Those with money barricaded themselves away, refusing alms to the beggars who gathered around the gates of their town houses and their estates. Those seeking food became more desperate, breaking into the houses of the rich, raiding larders, spreading germs. The new enemy was those with the means to avoid the squalor which begot the malady. The landowners, in turn, became more militant, keeping for themselves their dwindling supplies, defending by whatever means they could. And so, groups of citizens roamed the streets and the suburbs. The outcome was that many died of the plague, others of starvation, and others at the hand of those bearing arms in a vain attempt to protect their property and their lives. Lawless and uncontrollable justice was practised by the desperate hoards and the terrified gentry, illustrated in startling terms one morning by the spectacle of the lord of the manor strung up from an apple tree in his bountiful orchard, legs dangling in the gentle breeze.

A curious effect of the illness in some was that it caused a riot of involuntary movements to occur, arms and legs flailing with no purpose. In many, it led to the appearance of a frenzied dance. Groups of the infected frolicked their way through the streets, exhausting themselves yet having no power to desist, such being the power of whatever force had taken hold. A curious accompaniment to the dancing crowds – depicted in the few woodcuts generated by the city's artists of the time – was the sight of musicians, who would accompany the furious dances, playing on rudimentary bagpipes fashioned from the skins of sheep and producing the most ominous of drones. Whether these musicians were themselves infected with the plague and the clinical manifestation of their disease was the generation of an involuntary cacophony, or whether their music was their means of justifying the dancing, perhaps to make it less unholy, is not known.

It was a hopeless situation. The Church looked on. Most of its officials had retired to the monastery beyond the eastern hills, self-sufficient – for a time, at least. The bishops would watch through the windows of the central high tower, expecting at any moment a delegation of the infected peasants. Cowering and the clutching of icons were practised in equal measure. All vows were reinforced, particularly those of solitude. This immoral choreomania was, for sure, an indication of the Devil's work, so they had no qualms about locking the monastery gates.

The city had become a godless place.

Into this was born John Corn.

42

REUBEN CHRISTIAN SPEAKS his first words since emerging from his psychosis.

'Someone has been telling lies about me,' he says to the nurse who brings him his morning medication.

A bright light floods the room, reflecting off the clean plastic surfaces.

'It's all fine,' she says, speaking in a deadpan, calming voice. She is familiar with the many and varied paranoid revelations of her patients and is seeking not to provoke him.

The male nurse who accompanies her senses an anger rising in the patient and is on guard. His nature, of late, is to be combative, more willing to challenge – even when it comes to those he is employed to look after.

'Lies,' repeats the patient, looking at the male nurse, who supposes the comment is directed at him.

'Relax, Reuben,' he snaps back, more an order than words of calm, using the man's name for the first time since he arrived in the hospital. Staff are now aware of who he is, having been briefed by the police. The psychiatrist has urged them to use his name to help return his identity to him.

'You're a liar,' Reuben spits out, his gaze still upon the male nurse.

The two nurses ensure that he takes his medicine before filing out of his room. They lock the door behind them.

The male nurse hesitates outside the door, then looks through the peep hole. Reuben is looking directly at him, or, rather, at the other side of the peep hole, behind which he knows the nurse is standing. The nurse moves away from the door. He is disquieted by their interaction. He is an experienced psychiatric nurse and knows not to be offended or take at face value the disclosures of those with an altered mental state. Yet he *is* a liar. The interaction, albeit brief, and not unusual in such an establishment, has touched a nerve, a spoken truth from the depths of a muddled mind. He has lied to his wife for several months, making up stories about overtime shifts while really engaging in a new relationship with a former patient on the unit. He has lied to his colleagues about the affair; has lied to his profession, which considers such actions unthinkable and not compatible with continued employment. Of course, the man in the room, whose name he now knows to be Reuben Christian, has no knowledge of his private life, but words are words, accusations are accusations, truths are truths.

It is the latest in a series of events that has pushed the nurse to the extremes of his tolerance. A few days back, an old woman at the end stage of dementia had attacked him as he changed dressings on her self-inflicted wounds. She had scratched his arm violently, just as she had scratched her own. He had pulled back, but not before she had latched her nails deep into his skin. He now bears three fingernail tracks of clotted blood, three parallel lines. He had shouted at the woman, expressing his outrage at the assault and at her violence. The colleague who had accompanied him had been disturbed at his outburst. They both knew that the woman had lost all idea of social properness. Any notion of societal norms was now buried in her tangled brain, never to resurface. She had acted on an instinct, a primal urge to prevent pain as he cleaned and dressed her wounds – an instinct that years of development had supressed, only to be released by the decay of her brain. Did he have any right to be outraged? And why was he now so disturbed at the accusation of the man in the locked room?

He continues his work, putting up a barrier, telling himself not to think about these events. Yet, after a few minutes, he returns to the peep hole and, once again, looks through. Reuben is still looking in his direction. What had he expected? What made him check back on the man? Guilt rises in him like the outlet on a pressurised chamber, but his mind directs it towards the man in the room. *You're the guilty one, mate*, he thinks, moving away from the door. The policeman who sits outside the room is testament to that.

The hospital staff are aware now not only of the man in the room's name but also his identity as the man suspected of carrying out the atrocity on the bridge. They have had murderers in their midst before, but the notoriety of the recent event holds a significance, causing a heightened sense of apprehension amongst those working on the ward. Against the policies of the hospital, a few – most, in fact – have told their loved ones that they are looking after the bridge killer. They will not go into details, and their loved ones are not sure they want to know any more. Not being immune to the high levels of anxiety within the population over the incident, they justify their confiding of this fact as being necessary to alleviate the pressures of the job. And anyway, the papers have reported that a man 'wanted in connection with the killing' is being held in the city's secure psychiatric unit.

The nurse pauses for his tea break. He sits in the staff room with the words of the alleged bridge killer echoing in his mind. He looks down at the scratch marks on his arm, one of which has started to bleed afresh. He thinks back to the incident with the old woman and, at the same time, hears her calling from her room further down the corridor. It is a wail, perhaps another accusation. He has wronged her, just as he has wronged all the people who are close to him. He feels the need to scratch further, to excoriate the marks left by the deranged woman. He forms the fingers of his left hand into a claw, bringing it down on the injured forearm. With a frenzy he scrapes his fingernails back and forth, creating deep welts in the skin, blood oozing then forming a thick crimson line. A colleague seated opposite, a trainee nurse in her first psychiatry assignment, watches in horror, dazed initially, before the confusion of identities of the strange establishment overcomes her.

'Stop!' she shouts, before going to the door and crying out for help.

Two other nurses arrive, then the policeman who guards Reuben Christian. One restrains his colleague, while the other dons gloves, aware of the risk of bodily fluids. The student nurse is fixed to a spot in the corner of the room.

Blood is smeared now on the tunic of the nurse who restrains her colleague, but no resistance is met, and she slowly releases her grip on the scratching hand. The male nurse falls back into his chair and looks at his bloodied arm, almost in disbelief.

'What's happened, Joseph?' asks the nurse who has put on the gloves.

Joseph is impassive, staring forward, silent.

The student nurse runs from the room and the policeman looks back at the door of Reuben Christian's room, perhaps considering whether the event that has just occurred is linked to the crime whose perpetrator he now guards. It is an irrational thought, but one which sits firmly amongst the plethora of ideas and theories that have arisen over the past few days.

A doctor comes and the nurse with the bleeding arm is bandaged up. He is sent to rest in an empty side room, where a mental state examination will be performed by the consultant psychiatrist, called in from home to assess his longstanding colleague, who is calm now, committed to his fate, resigned to his guilt.

The other nurses, save for the student nurse, who has been sent home, get back to work. They are shaken, but they have seen occurrences of this nature before. The head nurse of the ward, herself approaching retirement and a good pension (which is granted at an earlier age for those working in the field of psychiatry), has lost count of the number of colleagues who have, over the years, traversed the line from carer to patient. In her early years of nursing, she would often reassure families that mental illness was not contagious, but she no longer offers this guarantee.

We are all just a few steps away from it.

43

A DAY AFTER unsubstantiated and untraceable reports of a gunman, or maybe several, roaming the streets, seeking some kind of recurrence of that murderous event, thought to be the nadir of the city's history, the people take to the streets. An impromptu gathering of forces rallied by mobile phones and touchscreen devices appears in Cleopatra Street. The instruction has been to come together at 10am and then march over Galahad Bridge. Beyond that, the details are flimsy. Bring placards, anything visual to demonstrate that we will not be cowed into hiding. *This is our city. These are our streets.*

The police have got wind of this, since mass communication tools are used by all in society, including those whose job it is to control and suppress any form of subterfuge. They summon up a team of uniformed officers, weary and unimpressed, imagining their time might be better spent in other ways. They expect trouble and have called for back-up from neighbouring forces. An armed response team has been summoned, and it arrives in an unmarked van with blacked-out windows. Intelligence has determined that a militant faction of a right-wing extremist group is travelling to the city to provide their own interpretation of the killing on the bridge. They will blame the people whom they wish to blame. They will use the demonstration as a perfect opportunity to expose the lies of immigration that have been peddled by successive governments, appeasing the liberal and the weak. Their rhetoric is of taking back power, and of returning England to a time of decency and a pure bloodline. The police will need to tread a cautious line, neither enraging the warlike throngs nor failing to act when lawlessness prevails.

In addition to this motley group of extremists, another group protesting the presence of such a group of fanatics is being mustered from the shires and villages. (Who will protest against the protestors?) They oppose the perceived bigotry and intolerance of the anti-immigrationists, yet bizarrely they share a common drive to return to a more decent time, when there was equality and capitalism hadn't taken its dirty grip on the ailing world. Whether the era each other imagines ever existed is uncertain, and they have no time machines to take them back to check. Nonetheless, neither side is deterred from protesting, with goals that become more distorted on each outing.

Constables Tomaris and Banner are positioned on the northern side of the bridge, approximately twenty metres from the site of the killing that has been the catalyst for today's events. The march has not yet reached the bridge and at the present time seems more of a disparate bunch of the unherdable. They can see them gathering on Cleopatra Street, waving flags and symbols of whatever cause they espouse.

'Colourful lot, aren't they?' says Constable George Tomaris, legs wide apart, hands on hips.

Constable Banner does not reply but looks on at the crowd apprehensively. In this time when nothing is predictable, she feels deeply uncertain about how the morning will turn out: either the masses will all walk peacefully and then disperse to various pubs, or else something more disturbing will develop.

'They're on the move,' says Constable Tomaris, pointing at a group approaching from the right. They are distant, herd-like in their form, yet their movements are chaotic, lacking a common purpose. Over the course of a minute, however, it is clear they are gathering at the far side of the bridge, ready to cross. A man with a loudhailer is marshalling troops, and the constables hear the tone of his amplified voice but not the content of his speech, which is muffled by distance and a strong breeze blowing down the river. They hear a cheering and then a clapping, followed by further indistinct sounds on the loudhailer.

The DI in charge of the police operation issues orders via police radio, which has the effect of drawing the uniformed group into a closer formation, strengthening the lines on either side of the bridge. None shall pass, other than through the defined channel flanked by the police.

George Tomaris looks behind him to the collection of police vans parked at the entrance to a closed-off side street. An officer in a bullet-proof vest and helmet is unloading riot shields from the back of one van. Other officers settle into position, cradling stubby black guns.

'The cavalry are here!' he jokes with Fiona Banner, who has also spotted the activity behind them. He is in his element, his senses sharpened by the imminent conflict; she is more conservative, wishing for a resolution without locking horns.

The noise from the other end of the bridge intensifies, and the two constables turn their attention back to the advancing throng, who span the bridge, forming a phalanx reminiscent, one might imagine, of barbarian invaders from the city's past. A trumpeter heads the group, playing a tuneless rally call that floats in the air and down the river. An ensign is raised. The gauntlet is thrown down.

The wind picks up overhead, almost blowing over a makeshift barrier the police have placed around the site of the scientist's death. More messages are issued to the lined-up police officers: they will let the marchers pass, then shepherd them into the marketplace, where they can be contained. They will have their say – a few speeches on the makeshift podium – then will be, politely, asked to disperse. If they do not, then who knows what will happen.

The constables lining up on the bridge relax their formation, not wanting to intimidate or agitate. The marchers come closer, shouting chants which are, at the distance the police stand, indecipherable. Keep them away from the site of the murder, orders the DI leading the operation. He offers no reason for this.

Constable Tomaris looks up at the windows of a tall building overlooking the bridge. He spots a marksman, all in black, looking through binoculars. But then his attention is drawn to a flock of crows that fly erratically above the building. One crow appears much larger and is the bird leading the others in their chaotic flight path. It swoops, falls and then reclimbs, leaving much of its course to the whimsical might of the wind that blows powerfully, a hidden force dictating the strange corvine ritual. Others in the flock follow, keeping their movement as one, as much as they can in the ferocity of the elements.

Fiona Banner nudges her colleague. *Pay attention, man* is the meaning of her intervention. She finds it hard to understand how he could be distracted by commonplace birds in the sky at such a time. Constable Tomaris focuses on the group of marchers, who are now close enough to be recognisable, should any of them be known to him. He tenses.

'Reclaim the streets!' is the chant, which is now recognisable to the police officers. *An odd thing to shout*, thinks Fiona Banner. She is not clear from whom they are reclaiming them, or if they have been claimed at all.

The marchers now reach the level of the police. Theirs are combative stares, interspersed with more slogans, shouted with as much force as they can muster. The police hold their ground. One protestor, clad in a brown waxed jacket and a knitted woollen hat, breaks from his compatriots and strides to the nearest police officer. A few inches from her face, he starts to shout the same slogan, flecks of spittle expelled with the might of his words. The female officer recoils a little, and her colleague, a burly officer who stands next to her, puts out a hand to prevent the protestor from coming any closer.

'Come on!' shouts the protestor, puffing out his chest and dropping his arms to his side, palms forward, fingers splayed. 'Do you want some?' he shouts, imploring a reaction from the officer, who keeps his hand outstretched.

Several other officers then pounce on the man, bringing

him to the ground and pinning him in a regulation hold. This provokes others in the marching group to advance on the police, shouting and gesticulating. None, however, replicates the action of the pinioned man, since an officer yielding a gun, jet black and reflecting no light, has now joined the line. 'Get back!' he says, superfluously, since the gun has indicated the sentiment more effectively than words.

The man on the floor looks up at his colleagues, issuing expletives, advocating full revolution.

'We will not be supressed!' he shouts, still struggling against the officer who is holding his arm behind his back and pressing a knee into his spine. His colleagues back off. There is a mass of expectation from those pushing from behind, a mass which imparts a force greater than the pleas of the man on the floor, and the crowd is propelled to the market square and the rhetoric that awaits. *Words for the masses are heard more loudly than single acts of retribution.*

The man on the floor, subdued now he is aware of his colleagues' fickle nature, quietens down and submits to his subjugation. Two police officers lift him to his feet after the application of handcuffs. He stands, his feeble frame cast against those of his two captors, a pygmy between giants. Initially he refuses to walk as the two officers move off towards the police van, resulting in him being dragged a few paces, but the discomfort of his feet scraping against the hard ground is such that he meekly makes his way to the open door and from there into the cramped confines of the vehicle. An inner door of steel mesh is closed after him, but the outer door remains open, and he can see the people continuing their march towards the market square and their own form of liberation. One or two cast their eyes in the direction of imprisoned man, their glances betraying a feeling of relief that it isn't them in the van.

In time, the procession passes, and the majority of the police officers follow in the direction of the square. Muffled sounds of speeches and outbursts of applause are heard.

Two police officers stay with their prisoner. Against predictions, they have only apprehended one person. Several lock-up vans remain empty.

'They are clearly well-behaved sorts,' jokes the older officer, knowing, however, that things could yet get ugly.

The younger officer, who has a neck tattoo that pokes out above the collar of his shirt, is a serious type and prone to acts of aggression, which has got him into deep water before now. He views the marchers with utter disdain and can't stomach the flippancy of his colleague in moments like this.

Sensing the mood of the younger officer, the older policeman will lead the initial interview with the detained man. It could be a long day, and there is no point in rattling the cage of the captured, at least not now. There will be time for that later.

He approaches the back of the van and peers into the darkness, from where two eyes glint back. He is reminded of a fox caught in a trap; a helpless free spirit displaced from its natural habitat. The protestor shrinks back into the shadows of the enclosed cage.

The policeman unlocks the cage and enters. There is a familiar smell to the cage which, despite the daily washing and fumigating, never goes. It is the stale cocktail of all the days and nights of bad behaviour. The policeman has never got used to it, and, in some way wishes that he never will; it is a reminder of the end product of criminality, an olfactory imprint which, he hopes, might repel those detained therein from repeating their misdemeanour.

'Can you take these off?' asks the protestor, pushing forward his shoulder, attempting to bring the cuffed hands into view. They are restrained behind his back, which makes sitting difficult. He perches on the narrow ledge of the van's interior, unable to get comfortable.

The policeman sits opposite and takes out a notepad, ignoring the request.

'Did you hear me?' barks the protestor, banging the cuffs against the side of the van feebly, being unable to generate much force due to the angles and leverage of his position.

The policeman looks up from his notebook and licks the lead of his pencil, a habit he has had since childhood, born of the erroneous notion that graphite in a pencil requires the action of saliva to work. He has the manner of someone who has been in this position a million times before. He has heard all the pleas, the abuse, the excuses. He checks his watch for the time, which he writes down in scrawled figures at the top of a fresh page.

'Do you understand why you have been arrested?' he asks.

The protestor bangs the side of the van with his cuffs again, like a zoo animal, unforgiving and irate.

From outside they hear the faint noise of cheering, followed by clapping.

'Let me tell you again, then,' says the policeman. 'You have been detained for incitement to violence and assault of a police officer.'

'I never touched him!'

'We have witnesses to your behaviour,' the officer replies calmly.

'Police state!'

The policeman again licks his pencil and writes in his notebook.

'Look, son,' the policeman says, pausing his writing, 'this doesn't look good, and you're in a lot of trouble. If I were you, I'd stop this nonsense and co-operate.'

The protestor rests back, his arms and hands uncomfortably positioned between his back and the van. He squirms, feeling a searing pain in his left shoulder, the recurrence of an old sporting injury. The policeman is old enough to be his father; his face is kindly, softened by the poor lighting in the vehicle. The captive man himself has a kindly father who raised him through his happy childhood, his law-abiding youth. The policeman's face emphasises the contrast of his former life to his current predicament, cooped up a police van, arrested and humiliated. Shame overcomes his protestations. A new emotion overwhelms him, and tears come to his eyes.

'I'm sorry,' he says meekly, 'I behaved badly.'

The younger police officer appears at the open door.

'Orders are to return to the police station,' he says holding open the door for his colleague to exit the back of the van.

'I'll ride in the back, constable.'

The younger colleague is surprised at this protocol breach, but doesn't question the decision of one ranked above him in the hierarchy. 'Suit yourself,' he mutters, closing the cage door and then the van door.

The policeman and the protestor sit in near darkness for a few moments until the van's motor starts and a light comes on in the back. They feel the motion of the vehicle, and through the small back window see the buildings surrounding the bridge retreat into the distance.

The van makes two ninety degree turns, and the marketplace is now visible. Banners and flags rise above the masses, bobbing up and down and fluttering in the wind.

'What exactly is everyone protesting against?' asks the police officer, addressing no one in particular as he watches the receding scene.

44

John Corn's childhood was marked by illness and suffering, almost ubiquitous at the time. His mother had died giving birth to the tenth of her brood, the runt of the litter who perished himself two days later, unfed and unloved. Childbirth, being such a dangerous event in those days, was the commonest cause of death in the country for women of her age. Her death, shortly after John Corn's third birthday, naturally changed the dynamics of the family, and its hardships were magnified by the removal of maternal compassion, the bond that held them together even through hunger and despair. His father had been a labourer for a large country estate and had done his best to provide, but grief overtook him and he became a distant figure, providing little discipline and even less food for the children who, for the most part, slipped into lives of truancy and petty criminality. Only three survived to adulthood, the rest succumbing to diseases of poor nutrition or to illnesses arising through absent sanitation. Of those who reached the age of fifteen, John Corn stood out as different. He had worked alongside his father on the country estate for several years by this point, and the wealthy landowner had taken an interest in him, no doubt enraptured by his golden hair and his pure nature. He was naturally a kind and friendly boy, an attribute which contrasted with the misery around, magnifying it and making it seem unreal.

The landowner, a progressive type, took a philanthropic interest in the motley band of peasants who travelled the four or five miles from the city, and was undoubtedly distressed by the ravages of poverty and the inequity of birthright. He made sure that John Corn received an education, enrolling him at the age sixteen in the local choir school attached to the city's cathedral. The rich landowner was a generous benefactor to the cathedral and liked nothing better than attending choral evensong, which he did every Sunday with his ageing mother. Being childless, he heaped attention onto the growing lad, shaping him in the manner he thought appropriate. He dressed him in fine clothes and paraded him in his carriage on a Sunday afternoon. John Corn even took up residence in the manor house and had access to his own servants. Some of them resented the elevation of one of their type to a life of luxury. His nature was such, however, that most did not begrudge his good luck.

His education in the Church, consisting of divinity, Latin and music, was all-consuming, and he became distant from his natural family. On occasion, he would spot his father repairing the perimeter wall or pushing a barrow, but the separation did not unduly bother him. Being young and, at this stage in his life, unquestioning, he supposed this to be the nature of childhood, the rich tapestry of ups and down, chance and jeopardy. He simply accepted fate and imagined all those around him would do the same.

But then, shortly after his seventeenth Christmas, his life changed once again, and almost overnight his outlook on the world was transformed. The estate owner was arrested for 'lewd acts' (the nature of which has been lost in the city's archives) and thrown in jail. His trial lasted for months, and the verdict and sentence were delivered as the bells of the cathedral chimed to herald the first evensong of Lent. The wealthy landowner was stripped of his assets and exiled to an unknown kingdom, never to be seen again. John Corn became homeless and without a patron. His relationship with his father had long since disintegrated due to his father's jealousy and obsessional suspicion with his offspring's new life, and his two remaining siblings had left the city to find their riches elsewhere, driven out by poverty and a lack of regard for their worth, which they saw as evident in their father's brooding over his learned son. John Corn was alone in the world. There was only one place for him to go, and that was the monastery associated with the cathedral, where, at least, he would find a bed and sustenance.

45

Rain is forecast, and the black clouds gathering above the police station will validate the prediction. DS Hameed arrives by bicycle, a folding type that is employed by commuters who are using a number of modes of transport. Her journey does not include the use of confined public transport vehicles, yet she feels that the ability to stow the bicycle indoors, rather than tied to a railing outside, outweighs its shortcomings as a mode of transport. There are many thieves about.

Her journey has been affected by the impromptu demonstration in the centre of the city. Several roads remain closed, and her diversion takes her to a part of the city with which she is not familiar. She has lived in the city for many years but is still uncertain how certain roads connect together; it is a higgledy-piggledy jigsaw of highways. She has passed several people carrying placards, looking bedraggled, like the remnants of a defeated army.

She carries the collapsed contraption of her commute into the large open plan office and places it beneath her desk. A square of yellow paper has been stuck in the middle of her computer screen which reads: 'He is ready to talk.'

Immediately she looks up in the direction of the DI's office, recognising his handwriting and his unique method of communicating. Others would use text or email. The light is on, and his form is visible behind the frosted windows. She walks the few paces, knocks on the door and enters without being invited.

'Let's go!' says DI Price, grabbing his coat and car keys from his desk. She follows without question.

They drive the few miles to the secure psychiatric unit, through country lanes and past the outer fringes of the city where the gardens become larger and the plaster on the houses looks cleaner. They approach the old mansion house that houses the psychiatry services for the county. Previously an impressive country estate, it is now battered, surrounded by quickly constructed brick extensions and makeshift portacabins. The space required to house the psychiatrically unwell is ever-expanding.

They park and make their way to the entrance, retracing their route to the ward, improbably named *Sunshine*, where the patient is held. It is situated on the ground floor, the preserve of the most challenging patients, giving them one less option for self-harm. The windows are barred, nonetheless.

'Detective Inspector Price and Detective Sergeant Hameed here,' the senior police officer says into the intercom outside the ward. A buzz sounds and the door clicks open.

They enter the ward to sounds of shouting, but the atmosphere is curiously calm. The nurses and doctors sit in the meeting room, formerly the drawing room of the house, engaged in their morning ward round, talking about their charges without the distraction of their presence. The two police officers are beckoned in to join them. A strong smell of coffee fills the room.

'We were just talking about Reuben,' says the doctor who sits at the head of the table, peering over half-moon glasses. Beside him a large pile of notes rests on the table, ready to topple with the slightest lateral force. The various therapists, nurses and administrators huddle around the table, waiting their turn to opine on matters concerning the disordered mental states of those in locked cells a few paces down the corridor.

The detectives remain standing, eager to get on with the task in hand.

'He's not out of the woods yet, but his delusional thoughts have settled,' continues the doctor. He flicks through the file in front of him, then pulls out a card which lists his multiple medications. 'He's on heavy-duty meds now,' he adds scanning the list.

'What is his diagnosis?' asks DS Hameed, aware, as soon as the words leave her mouth, that the complexity of the human mind may defy pigeon-holing into a single word or two.

'Acute schizophrenia.'

DS Hameed nods. 'Has he had it before?' she asks.

'He was diagnosed with a schizoid personality disorder a few years back, so has had psychotic tendencies before, if that's what you mean,' he replies, resisting the urge to point out the naivety of her question. Mental illness isn't like chicken pox, he might have said to a medical student if they were to ask such a question.

'So, he's known to your services?' asks DI Price, taking up the baton from his junior colleague, who is feeling some intimidation from the doctor.

'He was last seen a few years back. He was on anti-psychotic medication and was meant to be under regular review, but he's not been in the system for a while,' replies the doctor. 'It's not uncommon in people with personality disorders,' he adds.

'So, he wasn't taking his medication?'

'No. He was prescribed it for three months, then should have continued the prescription but didn't engage with his general practitioner or with us, so was lost to the system. Who knows if he ever took the meds?' He pauses and wipes his glasses on a cloth from his shirt pocket. 'I very much doubt it.'

The police officers comprehend the difficulties of the doctor. Trying to put right the very clients with whom they both come into regular contact can't be the easiest of jobs. Even if there were a cure for the bizarre illnesses of the mind, engaging with the afflicted must be nigh-on impossible. And anyway, sorting the sociopaths from the psychotics, or the delirious from the wicked is difficult enough, as they decide which form of incarceration – a psychiatric hospital or a prison – is appropriate for a person who has done wrong.

'Can we see him?' ask the DI.

The doctor looks at the nurse to his left. 'Are you happy for them to see him?' he asks him, relaying the question.

The nurse has a shaven head and a nose-ring. He takes his glasses off and considers the request. There is a need to protect his patient from psychological harm, but, at the same time, a desire to facilitate the police in their enquiries concerning the terrible event. He has lived in the city all his life and has been deeply affected by the murder and its ramifications.

'I think so,' he says. 'Maybe just for five minutes or so.'

The two police officers get up, and the nurse accompanies them to the patient's room. The police constable positioned outside the door stands when the two officers arrive. DS Hameed smiles at him, and he resumes his seat and his vigil.

The nurse unlocks the door, and they enter. Reuben Christian is lying on his bed, awake and staring at the ceiling. He turns his head as the delegation enters the room, looking upon each person in turn. Then his gaze rests on DS Hameed, who sits in a chair at the opposite corner of the room.

'Reuben,' says the nurse, 'I've brought some people to see you. They want to talk to you.'

He sits up and shifts his attention to the nurse, who now picks up some clothes from the floor. He studies this domestic activity intensely.

DI Price takes a step forward, as though he were a participant in a childhood game where those wishing to achieve the goal of capture do not wish to disturb lest they be chased away.

'Reuben,' he says, 'how are you today?'

Reuben turns his head away from the voice, towards the blank wall, then shifts his body so that he faces it with his whole body, his legs crossed, his spine askew. The DI takes another step and grabs the back of a chair situated next to the bed, turning it. He sits and continues: 'Reuben. We need to talk to you about what you were doing before you came into hospital.'

Reuben continues his silence. He rocks gently on his hips, making the bed produce tiny squeaks. The nurse interjects; 'Come on, Reuben, talk to us.'

The nurse walks closer and places a hand on the patient's

back, a friendly gesture to indicate a connection with a fellow human being, one meant to soothe.

Reuben turns his body sharply, and then stands and walks to the corner of the room, freeing himself from the unwanted tactile signal. He looks out of the window, to the fields and the horizon far off. Geese fly above in a V-shaped formation, their cries inaudible through the reinforced glass of the hospital. He watches their gentle flapping as they disappear from view.

'Reuben. You're not in any trouble, but we need to talk to you,' says the DI. It is clearly a lie: he is in trouble. He is the chief suspect in a murder case. What more trouble could he be in? It is the kind of thing he would say to a child to draw out a confession of a minor infringement of household rules. It is a phrase with no meaning, other than to put him at ease, to get him to talk. DS Hameed coughs, quietly, an involuntary expression of surprise, perhaps. She cannot understand why her superior officer would say such a thing.

The nurse picks up a pillow from Reuben's bed, which he carries to the door, glancing at the DI as he passes. He too is incredulous. The last thing they should do is lie to their patients. That breaks all codes of psychiatric practice. He places the pillow and the dirty clothes on the floor by the door, ready to be removed and taken to the laundry.

There is stalemate in the room. The questioning of the suspect has faltered with the most benign-sounding of statements.

'Perhaps, we should leave Reuben in peace now,' suggests the nurse, doing little to hide his annoyance at the police officer.

DS Hameed stands up and pushes her chair back against the wall.

'The geese are flying to their feeding grounds,' says Reuben, still gazing out of the window. His utterance surprises all in the room. DS Hameed instinctively looks out of the window, up to the broad grey sky, scanning what small space can be seen from where she stands.

The other police officer steps over to the window and stands next to the patient. He too scans the sky to confirm the presence of the birds.

'They've gone now,' says Reuben.

DI Price nods. 'They roost overnight in the salt marshes out west, flying inland to the fields to feast on sugar beet and grain.'

Reuben Christian shakes his head. 'But this year it's all wrong. The birds think it's winter. They shouldn't be doing this in the spring, not now,' he says continuing to scan the sky, looking for more evidence of the chaotic happenings of nature. 'It's all wrong,' he repeats.

The two men stand at the window for several minutes. No more birds fly overhead. The sky darkens and grey clouds roll in from behind a sparse patch of trees bordering the hospital confines.

'Shall we sit down?' asks the DI, pointing to DS Hameed's vacated chair. He pulls another chair closer as Reuben sits down.

'Tell me about your time in the woods.'

A flickering appears beside Reuben Christian's left eye, an involuntary muscle spasm.

'It was cold,' he starts, 'and wet. Lights shone in the night's darkness, but I hid beneath an old fallen tree. A trench had formed beneath. It was boggy, but warmer than on the exposed earth. I remember dogs and then the trees became …' He breaks off, in the manner of one who is searching for a memory, or perhaps not wishing to remember.

'Why were you in the woods?' asks the policeman.

'I was escaping.'

'Escaping from what?'

Reuben Christian points to the door. 'From him.'

The door is closed.

'Who?' asks the DI.

'Him,' he continues to point.

The nurse restates the need to terminate the interview, but the DI is keen to continue.

'Who is at the door?'

He turns away. It is a question without meaning.

The nurse at the door grabs the handle, making to usher out the delegation, who have overstayed their welcome. A rising tension occupies the stale air of the tiny room.

'Tell me about John Corn, Reuben.'

Reuben Christian, failed jewel thief, now murder suspect, puts his hand to his ears, covering them, curls his head down into his chest, then contracts his whole body, twisting and writhing in a demonic dance. It is as though the mention of something so vile has caused a convulsion of his humanity.

46

THE MONASTIC LIFE initially suited John Corn. His diaries from that time indicated that he enjoyed the rituals of a simplistic life. Furthermore, the deprivations expected of the lifestyle were not challenging for him to tolerate given his early years which were, in fact, more restricted than anything he would endure in later years. During those first years of life he had existed on the verge of starvation, so any way of life encompassing even a modicum of comfort was seen as a luxury. He particularly enjoyed his chores in the monastery garden, tilling the rich soil and sowing the crops. For reasons he could not fathom, the land surrounding the monastery was particularly fertile. Perhaps they had received a divine preference in return for their devotion to His duty. The monastery had a fine, established orchard from which the apple harvest was bountiful. Raspberries, blackberries, and wild strawberries grew among the squat trees, and the crop was greeted with great excitement when harvested and presented before the monks. He learned the art of cider-making and preserving of fruits for the barren winter months. A whole field of beehives provided enough honey for their own use and also to sell to the pilgrims who visited from the city and beyond. The monks sold wool from their flock of sheep and smoked meat – the tastiest of victuals in the county, it was claimed. In the years leading up to John Corn's admittance, the monastery had become a profitable industry. The collapse of the disgraced landowner's estate only increased their profits, since his erstwhile land lay fallow for years after his transgressions were exposed. The monks grafted tirelessly, rejoicing in their ability to provide (albeit at a cost) for the down-at-heel, and praised the bounty of their gardens as the true work of God.

But, over time, the commercial aspect of the organisation rankled with the young monk. He wrote in his diary of his daily chores and the increasing reliance of the city dwellers on the monastery's produce. He noted the line of people who had trekked for miles up the rocky hillside and through the deep forest, waiting for whatever was on offer, and, more importantly, what they could afford. He described hearing of one boy, no older than ten, who had appeared late one evening at the door of the fratry, barefooted, with the thinnest of rags protecting him from the wintry night. The boy had come from a farm on the far side of the city. His family's crops had failed and their livestock had been struck lame, so he had travelled the farms and the markets of the region begging for food for his ageing father and sickly siblings. His last hope, so wrote John Corn, was the monastery. As the monks sat down to eat, they were told of the arrival of the boy: *a wretched urchin on the point of collapse* were the words used. The abbot, a stern leader of the men, had immediately left his table and attended to the boy. Assuming that the boy would be offered food and a bed for the night, John Corn wrote in his diary of the humanity of the man and prayed harder for the monastery and its good work in evening prayers. The next diary entry was altogether different, however. He had learned that the abbot had turned the boy away into the dark night without even a scrap, nor shelter from the cold. His diary entries became increasingly questioning, more critical of the abbot, whom he regarded with burgeoning contempt. The abbot and those who did his bidding were, he concluded shortly before leaving the monastery, no better than the swindlers and conmen who lurked by the river's edge, preying on the hopelessness of those entering the city by boat, refugees from the civil unrest in the neighbouring counties. The monastery had become more of a business than a place of succour. Profits, rather than charity, drove the ethos. Again, he became isolated from the men who surrounded him. He resented the lifestyle, which, he wrote, served no purpose other than the survival of the men who live encircled by the red sandstone walls of the monastery.

Thus, shortly after his twenty-third birthday, he left the comfort of the monastery, determined to live a life that was purer; a kinder life, one more in keeping with his own version of faith.

47

IT IS A simple room, without pictures or ornament. The blinds on the window are closed. Two large screens sit atop a plywood table, connected to a keyboard, a hard drive and a printer. The chair facing the screens is hard-backed, functional. Green lights flash intermittently from among the wires and cables which snake around each other and around the table legs. These are the instruments of his labour.

The young man returns to the chair carrying a plastic carton of reconstituted soup from which steam rises, momentarily fogging his thick-lensed glasses. His sips his meal, then, finding it too hot, places it down on the only part of the table that is not covered in some form of technological debris. He grabs the computer mouse and flicks it, making the expanding and rotating cuboids on the screen disappear and the familiar web browser appear. In the short time he has been gone to rip the foil off the carton, boil a kettle and pour water into the lumpy powder, his inbox has filled up, a plethora of messages from his followers around the world.

He opens the most recent. Its message is pictorial, a grainy image of a man being held hostage. He wears an orange jumpsuit, so familiar to those who watch the evening news, and is flanked by two men, masked and holding rifles of a rather old-fashioned variety. A subtitle at the bottom of the screen displays a message, most likely in Arabic.

The young man types: *This is happening* on his keyboard, then adds *NOW* in uppercase. Immediately a thumbs-up sign appears by the comment. They are waiting on his every word.

He moves on with his perusal down the message thread. He has a lot to get through.

Next is a missive continuing the thread on the scientist's murder that has been running for a few days. There are thousands of messages: responses and counter-responses. Two conflicting themes have emerged: one side espouses a government cover-up of both the crime and its clearly apparent perpetrators; a second side claims the crime was never committed and is a fabrication concocted by forces who are using the spread of misinformation to control a frightened populace. The young man reacts forcefully against the latter. The crime was real, he tells those who are reading.

He sips the soup, now cooler, keeping hold of the computer mouse in the other hand. He scrolls down the message and the numerous responses. For the most part they concur, the occasional dissenter put in their place, their arguments discarded and disproven. The scientist was killed by order of the chairman of Rubica, a vast multinational telecommunications business which has its finger in a wide array of companies and governments. It has become the dominant business enterprise it is today by manipulating events to influence government policy and the opinions of the general public. The scientist had been carrying out work contrary to its mission. Success for his research programme would have unleashed carnage on the markets and dented the profits of the company, which is, as pointed out by the message board contributors, a monopoly.

There were other examples of murders and disappearances of those whose life work was detrimental to Rubica. Take the case of murdered environmentalists in the South America jungles who opposed the laying of telecommunications cables, or the so-called freedom activists who fought the government of a tiny Pacific Island state that had sold land to the company for secret testing. Or the man who is now locked up in an Indonesian jail for breaking into the company's headquarters in that country and stealing documents relating to government-backed surveillance of the entire population. All had been dispatched, never to protest again.

Yes, the events in a small city in England were linked to a multitude of other murderous transgressions carried out in this megalomaniacal crusade.

The young man types in the comment box: *Rubica is the Bridge Murderer.*

Another comment appears: *All the internet we use in this country is controlled by Rubica.*

Then: *They are reading THIS.*

And that is not all. Not by a long shot. He, and the masses of those who support his cause, have evidence as long as the internet threads. And longer. Even the feelings (some might say paranoia) generated by the exposé of the company are part of Rubica's plan to suppress an uprising. The streets are not safe.

He hears a knock on the front door. He glances up from the computer screen at the blank wall behind, then back to the keyboard on which he continues to type: *We are not safe. Rubica is sending round people to take you away.*

Another knock. He sits bolt upright. He knows he cannot be detected from the confines of his back room, provided he remains silent. He waits. No more knocking, but then he hears the sound of the letterbox opening and closing. Cautiously he gets up and slips into the hall. Through the frosted-glass window he sees a distant man, his unsuccessful visitor, bag slung over his shoulder, approaching the opposite house in the quiet cul-de-sac. On the door mat, beneath the letterbox, is a piece of paper, coloured purple with blue writing, the size of a postcard.

He picks it up.

FASTER BROADBAND IS COMING TO YOUR AREA.

48

IN THE CAPITAL city of this great country, a mass rally is being held. It is a show of strength put on by those who say they wish for their voices to be heard.

Not two days have passed since the demonstration that traversed the Galahad Bridge in New Canterbury, the site of the murder that has triggered such widespread alarm in an anxious populace. That gathering has been deemed a great success by those who marched and those who sought solace from it. Speeches from local politicians and leaders of local community groups have galvanised the people. *We will not be frightened into hiding*, they have concluded. *The streets are ours.*

The Galahad Bridge demonstration was, for the most part, orderly, and only one man was arrested. The police presence was discreet, by all accounts. Neither side had the stomach for agitation, as it turns out, despite the warring cries of the placard bearers. The arrested man was released without charge, his good character having been taken into account. He received a caution, promising not to transgress in future. He has stayed away from the capital city march, citing prior engagements. He is there in spirit, as he told his comrades over a pint in the pub where they met after his release from the police station, garrulous in his manner, yet shaken that he now has a police record.

The leaders of the capital city demonstration, which has been planned to follow a similar structure to the Galahad Bridge event – a march over one of the capital's iconic bridges, up the streets near to Parliament, ending in the main square with its looming statues and deep-rooted history – gather early and hand out pamphlets and instructions. The crowd is huge, even at this early hour, and the capital's police are out in force. A large delegation from New Canterbury has arrived and taken centre stage in the proceedings, reusing their banners from a few days ago. Television and radio crews have arrived in force, parking white vans with radio antennae at strategic points along the march, transmitting images to a waiting world.

Brian George, self-titled procurator of the city of New Canterbury, watches their images in his cell. His television is screwed to the wall, and the picture is grainy. The news channels have declared that they will follow the story all day, it being of such importance: the largest act of protest since the march against the wars in the Arabian Gulf, they say. The journalists are already in their stride, and they comment on the likely course of events before anything has happened. Helicopters are deployed to assess the size of the crowd. The streets are crammed with a seething mass of people which, seen from high above, looks like a slovenly snake, unlikely to catch its prey.

The images on the screen cut to a man dressed in a combat jacket and dark glasses. Under his image is the television description: *ORGANISER OF THE EVENT.* He is asked the numbers of people who are thought to be attending, then the reasons for the demonstration. The procurator struggles to hear his words, since a commotion outside his door has escalated into a shouting match, which, in turn, has set off a commotion in the surrounding cells. A rhythmic banging of pipes and the staccato screams of his fellow inmates continue for a minute before subsiding into the occasional protestation.

The images on the television move away from the organiser and pan down the street. The people march towards the camera, like a bedraggled army, lacking discipline or uniform. They carry flags of colours that may hold a special significance, and banners with slogans. The only one discernible on the tiny TV screen asks: *ARE WE SAFE?* The placards bob up and down, and the people surge forward with gusto. The camera pans in for a close-up of those leading the procession, resting on a man in a black raincoat and matching hat. This man, states the television commentator, is the MP for the city of New Canterbury, who has called for unity in the face of the murder that occurred in the heart of his constituency.

Television images of the march are interspersed with archive footage of the scene on Galahad Bridge shortly after the murder. Police officers and investigators in forensic suits walk past barriers and police warning signs. A dark patch on the brick street is being inspected by a man dressed in a white jumpsuit. His head is covered and his face is obscured by a mask.

There is a rattle of keys in the door, and a prison guard enters the procurator's cell. He has been there for less than twenty-four hours and yet is checked upon every hour or so. He has been moved from the police holding cell to the prison, an indication that he will be incarcerated for some time. The prison guard looks at the procurator, then at a tray of uneaten food.

'I'd eat if I were you,' he says gruffly, before leaving, locking the door behind him.

The procurator gets up from his bed and approaches the tray of food. He picks up a banana and eats it before lying back on the bed.

The television plays on, showing an interview with another demonstrator. This man is more animated than the previous interviewee and gesticulates forcefully.

'We are the people!' he says, shaking his fist without elaborating on the statement. Around him the crowd is becoming rowdier, and the interviewer is struggling to hear or be heard. The man is jostled, and the images become shaky. The cameraman, it would appear, has been pushed and cannot hold his focus on the interviewee. For a moment, the television transmits black images, before they cut back to a studio, where an older man in a suit and tie apologises for the loss of coverage. 'This is a rapidly developing story,' he explains, staring into the camera before the images return to the streets.

The procurator presses a button on the TV remote control but finds more coverage of the march on the next channel. People sit in a television studio with images of the demonstration running on a screen behind them.

'I think what we are seeing is a reaction to all forms of hate crime,' says a woman who sits on a black revolving chair, her legs crossed. She spins to look up at the screen. 'The murder in New Canterbury was just the tip of the iceberg, but it was a spark that lit the flame for uprising,' she concludes, pointing up at the screen, which, fortuitously, displays the image of a masked man carrying a baseball bat and lighted torch.

The procurator turns off the television and returns to his bed. He lies staring at the ceiling. He thinks back to his first meeting with the man he called Peter. This was the start of all this, the catalyst for what he has seen on the television: the crowds, the disquiet, and the fury; all that he now observes, helplessly, from his uncomfortable bed in his isolated room, being now confined for a time unknown.

What was it he asked Peter to do?

49

JOHN CORN ARRIVED in the office of Hammond Scar after travelling all day from the monastery. His mission was to secure employment and influence in the city. The city was vast and noisy in comparison to the tranquil setting of his previous few years, but the company of so many people who thought in non-uniform ways thrilled him. His arrival at the door of Hammond Scar was, by all accounts, influenced by his dealings with the procurator's deputy, who had sought refuge in the monastery a year before. He had told Corn of the despotism of the man and, rather than be put off by his reputation, Corn had been attracted to the court of a man who had achieved so much from so little. These were the early days of the procurator's tenure. Still a young man, he had been appointed to a role which sat in the middle of the feuding twin brothers, both of whom sought a claim to rule the city. Their father was declining in health and the battle for who would succeed him had begun in earnest. Scar was initially firmly aligned to the gathering northsiders and the bellicose twin, being of the opinion that the might of the sword will always win. Yet his meetings with John Corn caused a change of heart. Corn himself had already communed with the peace-making twin, a man who spent time at and gave alms to the monastery, and even by then, Corn had become his adviser.

So John Corn, still barely out of childhood, now had his feet in both camps. There was, naturally, a conflict between his attraction to the procurator, with his aggressive band of enforcers, and his preaching of a utopian lifestyle, to which he was hoping to attract followers. But he was very much of the opinion that the ends justified the means. Converting the people to his developing philosophy was his sole aim, even then. In many ways, he shared a metier with Scar, both men believing that they would achieve whatever they set their minds to. Scar had no problem in changing allegiance. Vacillation was a key attribute for survival in those turbulent times.

In a short period, John Corn had risen to the top of the pile – albeit a pile that consisted predominantly of henchmen with little intellect between them – and had become Scar's chief adviser by Christmas of the year he had returned to the city. Many negotiations were left to him; enforcement was left to the aforementioned band of men, hungry for violence and their own brand of thuggery.

At the same time, Corn continued to minister to his growing congregation, who aligned themselves to the principles of peace, tolerance and divinity. He helped to establish funds to build a new church on the south bank of the river and preached his own brand of religion, steeped in mysticism and allegory. He began to write for the first time, putting down his thoughts on the new moral order that had been brewing in his mind all his life.

Over time, Scar too placed his significant influence behind the succession of the peaceful twin to ruler, not out of a philosophical or moral stand, but more out of his reading of where the balance of power lay. The warring brother had become increasingly erratic, fuelled by drink and the ravages of what was in all probability tertiary syphilis, which had caused a rapidly progressive dementing illness and epileptic fits. Scar passed laws to restrict the power of the twin, who could do little to prevent his influence and his supporters from dwindling. Those who did remain loyal eventually took the man, a paralysed and haunted shadow of his former self, into exile in the mountains, never to enter the city again.

It was, however, the illness of the warring twin which first caused the citizens of New Canterbury to become suspicious of John Corn. Up until that point, they had seen him as a saviour of their city, as one who could do no wrong. Epilepsy was poorly understood, and its manifestation was so bizarre that they felt it could only have been wrought on its sufferers by the hand of the Devil. This strange preacher, who had brought his own brand of spirituality, novel and full of imagery of fiery pits and eternal damnation, had effected a highly unlikely victory against the might of the stronger son. He had formed an allegiance with the thug Hammond Scar, yet preached peace and love. His conflicting personae confused the city dwellers, who suspected unholy pacts more deep-seated than those between men of power. The perceived wisdom was that he could only be gaining the upper hand by foul means, and the notion that John Corn was dealing with the Devil himself was whispered in the streets and in the taverns in the outskirts of the city. Had he cursed the brother and caused his diabolical affliction?

Despite this, many thought Corn's influence was, on balance, for the good, so he was tolerated and these suspicions kept largely suppressed, lest a return to lawlessness should occur. Many were concerned, though, and, they feared that it was only a matter of time before the true allegiances behind the shift in power would become apparent.

50

LOCAL NARRATIVES FROM the time of John Corn tell of a man, Jared Eden, who resided in the shadow of the Black Hills, a day's ride from the burgeoning city; a man intent on discovering the most potent of elixirs and restorative potions. He had made his wealth by importing and exporting medicinal herbs and, being trained in the science of the apothecaries, had set up a laboratory in his mansion house to discover combinations of herbs that would rejuvenate the body and alleviate suffering within the three score years and ten that most were fortunate to achieve. He had taken a particular interest in the herbs of the Orient, expensive commodities that had reached the city courtesy of the expanding trade routes through Europe and across the English Channel. Strange plants arrived on the shores, and their mysterious appearance led to an expectation that at least one would provide an antidote to the various illnesses of the time. Arrowroot from Polynesia, pungent herbs brought to the shore in terracotta pots from Chinese trading boats, fantastically coloured peppers that burned the skin just to touch, acrid smelling pinecones, spidery leaves as large as ponds, and pods of ancient vanilla trees known to grow only one remote island of the vast Pacific Ocean: all these, and more, were imported for pharmacological manufacture by the man in the mysterious mansion.

But the industry of Jared Eden, in time, became geared purely to the discovery of that combination of roots and leaves that would prolong life, and, more specifically, his own life. He had been orphaned as a youth and had used his meagre inheritance to travel to the capital city, where he had enrolled in the Royal School of Apothecaries, gaining a distinction in the final examinations. He had then gained passage on a trading ship to the East Indies and beyond, having persuaded the captain of the vast wealth to be obtained from the trade in oriental plants. He had returned a year later with enough specimens to keep him going for a lifetime of research and the manufacture of endless new therapies. His shop in the East End of the capital, which he had purchased in partnership with the ship's captain, was a huge success, and he opened branches throughout the south of England. The local clientele couldn't get enough of his wares as they sought remedies for the effects of pestilence and unhealthy living. Jared Eden settled in New Canterbury, the location of what had turned out to be the most profitable of his shops. He purchased a manor house half a day's carriage ride from the city and there set to work on his experiments to discover the ultimate remedy.

It is recorded that Hammond Scar, the all-powerful procurator of the city of New Canterbury, was unhappy regarding the activity of the self-fashioned lord of the manor who traded in the city and was amassing even greater wealth than him. Taxes were raised, and the procurator passed a new levy on the trade of medicinal herbs, but this did not deter the man, whom most in the city now viewed as some sort of miracle-worker, protecting them from the ravages of arthritis or the pains of gout. He even gave away some of his fortune to the almshouses and to those who resided in the city's Hospital for Incurables. On the rare occasions he ventured into the city to check up on his shop or negotiate passage for his fleet of ships, he was treated with a reverence bordering on that afforded to royalty. All this increased Hammond Scar's resentment of the man, whose wealth he did not begrudge, but whose influence (albeit one he didn't court) was now great within the walls of the city – so much so that the procurator felt a threat to his hard-earned omnipotence. Yet Jared Eden took on an increasingly mysterious persona, to which his reclusiveness only added. His lack of interest in wielding his fortune for power was unfathomable to Hammond Scar, and equally as infuriating. He had become untouchable.

In his rudimentary laboratory, Jared Eden cared little what the procurator thought and spent very little time considering the man, despite his assault on Eden's business in the form of taxes and levies. Jared Eden had become obsessed with one thing and one thing only: the search for the elixir of life.

51

THE NEWSPAPERS CARRY stories of the arrest of Reuben Christian and Brian George, two men residing in the city of New Canterbury and now accused of the murder of the eminent scientist nearly two weeks ago. The police have released a statement to a press eager for any news on the mysterious crime that has filled acres of newsprint with a combination of speculation and scaremongering. There is, it must be said, something of an undercurrent of disappointment in the breaking stories. In the days after the killing, theories of international plots had been conjectured: networks of terrorists spreading across the globe, nefarious masterminds holed up in subterranean lairs, and threats of repeated actions reputed to be around the corner. The news that two local men – one a lawyer, the other a petty criminal – were in custody was deflating to the imagination of the journalists. There was only so much sensationalism to be generated from suburban disaffection, as it was considered to be by many of those writing. It didn't stop further narratives emerging, however. So-called investigative journalists were unearthing links to Irish republicans and far-right European dissident groups. The conflicts perpetuated by these groups were well-known to regular readers of the papers, which drip-fed their readers with a diet of half-truths and complete fabrication.

The lives of the two men are pored over in minute detail. Of greater interest, of course, is the lawyer who practises in offices a few streets away from Galahad Bridge. His life story, as much as is known for the time being, is laid out in dense type on the inner pages of the papers, some of which devote twenty pages or more to the story. Pictures of the arrested men have been released by the police and their mugshots printed above captions that are heavy with startling adjectives to describe their deeds. Brian George, it is reported, has been previously censured by the Law Society for unprofessional behaviour. He received a caution several years ago for abusive behaviour to a client, the report runs, and was warned that further transgressions would be more severely punished. More stories will emerge, no doubt. The journalists have only had a few hours to dig the dirt before the print run.

Other newspaper columns write of a putative connection between Brian George and religious extremists. Minutes from the ethics committee meetings are freely available and easily found with a few taps on a computer keyboard. It is easy to discover that he was ejected from its membership and barred from future committees. The precise details are rather cryptic, which fuels the journalists' imaginations. Coupled to this, his allegiance to the followers of John Corn is reported. Promotional documents produced by the 'cult of a bygone prophet' (as one of the papers dubs it) have been found on the internet with George's face, young and determined, staring out from the computer screen alongside his words, welcoming newcomers to embrace his faith. It's not hard, therefore, to put two and two together and imagine he killed the scientist because of his long-held religious zealotry.

Less attention is garnered to the younger accomplice in the crime. Reuben Christian is clearly more of the criminal type, so perhaps his involvement in the murder is of less importance to a readership that demands titillation as much as (and possibly more than) information. He already has a criminal record for a bungled jewel theft and has spent time in youth detention centres. His background and upbringing follow all the stereotypes of delinquency, well-known to the readers of the newspapers, so there is little to fascinate. His psychiatric history is, as yet, unreported. One newspaper has already found Christian's older brother and carries an interview with the man, deep in vitriol and uncensored hatred, fuelled, the reader discovers, by an argument over his car, which the younger brother had crashed into the canal under the influence of undefined chemical substances. Readers are left in little doubt concerning the nature of the man. His guilt cannot be argued against.

But who or what is behind the two men? This is the question asked by many of the newspaper editorials. It is impossible to believe that they have acted alone, runs the argument. Just look at the calibre of the people accused compared to the terror they have unearthed. How could two local misfits cause this degree of panic? There is no doubt that some mastermind is pulling the strings, and the act on the bridge is just the start of a tidal wave of atrocity. One article links the lawyer to a jailed nailbomber who waged a campaign against the heathen, but shies away from any detail or proof of a connection. Another suggests that George was on covert operations for the group behind the recent attack on the capital city's train station, which was only foiled because of the vigilance of a train guard, a man who was later decorated by the Queen and declared a national hero by the papers.

The facts are emerging, say the editorials, but, for now, a combination of rumour and inference will have to do. The public will lap it up, anyway, and anything written can be redacted at a later date.

DI Price reads the morning papers in a break from his paperwork. The colossal effort required following any arrest has made him consider on certain occasions whether some arrests are worthwhile. He knows that some will come to nothing, thrown out by magistrates as soon as they are brought to trial, so the effort of filling in the twenty or so forms he is required to submit is not appealing. In this case, however, the enormity of the case means he will have no such doubt. They cause a headache nonetheless, and he takes regular breaks.

Opening the local newspaper, he reads the editor's version of events. He knows the man well and has respect for him, as he is less underhand than many in his profession. The local newspaper exists in a stable equilibrium with the police, each using the other for its own gains, and, as such, the reporting of the Galahad Bridge murder is more subdued than in the national rags. This morning (which is the first morning when the identity of the arrested men has been declared), the editor has focused on the implications this revelation will have for the city of New Canterbury. These 'self-grown terrorists' who have, presumably, been radicalised within the city walls present an unpleasant disclosure to those already looking over their shoulders and checking their doors are locked more times than is strictly necessary. Terrible deeds carried out by those entering the city from afar, perhaps akin to a travelling circus, are easier to compartmentalise in the mind as being random: bad luck that the men happened to descend on the place, choosing it as a location for their actions, maybe for no reason other than chance, which in itself is not really a reason. The editor paints a dire picture of likely similar actions, asking how many have been radicalised, how many are planning attacks, how many are taking up arms against the decency of the city. DI Price is alarmed by the tone of the writing, since the editor is usually more sober in his assessment. Indeed, he occasionally reads the paper's reports of crimes he is investigating in order to define a different angle on the case, and is generally struck by the rational dissection of the case that the man conducts. Not so today. Gloom and despair seep through the words and infiltrate the reader's already fragile psyche.

52

OUTSIDE THE LAWCOURTS stands a doorkeeper. He is dressed in clothes more suited to pageantry: a top hat, shoes with sliver buckles, and a fur-lined coat upon which he displays the emblem of the legal society to which he is affiliated. Even those charged to keep order among those accused of disorder are regulated and allied to a common cause. The ancient Order of Court Executives has been in place for generations, formed as a reaction to the lawless nature of the courts that existed in the Middle Ages – a shocking necessity, given the nature of the institution in which the iron fist of regulations is mandated to rule the roost. But bribery and fracas were rife in those times, and even the judges slipped into a life of corruption, deciding that tolerating the common ways of criminality paid more than upholding the practices for which they had been trained.

The doorkeeper is stony-faced and not to be distracted. He has seen it all in his twenty-two years of service and tells a good tale to his colleagues and to his friends, whom he meets every Thursday after work, Friday being his day off and a day when the courts do not sit. He keeps the names of the lawless out of his tales, having sworn himself to a code of confidentiality, although his listening friends work out the identity of the people he speaks of through his colourful descriptions and by reading the court proceedings, of which they are avid readers.

Beside him stands the lawyer for the accused, a surly man in thick-rimmed glasses who sniffs at regular intervals, and in front stands Brian George, the accused. DI Price and DS Hameed loiter some way back, not wishing to get too close to the man they have been interrogating for several days. They wait patiently for the doorkeeper's say-so to enter the courtroom: room number 3 in the High Court of New Canterbury.

The procurator's lawyer sniffs once more and then sneezes, which causes him to drop several of the sheets of paper he is carrying. He drops to his knees and attempts to pick up the papers in some kind of order. At the same moment, however, a buzzer sounds and a red light flashes from above the courtroom door, causing the doorkeeper to spring into action, placing his hand on the shoulder of the accused man who stands before him. Automaton-like, he exerts force with his rigid arm and propels the accused through the doors, which have opened automatically. The procurator's lawyer, however, is still scrambling around on the floor, picking up the papers, which have become muddled; some are creased and one has been trampled by a court official, who overtakes the assembled party in the manner of one who wishes for access to the best seat in the house. The doorkeeper, disgruntled by the ineptitude of the procurator's lawyer, stops and pulls the accused's shoulder back, almost toppling him. The procurator takes a step back to prevent his fall, and, in so doing, steps on more of his lawyer's papers. A passing court official, clearly not as bothered by winning the race to the courtroom, stops to help collect the papers, which are gathered up in a higgledy-piggledy state by the flustered lawyer, save for one which resides firmly under the leather shoe of the procurator.

'Excuse me!' says the lawyer, who is still on his knees, directing his words to the procurator, who looks down and, noticing he is standing on a piece of paper, perhaps a vital part of his case for acquittal, shifts his stance away, revealing a dusty brown footprint on the page, which is, in fact, blank.

The farcical theatrics now concluded, the doorkeeper grabs the shoulder of the accused again and continues the march forward into the courtroom. 'God help you,' mutters the doorkeeper under his breath, a phrase directed to the procurator, who does not hear it, yet thinks similar thoughts, having witnessed the shambolic display of his legal counsel.

Once in the courtroom, the procurator is aware of the brightness of the lights, which contrasts with the dinginess of the corridor in which they have been standing for fifteen minutes. He squints as he looks around. The figures who are seated in the bench opposite him appear as thin black silhouettes, blurred around the edges. They sit in two rows, on a bank of seats similar to that in a theatre, an amphitheatre even. Scanning further around he sees, as his eyes become more adapted to the light, the judge, unmistakable in his red gown and black hat, seated high up in a galleried seat, alone, looking down up the proceedings. The judge's assistants, considerably lower than him in their own wooden booths, flank him. Due to the judge's elevation in the courtroom, when they wish to speak to him they are required to scurry up one of the two sets of steep stairs that run either side of the judge's lofty throne. In some court cases – those of the utmost complexity – they will spend their day running up and down the stairs, providing for the needs of the man who requires information to be received and dispatched with alacrity, thus filling the court with an unceasing rattle of feet and creaking of timber – a sound emanating from the ancient structures, installed centuries ago and maintained to indicate to those entering the courtroom the weight of history behind the decisions being made.

The procurator is instructed to sit while the remainder of the courtroom party file in. His lawyer, who is still shuffling his papers, sits beside him, paying him little attention. He takes off his glasses, which have misted due to the differences in ambient temperature and humidity between the courtroom and the corridor, and wipes them on a cloth he has produced from his jacket pocket. The two police officers sit at the back, out of sight, for the moment. They have worked hard to secure a court case, and both feel a nervous anticipation around the event. The experience is, perhaps, akin to that of a parent watching a child perform in a school play – although in the present scenario, the child is one whom the parent wishes to fail and be sent away for a long time.

The judge, having been instructed by the stair-climbing minion to the left that all who need to be present are present, rings a bell, which gives out a single low clang. This is the indication for all to stand, causing a scraping of chairs, a shuffle of feet and a creaking of wooden benches.

'For those about to be tried, may God Have mercy,' says the judge in a slow, lugubrious manner, lacking conviction, before the bell rings once more.

All sit. The procurator's lawyer continues to shuffle papers, his angst rising by the moment, knowing that his work, for which the dropping of papers has rendered him unprepared, will commence in a matter of minutes. This causes a court official seated on the ground level directly beneath the judge to bang a gavel on his desk and shout: 'Silence!'

The lawyer puts down his papers, sheepishly meeting the glare of the court official through glasses which have steamed up once more.

The judge, despite his years of dealing with misdeeds of greater magnitude than a man shuffling papers, appears affronted by this disturbance in his court and also glares at the lawyer. He has met the man before, having been witness to his previous court appearances, and makes no secret of his disdain for his way of working.

'Let us begin,' he intones, his eyes still on the procurator's lawyer, who is now still, too intimidated to move.

A man stands and holds a clipboard up to eye level, from which he reads a series of charges levelled against the accused and which are to be considered in the courtroom by the learned gathering. After reading 'incitement to murder' he pauses and peers over the top of the clipboard as if to emphasise the severity of the charge. He continues. The charges are several and relate to the events on Galahad Bridge and the aftermath. Not only is the incitement to murder to be tried, but so too are the actions of the accused in the days following the event and before his arrest. Crime begets crime. Justice demands reverence, and thus it is possible to pervert its course merely by the act of not presenting oneself for punishment – a concept that the procurator has always thought anomalous, since the act of committing a crime is naturally (for the most part) associated with a desire to evade justice, and thus should be considered as one entity. The police like making up charges, nonetheless, and seem most happy when they have come up with a long list of transgressions. The cynics would say that they are judged on their conviction rates. Thus, if they can convict a man of three or four crimes sprouting from the initial misdemeanour, that must be considered a bonus.

The man with the clipboard, having finished his list, sits, which prompts another man to stand.

The case for the prosecution commences.

53

FOREBODING DAYS OF summer turn to rust. Open windows close. The rituals of an incarcerated life continue on an orbit, mirroring the path of the earth around the sun.

Reuben Christian, a man known by multiple pseudonyms but one who now shrugs off the mantle of enforced nomenclature in his haze of thinking, sits observing the gentle fall of leaves that form a carpet of brown pendants on the sodden lawn. A man came yesterday (or maybe the day before) to rake away the fallen leaves, he recalls. He raked furiously for an hour or so, forming four large, glistening hills of brown and orange, one in each corner of the rectangular patch of land, before gathering up his harvest in large brown bags – dirty shrouds that were lifted onto a trailer hooked up to a tractor and driven away. Already the lawn is covered again. The man will not come again, defeated by the actions of the passing seasons and the budgetary constraints of the psychiatric hospital that deems gardening services a luxury. They will rot and decay to produce a mulch, slippery and fetid, nourishing the earth, as they were destined to do.

A bell sounds and Reuben stands. He understands that this is the cue for something to happen. If he were a dog he would start salivating, or clawing at the bars of his cage. Instead, he walks over to the door, where a man in white overalls stands fingering a set of keys that hangs from his belt.

'Come on, Reuben,' he says, ushering him out of the room and into a whitewashed corridor lit by bright strips of phosphorescence. He locks the door behind him, then trudges down the corridor. Reuben follows, a hunched form, festinant and furtive, his shoes scuffing the floor, his arms stuck by his side without swinging, as though they were tied to his trunk by an invisible bond.

The door at the end of the corridor is open, and soft voices are heard. Reuben thinks of a recurring dream: a visit to an unknown school friend; a family eating together in a heated room, light-hearted conversations and warm food; the trepidation and the fear of entry into the family's kitchen.

'Come in, Reuben,' says the man, who leads him by the hand over the threshold and guides him to the chair before leaving the room and shutting the door behind him. The room is capacious, one side lined with bookshelves that hold leather-bound old tomes bearing such unlikely titles as: *Treatments of the Criminally Insane*, and *Handbook of the Maladies of the Mind*. An oak sideboard stands against another wall on which a lone glass tumbler sits, half-filled with water.

Reuben slumps down in his chair. A silence is observed, a minute of remembrance, perhaps, broken by the shuffle of papers and the cough of the doctor, who brings the group to attention. There is no time for solemnity, his interjection implies: we must get on with the treatment of troubled minds.

'Reuben, how are you today?' is his opening gambit, uttered quietly yet authoritatively. No answer is expected, but the burden of expectation works both ways and in medical parlance this is as good an opening as any.

Reuben's neck remains bent and his gaze directed at the floor. He has not looked upon the panel of people who sit behind the large wooden desk and who hold information on him in written notes and in the inner encryption of their computers upon which they type, episodically, when a thought comes to them or an observation is deemed important enough to minute.

If he were to look up, he would see the same group of healthcare workers who have been continuing this ritual for several months now. An elderly doctor, a few months off retirement, who has spoken already to enquire about the status of Reuben's health; two psychiatric nurses – one who is in charge of the unit and reports the latest developments to the doctor like an eager schoolchild to her pedagogue, the other who sits meekly, afraid to say much in the presence of such august company; a social worker, who reeks of cigarette smoke, offending the sensibility of the senior nurse who sits next to him; and a student nurse, who has been sent to the unit as part of her training and who watches with a kind of horror at what is being wheeled before her. She has already decided never to become a psychiatric nurse after the bizarre circus she has witnessed for the past four long weeks.

The older nurse taps on the keyboard and then pipes up: 'Reuben has had a good week.'

The doctor smiles. 'Good,' he says, shifting his gaze from the patient to the nurse.

At the same moment, the student nurse sneezes, making the patient look up for the first time. She apologises, blushing at the untimeliness of her interruption. Reuben continues his stare at her. She looks down at her hands.

'Reuben,' says the doctor. Noticing the discomfort of the nurse, he attempts to distract him.

'Reuben,' he repeats more loudly.

The student nurse experiences a hot feeling rising up her body and a clamminess in her hands. The gaze is encompassing her, and it is as though Reuben's being is surrounding her, smothering her. She has no thought other than to flee, so gets up and runs to the door, whimpering, pulling at the handle several times before it yields. It closes with a loud thud and the patter of feet is heard from beyond, urgent yet diminishing.

The doctor exhales loudly, and once again looks at the senior nurse, encouraging an explanation concerning the actions of one of her charges. She apologises and promises to talk to the young woman later.

Eyes turn once again to Reuben, who has adopted his former position, head slumped, looking at the floor.

'What happened there, Reuben?' asks the doctor. There is no reply.

There is a commotion outside the door, and the white-overalled nurse enters in an agitated state.

'Can we have some help out here?' he implores, causing the two nurses to stand up and head to the door. The senior nurse looks around before she exits, realising that a protocol will be breached if the doctor and the social worker are left alone with the patient. The call for assistance is repeated, more imploringly this time, and, considering this an exceptional circumstance, she leaves the room and runs down the corridor.

Reuben stands, awoken by the events in a different room, and walks over to the sideboard. Picking up the glass tumbler, he smashes it down on the solid wooden top of the sideboard in one swift movement. The social worker, sensing danger, runs to the door, calling for help, seeking those who have just left. The old doctor attempts to stand, yet his chair is wedged under the table somehow and the friction of the chair legs against the floor is such that he cannot extricate himself from his seated position. He leans back, hoping somehow to slither out of his trapped position, but the patient is already approaching, brandishing the remains of the glass, jagged shards protruding from the base.

'Reuben, no!' shouts the doctor, who has now managed to slide the chair back and stands viewing his exit. His path is blocked, however, by the hulking form of Reuben Christian, who approaches, animated, intent.

'Don't do this!' shouts the doctor, before himself imploring for any form of help which may be available in this time of so many crises.

Too late, however, is his cry, which fails even to reach the end of the word *help*. Reuben Christian forces the broken glass into the wrinkled face of the psychiatrist, who screams for the first time since childhood, a call back to a time of innocence, before he had encountered all this madness.

53

THE NEWSPAPER JOURNALISTS write with a frenzy reserved for moments they consider most noteworthy. They write of incidents judged important not by their historic potential, but by an imparted significance generated by an excess of opprobrium, a sentiment in the readership that sells papers. The journalists are reminded on a daily basis of the importance of this concept: the unwritten mantra that they are here to generate income rather than document the precision of the news. The editors are hardened to the realities of modern-day journalism. The internet has exposed a fragility in their income stream and opened up new competition from the most unlikely of sources. People can find whatever information they require from the recapitulations of events, told through the eyes (or rather the brief limited-character missives) of the bigoted and the unhinged. The truth is often discarded for a good story, the facts are stretched out of recognition. It is apparent to those who have been in the business for a long time that readers want to be confirmed in their long-held beliefs; they wish to be fed their own version of the truth to wrap around themselves like a comfort blanket. Journalists must oblige, writing in terms that express such opinions – extreme and polarised ones at that – but always covering their tracks so that allegations of libel can be rebuffed, quashed before the lawyers have had time to prepare a draft. It is what the people want.

And so, the back story of Brian George is published in numerous newspapers. Where a gap in his history exists, a filling paragraph is written, one that skirts the edges of what may be true but that broadly fits the possible experience of one who may have lived a life in parallel. He is a man who has been shunned by his profession, they write, one who now practises his version of the law on the edges of conventional practice – if indeed it is a profession with conventions or morality, solicitors often being the target of scathing articles about their underhand practices. The owner of one newspaper, himself embroiled in legal proceedings as lengthy and complex as that most memorable of Dickens' creations, uses his broadsheet to vent spleen on the despicable practice of those who inhabit plush offices in the capital's trendiest of streets, and the judges who are, it is claimed, as detached from sense as it is possible to be. The former procurator is defined, therefore, as one who has sunk so low as to have been rejected by the sewer rats.

His early life is pored over, the journalists becoming amateur psychologists and gathering evidence to unravel the root of George's evil. If Freud – or Jung, or any other psychoanalyst – had inferred so much from so little, their field of learning may have been very different, one imagines. His boyhood, his privileged upbringing in a quaint market town, is described in details both idealised and stereotyped, designed to contrast with the actions performed by the man that boy had become. His parents' professions, the private school, the comfortable route into university are details all exhibited to a particular readership; many of them have not shared these advantages, and not one of them has grown up to be such a reprobate. They carry interviews with people who have known Brian George, an irregular and fragmented patchwork of mostly pre-pubescent relationships from anyone who will talk. One paper has an interview with his former schoolteacher, now retired, an old man who may, one suspects from the responses written in the paper, be a little way off full cognitive function. It matters little to the journalist, who juxtaposes the words of an old man with descriptions of the wounds inflicted on the scientist and the ensuing unrest on the streets of New Canterbury. Mr Fred Proudlove, retired science teacher, describes the boy he taught several decades ago as 'not up to much' – a statement capable of being interpreted in a variety of ways, suggesting both inertia and incompetence.

Another newspaper has rounded up clients of the procurator, displaying their pictures in a checkerboard of the accused and the (mostly) convicted. How much these men and women have been paid for their insights into the legal practice of Brian George is not disclosed, but the sense from the article is that most would have done it for free, having been given a mouthpiece to denigrate the man who failed to get them off their unjust charges. Indeed, it would appear from the dialogue that most view the former procurator of the city of New Canterbury as the cause of their criminality, or at least their continued criminality. Charles Moore, bespectacled and bald, with a gold earring hanging from his left ear, stares out from the centre of the page. He has used the services of George twice, he says, and both times he has been convicted, once for fraud and the other for handling stolen goods. He claims an acquaintance of his (unnamed) was acquitted from similar charges thanks to the actions of a 'proper lawyer'. Furthermore, he claims that George was unwilling to listen to the details of his circumstances – his ailing mother, his mounting debts and his fibromyalgia that had become 'acute' thanks to the time he had spent in HMP Dovestone. If only he had used another lawyer, his life may have been very different.

Another tale, accompanied by a black and white photo of a young woman with short hair, undoubtedly taken many years ago, tells of the lawyer's manner, his clear disdain for the client who passed through his door. 'He treated me like a criminal,' she says, reflecting that she had been warned off the lawyer by a colleague, but that he had been the only one available to her, provided by the legal aid system which states, erroneously in her opinion, that all are equal before the law. She had received a sentence of three years in prison and was released after ten months for good behaviour. She now runs a business making soap, employing former convicts with a grant from the government, which are keen for such people to reintegrate.

Most disturbing of all is the vignette printed in bold at the top of the article. The mugshot shows a man in shirt and tie, neatly preened. His hair is slicked back and shines in the light of the camera flash. He recounts his only encounter with Brian George, in which the lawyer branded him liar and a counterfeiter. The tirade of abuse, littered with offensive expletives, was constant, he recalls, so much so that he immediately changed legal practices and needed counselling from the effects of such abuse. At one point in their consultation, the lawyer threw a book at him, he claims, and, if it hadn't been for the actions of a beleaguered receptionist at the legal practice, he thinks he would have been assaulted by the man. The nature of the smartly dressed man's crime is not disclosed.

54

THE RISE OF Hammond Scar, the olden times procurator, was inextricably linked to the increasing prominence of John Corn's teaching. The two had formed an alliance, unwritten and unstable, one in which both parties were wary of the other yet knew their mission could only be achieved by the success of the other. The procurator understood the spiritual needs of a city reeling from war and plague. They were a populace looking for answers. The oppressed were looking to make sense of a senseless world. In John Corn they saw solutions. His religious beliefs and teachings had been shaped by his time in the monastery yet had diverged from the conventional since his arrival in the city. He recognised the gulf between the monks striving for an idyllic life and the harsh reality of barely scraping by on the streets and ramshackle farms. His brand of religion was more accessible to the common man, and he was, at least at the commencement of his ministry, less corrupt than the recognised Church of the ailing state, whose ministers syphoned off alms for their own gratification in a version of spirituality which necessitates luxury for its teachers. John Corn, having been raised in poverty, was content to live a simple life and thus be seen as a man of the people. His worn clothes and unkempt hair were not the turn-off the bishops had imagined. He had developed a magnetic attraction, a charm that entranced his followers as he preached atop a wooden box in the marketplace or in the parks. Great crowds would flock to his sermons, causing increasing disquiet in the churches of the city and in its fine cathedral. The council of bishops, rectors and vergers met to discuss the threat to undermine their hold on the spiritual needs of the city. They saw their position in society as having reached a point of jeopardy. At any moment, the stones of the cathedral could crumble; a revolution against centuries of tradition and power was a genuine threat, and one that the Church had not had to face in a generation. The idea that a boy born in poverty, a hoodlum in his youth, could shake the underpinnings of an institution as old as the hills was unthinkable. Where they had disregarded the threat of an uncouth vagrant a year ago, they now took note and planned for all-out assault. The bishops, in their vaulted palace and cold chancels, invoked unnatural happenings and prayed to their God for deliverance from this usurper.

Thus, the antagonism between the Church and Corn grew, pushing each faction to more extreme positions in their quest for the upper hand. John Corn attacked the bishops and their fold for their aloofness and their failure to recognise the good that their ministry could achieve. If only they were to renounce their riches and plough the money into farming the land, they would do more good than they could ever do in their Sunday morning ramblings. They had lost touch with what was happening and clung to an ancient way of living that existed solely to perpetuate its existence. The bishops retaliated by spreading rumours about the unholy alliances the preacher must have formed to hypnotise a population that had relied on the Church for generations. They actively encouraged talk of witchcraft and devilry, increasing their use in their sermons of the fiery terminology of the underworld. They warned of what would await those who followed this deviant religion of this man on the edges of society, a man living in caves – the Devil's troglodyte.

Just as the frightened people began to believe the stories of sorcery and it appeared that the Church's assault on John Corn was about to succeed, Hammond Scar stepped into the fight. He had weighed up his options, ready to ditch the rebel preacher should it be in his interests. Yet he had reasoned that the power of the Church would be too great, too much of a threat if successful and emboldened. He set in train a series of laws to reduce its secular power. He hit at the one thing the bishops had little influence over – the city's taxes. The Church had long since used its status as a charitable organisation to exempt itself from all but the most paltry of taxes. Hammond Scar, no doubt in cahoots with John Corn, passed a law stating that the Church (or indeed any other institution which claimed exemption from tax on the grounds of its charitable status) must give away at least half its income and assets per year if it was to qualify for such pecuniary immunity. *A charity which keeps all its money for itself cannot be considered a charity*, was how John Corn documented this policy in his *Chronicles*.

The Church had no choice but to pay large taxes on its income, forcing it to relinquish much of its land in the hinterlands beyond the city. The Church owned many of the houses in the vicinity of the cathedral, and the policy of Hammond Scar forced the Church to raise the rent it charged its tenants. This in itself further reduced the power of the Church, since those living in these rundown buildings, having no knowledge or interest in the policy of taxation that had been instituted, resented the rent increase, magnifying their perception of the Church as a greedy, uncaring organisation.

It being in his nature to subjugate others, Hammond Scar turned his attention in other directions once the Church was no longer a threat. He knew that, in due course, he would need to deal with Corn, whose power had increased dramatically since his undermining of the Church. But for now, he would keep him in tow, using the hold Corn had on the people to further his own ends.

55

GALAHAD BRIDGE IS quiet today. The throngs of people who would usually be found crossing the river at this point have stayed away for reasons undefined. The morning is crisp and the air under the bridge is dense, mist curling up from below and spreading out between the feet of the few who walk or stand to admire the view. Down below and just upstream, a lone boat – a dirty old tug – chugs slowly, emitting brown fumes that mingle lazily with the morning fog. A man stands on its broad deck and whistles a rapid tune, perhaps a shanty with a rhythmic beat and a time signature redolent of storytelling. He looks back at the bridge, its impressive arches and its palisades that border the walkway, and remembers, as he has done for the past few days when passing beneath, the murder of a scientist; an event that has redefined this construction of bricks and mortar. From the bridge his gaze shifts to the courthouses that border the southern bank of the river, nestled between restaurants and department stores, each vying for their place beside the rushing river.

In that courthouse, beyond the second-floor windows visible from the river, the trial of Brian George, self-titled procurator of the city of New Canterbury, is reaching its denouement. Already, electronic reams of rhetoric have been recorded by a team of court officials, who type silently on keyboards – recent replacements for the archaic stenography machines so commonly depicted in courtroom dramas. Grandiose justifications and exaggerated accusations have been argued in the curious game of law inside the high-ceilinged theatre where words of condemnation intersperse with those pleading leniency. The public galleries, packed out for the first few weeks in anticipation of the trial, are now only half-filled, and those listening do so with decreasing enthusiasm and increasing fatalism. Those in the press gallery continue to tap on machines that are capable of transmitting soundbites to the outside world in an instant, creating a running commentary on proceedings. Even so, the output of journalists has now reduced somewhat, having fewer points of interest to transmit. *What is being said has already been said*, writes one. *The case for the defence makes the same point again*, writes another. They too are beginning to wonder why it is taking so long. The arguments have been presented and they have informed their readers of their overwhelming conclusion. All each of them thinks about now is their article for the day the verdict is announced, which is already half-written.

The judge too is becoming impatient. The defence team, led by a lawyer who has irked the judge in previous cases, are making the same point on multiple occasions, he points out. Either say something you haven't said before, or say nothing, he tells the tedious man. Suitably chastised, the lawyer sits down, offering the defendant to the prosecution. Before the prosecution speaks, however, the judge puts a finite timeframe on the remainder of questioning. He will sum up tomorrow morning and dismiss the jury for their deliberations, he declares, an interjection that causes a scurrying of fingers on keyboards in the press gallery, accompanied, one might imagine, with a sigh of relief.

As though the moment needs to be afforded a greater emphasis, he also calls for a recess, a time for a break. A court official bangs a gavel on his oak desk and all rise from their seats as the judge makes his way down the precarious steps and out of the door at the back of the court – the one used during the course of a trial, since the main door is only exited at the conclusion.

Brian George waits for the courtroom to empty, then walks over to the courtroom guard, allowing himself to be handcuffed and taken away to his basement cell, where he will spend the next twenty minutes reflecting on what has passed.

He has, by now, resigned himself to his fate. The case is going badly, and the ineptitude of his legal team is absolute. *Why didn't I defend myself?* he now wonders. He would have done a better job, no doubt. But his awkwardness and the likelihood that he would have been found guilty of contempt of court, given his frame of mind, meant that he conceded to the legal team he was given. It matters little now, anyway. There is not much hope.

The door is locked behind him and the guard informs him that the break in proceedings will be longer than expected. No reason is given, but the procurator accepted a while ago that he is no longer a person who has any influence over the timetable of his life. He is one who is informed. Things are done to him, rather than by him.

He sits on his bed and then lies, staring at the ceiling, its cracked plaster forming an imperfect arc stretching from one wall to the other. His eye traces the curve from one side to the other, and then back again. The pillow on which his head rests is lumpy, made for discomfort. There is no repose anyway, not in this state of limbo, heightened by the impending decision regarding the rest of his life – a verdict that, when delivered, will not end the indeterminacy of his fate.

The door rattles and the guard re-enters, this time accompanied by the procurator's lawyer. The procurator can hardly bear to look at him – this incompetent fool who has put up such a shoddy defence. At least he has the look of one who acknowledges his ineptitude, although that is small comfort.

The lawyer sits and takes off his glasses, which he polishes on his tie, and speaks. 'You know, it's not looking good.' He pauses, listening for a reply, yet he does not take his eyes off his polishing. He talks with the nonchalance of one assessing the weather, rather than a life's miserable destiny. It is not the first time he has uttered this sentence at the end of a trial. It is a euphemism, at best. If something doesn't look good, it still has the option of not looking bad.

The procurator sighs deeply, not having the strength to reply.

The man is a fool, he thinks, yet no more than me or the many other robed clowns in this place.

'Tell me why you got involved in all this?' asks the lawyer, replacing his spectacles on his nose and pushing them back with his index finger.

56

HE IS ALONE again, the words of his lawyer buffeted and blown away, just as ephemeral words of a courtroom are tossed and reflected in attritional attacks on sensibilities presumed to be wrong. He awaits the verdict of a judge with a feeling both familiar and alien; one he has experienced before, since he has waited on numerous occasions for the fate of his clients to be read out by the man in his robes and wig, seated on the high throne. On those occasions, however, the verdict had little impact on him, save, perhaps, on his reputation. But that consideration had long since vanished as he became marginalised, becoming only required to defend the undefendable, existing on the fringes of a profession he had come to despise. The verdicts were predictable; even before each trial, he knew the outcome. The wait then was as mundane as a wait for a bus.

Now it is he who waits for judgement. The inevitable delays in the proceedings of a process burdened by bureaucracy and ceremony have stretched out far beyond the day, and his verdict will now not be delivered until tomorrow. He is in little doubt over the outcome. He is disquieted, nonetheless, the boot being on the other foot, as the expression goes. He imagines how a doctor might feel when he is told he has a terrible disease, having given the diagnosis himself to countless others. The rigidity of his professional career does not prepare the doctor for his own morbidity. Never in the procurator's courtroom appearances had he considered the future of his clients nor imagined himself in their predicament. They had become past problems, resigned to history, merely a concern for his secretary to chase the fees and tie up the loose ends as the law dictated. His complete lack of empathy, he reasoned, was necessary to survive in the atmosphere of criminality. To feel sorry for a defendant is to show weakness. It distracts from the execution of the law. There is no place for sentiment in the courts of law. Of course, the people he defended were victims of their circumstance: pigs rolling in pig swill will never be clean. Even he, the uncaring man that he was, knew that. Their subjugation was as much down to luck as it was down to any wrongdoing. The tenet of law suggests that each man has the ability to decide his own fate, but framed in the context of poverty, that decision is more prone to result in disobedience than if it were taken in a palace. To put it bluntly, rich and contented men don't need to steal.

Where does that leave him, Brian George, former lawyer of the city of New Canterbury, now defrocked? He had enjoyed all available luxuries in his youth; an education rolled out before him, a conveyor belt of opportunity upon which he merely had to step, then roll along with the tide to prosperity and a place in society. He watched as those around him rose to the heights of their career, driven by self-imposed ambitions and the burden of expectation. School friends (who were not really friends, more like children with whom he shared lessons) bought their high-end detached houses and personalised sports cars, took holidays in exclusive encampments, and sent their children to the same schools to which they had been sent, never imagining any other option from the moment the offspring uttered their first word. Yet he had stepped off that conveyor belt, declining the routine of a lifestyle defined from his birth. He understood counterarguments, sought out rebellious routes, and would not be drawn into convention. He drifted from his potential comrades, severing any weak bonds with other human beings he might stumble upon, repelling intimacy. Even in his dalliances with the followers of John Corn, very quickly he felt the desire to derive his own personalised convictions, considering his alignment to others abhorrent. He eschewed the company of others, defining his own set of rules, refusing to be drawn into the crowd. In time, he was expelled from the Church of John Corn, already seen by many as a cult. He had become too extreme even for a cult.

And from the moment of his rejection from an organisation he had initially considered to be his salvation, his need to prove his point was set in train. He was damaged by the denial of others and positioned himself on a limb, a radical decision burning in his mind that he should fulfil his destiny in one way or another. It so happened that his meeting with a man, an immoral man, now dead, on a committee in the drabness of the city's university, followed by the cryptic discussions he had had with the man called Peter, were the points at which his destiny was sealed.

And what of Peter? He has not been told the fate of the man he inadvertently instructed to kill, save for mention in court proceedings that he is now being treated in a psychiatric unit, unable to give evidence or to stand trial himself. He should have sensed the glimpses of his mental aberrations and steered clear of the man. Instead, he had ploughed on with his half-baked idea, an idea that had been interpreted in the most murderous of ways by a man who was no doubt subject to delusions and persecutory thoughts. He does not recall now what his idea was, save for preventing the work of the scientist. There were no details. He has told the court of this, but they do not believe him. His vagueness on the matter will convict him. His defence appears evasive, and the jury is unlikely to consider that this most heinous of crimes was constructed on the premise of ambiguity. He considered the man he called Peter to be a disciple in his battle against immorality but knows now that he was mistaken. *We must stop him*, he had said. *We must stop him.*

57

THE SKY IS grey, imbued with flecks of black, ominous in their distribution. DI Price and DS Hameed sit under the awning of a roadside café, drinking coffee and reflecting on the day in court. They await the inevitable deluge of rain but rest for a while, glad to be outside. It has been a tedious day in courtroom number 3, the senior officer is saying. They are both frustrated at the lack of progress: the machinations of the legal journey are taking an age, the deliberations are tortuous. At least the judge has now set out the timetable for the trial's denouement.

For the two officers who have investigated the murder, there seems little doubt concerning the culpability of Brian George. Today's deliberations in court have focused predominantly on exposing the underlying motive for the heinous act on the bridge. There is an unwritten mandate that those gathered in the law courts owe to the family the uncovering of a motive: a chance for them to make sense of what is otherwise senseless. How can they grieve, move on from such a terrible event, if the reason for it is not exposed? The police officers have observed before now that families of those killed in apparently random acts float around in the ether, restless souls, neither understanding nor living. Brian George, despite having become more accepting of his fate throughout the long days of the trial, is giving little away. He denied all but a fleeting acquaintance with the protagonist of the case in early exchanges, but his resolve, or perhaps his ability to keep up a ridiculous pretence, crumbled after a day or two. He has admitted to discussing the scientist with Reuben Christian, the man currently locked up in a secure psychiatric unit, fighting his devils with the aid of strong anti-psychotics and restraint. He has reported that, during discussions with Christian, he uttered the words *he must be stopped*, or something similar, the passage of time blurring the exact terminology. So much has happened, so many words spoken. How can he be certain of exactly what he said? Did he instruct Rueben Christian to kill the scientist? In what manner should his work be stopped? Why was he discussing these matters with a man who was clearly psychiatrically unwell? What had he hoped to achieve?

'It all boils down to ethics,' declares DS Hameed, feeling the first drops of rain blowing in from the side.

DI Price nods and sips his coffee. He is aware of his colleague's mission right from the start of the case to unearth the reason for the murder. As he has got older, he is more inclined not to think too deeply about motive, accepting the irrational nature of indiscretion, without which there would be less call for his line of work.

'They haven't really pinned him down on his religious convictions,' says DS Hameed, holding out a hand to feel for the incoming rain.

The senior officer shrugs.

'This precious gift of mortality. The copy of the John Corn book at the tow path. Research into immortality,' lists DS Hameed, recalling their hours of interviews with the man, all now recorded and regurgitated in court.

'He's keeping that side of his life quiet,' replies DI Price.

It is a private matter, thinks DI Price. Or at least it would be in any other circumstance. Religious intolerance is a thing of the past; that is what society has decreed. A man can no longer be shamed by his thoughts. Those days are long gone. And anyway, Brian George denies the connection to ancient prophets. He states that he is no longer a member of the Church of John Corn, having been relieved of his membership following a difference of opinion. He denies giving Christian the book found on the towpath or discussing the teachings of John Corn with him.

He is not clear how the book, which he admits belongs to him, ended up in the possession of Reuben Christian, despite his clear contact with the man.

'A religious killing: a purging of unholy science. That is what it boils down to,' states DS Hameed, continuing her musings while gazing into the far distance. 'But why does he refuse to talk about his religious beliefs? It is as though he is protecting his deep-seated opinions.'

'Protecting them from what?'

'I don't know,' replies DS Hameed in a soft, contemplative voice. 'Perhaps from scrutiny of an irrational belief system by trial?'

A waiter appears and places the bill for their coffee on the table. DI Price picks it up and holds up his plastic debit card as an indication to the waiter of his preferred method of payment. The waiter nods and heads inside.

From the direction of Galahad Bridge, a loud noise is heard; an explosion, too loud to be a firework. The two police officers look at each other with alarm. There has been too much going on in their city for things like this to be ignored. They remain seated, however, and there is a moment of calm before they spot a crowd of people running from the direction of the bridge, up the road and away from the origin of the noise.

'What the …' DI Price starts to speak but is interrupted by the ringing of his phone. He answers, the call lasting no more than ten seconds.

'We must go,' he says to DS Hameed, offering no further explanation. The waiter appears outside with the card reader to take their payment, yet is distracted by the unfolding chaos that ripples down the street, first a few souls running, then a stampede.

'We'll pay later!' shouts the police officer, holding up his badge of authority, before running against the direction of flow.

'What's going on?' shouts DS Hameed, running a few paces behind her boss, striving to keep up.

'Something's happened on the bridge,' he replies dodging the crowd of fleeing people.

58

IN FACT, WHEN the two police officers reach Galahad Bridge, they discover that the event that has caused such alarm has occurred under the bridge, not on the bridge as they have been told. Smoke billows from a boat, a blackened form, static despite the vigour of the river. From it, thick clouds rise up and envelop the now-empty walkway of the bridge. Police officers have sealed both ends of the bridge, and multiple vans are parked in the streets surrounding it; this is a police force on high alert. Officers walk around with a rapid gait, and those with authority to carry weapons have one hand on their gun holsters. Some have arrived in breathing apparatus and capacious overalls, wading through the thick black smoke as if it were a scene from a sixties science fiction film. The officers tread softly, restrained by the menace of imagined explosives and the heaviness of their suits. One man approaches a bin, then calls over another officer, who wears an even more elaborate outfit – one designed to resist both noxious gases and explosives. The first man retreats and leaves the inspection of the bin to his colleague. More cars arrive, their sirens chaotic, their lights appearing as an industrial aurora in the gloaming of the morning light.

DI Price and DS Hameed enter the police cordon after showing their badges. They spot Constable George Tomaris, who is guarding a barrier with some colleagues and preventing anyone from entering the walkway. People stay away anyway, so his task is simple. This is a scared population, on edge, willing to run away from a threat of which they have no understanding.

The two officers walk over to their colleague.

'George,' says DS Hameed, 'what's going on?'

She has not been filled in on any details by her senior colleague, the perfunctory telephone conversation at the café unrevealed.

Constable Tomaris points at the smouldering wreck on the water. 'It appears there was a bomb on the boat. It exploded when it was directly under the bridge.'

'Was anyone hurt?' she asks.

The constable shrugs. 'Some ambulances have arrived, but I don't think there were any fatalities.'

DI Price's phone sounds, and he steps aside to answer. DS Hameed thanks her colleague for the information, then walks a short distance to a line of police cars which delineate the safe area. The explosives expert near the bin has emptied it on the stone walkway and is pawing over its contents, which appear to be nothing more than the regular detritus of a wasteful city.

The smoke dissipates, the wind taking it downstream. DI Price heads over to a police officer who is questioning a civilian in a dark blue coat. He beckons his colleague to join him. The woman being questioned has dark eyes and a manner of one who has much to unburden. She holds a scarf to her face to prevent the ingestion of the toxic gases, and lowers it a fraction to talk.

'This is Marta Vanderland,' says the policeman addressing DI Price. 'She witnessed the event.'

'Vanderlinden,' the woman says, correcting the officer, at the same time as extending a hand to DI Price, whom she recognises as a man in charge.

'Apologies,' says the senior officer, who accepts her handshake, then takes out a notebook.

'Tell me what you saw.'

The thick smoke has now all but gone. The woman takes a deep breath and lowers her scarf. 'As I was saying to this gentleman,' she commences her story. Her accent is foreign but its origin unrecognisable to the police officers. She is one of the multinational, multilingual workers in the metropolis that embraces, for the most part, the diversity of nations. 'I was standing on the bridge waiting for my friend, and then I see this boat coming down the river. It was making a noise and came to a stop under the bridge – just where it is now.' She points to the smouldering black shape. A fire engine has pulled up on the bank, and a dinghy containing several firemen clad in yellow outfits and with breathing apparatus has been launched into the river. They cautiously approach the boat, shouting instructions and observations to their colleagues on the bank. The three police officers and Marta Vanderlinden watch in silence for a few moments before DI Price brings her back to her story.

'Yes, sorry,' she says, averting her gaze from the event on the river, which is not a rescue, but is, perhaps, the attenuation of further explosions. 'Yes, the boat stopped just there, and I think dropped a …' she struggles for the word.

'An anchor?' suggests DS Hameed.

'Yes, an anchor,' says the woman, looking back at the boat and its attendant dinghy. 'Another boat then passed by and pulled up beside it. The men then put on a sign on the first boat, and then they crossed over to the other boat. That boat then sailed away.'

At that moment a fire hose, unfurled from the fire engine, begins squirting a white foam in an arc from the bank to the smoking boat. Their first effort misses by some distance and the men on the shore adjust the trajectory of the stream of foam so that the boat is hit. In a matter of seconds it turns from black to white, the smoke ceasing instantly.

'Carry on,' requests the senior police officer. They have all been distracted from her statement by the actions of the fire brigade, just as young children marvel at the bravado of the emergency services.

'Oh yes,' she continues, 'the other boat goes away. Then I wait. My friend was late. Her baby is unwell and she was picking up some medicine. I think she was …'

DI Price interrupts her: 'Tell us about the explosion.'

She looks at the DI, appreciating the urgency of his enquiry. 'After the other boat had left, nothing happened for a few minutes, then …'

'How many minutes?'

'I don't know. Maybe two?' replies the woman. DS Hameed

notes this down in her notebook, cognisant that the perception of time in stressful moments, particularly those recollected at the extremes of threat, is typically well off the mark.

'Then?'

'Then there was a big bang, and the boat was up in fire,' she continues. 'I was right above it. I felt the heat on my face. I nearly burn,' she adds, taking a handful of her long blonde hair for inspection of its ends, which may have been singed.

'Is it burn?' she asks DS Hameed, pointing the handful of hair in her direction.

DS Hameed shakes her head, dismissively.

'Then what?' asks the DI.

Marta Vanderlinden shrugs her shoulders. 'Then smoke,' she says, uncertain of what it is she is meant to have remembered.

The young police officer receives a message on his radio and steps aside to answer. DI Price and DS Hameed thank their witness, taking her contact details should they have any further questions in future. She will be happy to help, she tells them. They instruct her to wait for the other police officer, who will take down her statement in detail and inform her of the next steps. They begin to walk away, but DS Hameed pauses, recalling a moment of their conversation. 'You say the men put a sign on the boat,' she asks Marta Vanderlinden, who is typing a number to unlock her mobile phone.

She stops tapping the screen. 'Oh yes,' she replies.

'What sign?'

'I don't remember exactly, but …' she pauses and again looks down at her phone. 'I took a photo of it.'

She taps a few more times on her screen then brings up a photograph, handing the phone to DS Hameed. She takes it, enlarging the image to focus on a banner that is draped from the masts of the boat.

DS Hameed reads the message written on the banner, then shows the image to her senior partner.

BRIAN GEORGE IS INNOCENT, he reads.

59

As a child, Brian George would often visit the ruined remains of the city's medieval castle on the southern bank of the river, downstream from the modern-day centre of power. It was surrounded by a wall, half of which had crumbled into the river, its stones carried away to the sea or sunk deep into the silt of the riverbed. He would walk over the rocks, imagining what life would have been like when the castle was the stronghold of the region, repelling attacks from the barbarians outwith the walls. Most noteworthy to a fertile imagination were the dungeons, accessed by a small stone staircase that opened unceremoniously into the ground – a dark pit lined with black stones whose surface was damp to the touch at all times. The dungeons were lit by a single light bulb that swung an erratic journey on its long cord from the centre of the dungeon's ceiling, flickering, casting otherworldly shadows on the stark stone walls. The orbit of the light bulb appeared to be generated by a breeze, the origin of which the young boy could not comprehend, the room being subterranean and not subject to the atmospheric conditions above ground. He had imagined it to be a supernatural force generating energy to move the bulb, perhaps the agitated motion of an imprisoned soldier from centuries ago fated to scurry around the dingy cell, attempting to find a way out; or perhaps the ghost of a petty thief, forgotten and starving in the darkness, clawing his fingers against the hard stone, attempting to dig his way out of the abyss in which he had found himself.

Even now, he recalls a blue plaque screwed to the wall in the corner of the main dungeon. It revealed the cause of smooth indentations in the wall, near-circular patches where the sandstone had been worn away by desperate prisoners who licked the damp walls to slake their thirst. The thought of it was horrifying, yet fascinating; how the circumstances of life can end in such a way, directed by the whim of others. One wall was fully covered in the discs, which reflected the dim light. How many men had had to endure these conditions was not revealed, but the evidence suggested hundreds, maybe more, had fashioned their gruesome epitaph in the wall, a testament to cruel times when punishment was absolute and redemption was impossible.

The deprivations of Brian George's incarceration are very different. Yesterday's guilty verdict delivered in all its pomp means that this will be his life now for the foreseeable future. Redemption (of a sort) will be offered, if he wishes; an early parole if he behaves in a manner acceptable to the courts and the prison service. He cannot begin to imagine how he will behave in prison. The alien nature of an existence cooped up with those who have transgressed is something he had never considered until a few days ago, when the inevitability of his guilty verdict became apparent. His behaviour in custody so far has been governed by the prospect of release after a while; a hope that the life he lives will be returned to its former status. But now the indefinite nature of his fate has struck him, knocking his feet from under him, forcing him into existing in a half-life of rules and subjugation.

The guard arrives at the door and unbolts the numerous locks that keep Brian George bound to the spartan cell beneath the law courts. Wordlessly, he secures handcuffs around the prisoner's wrist, then marches out of the cell, up a series of staircases and into the waiting rooms outside courtroom number 3. The defence lawyer is there already, sitting in the corner, studying some papers. He nods at the prisoner when he enters, a noncommittal gesture of a man lacking hope greeting one defeated. Brian George, holding his bound hands in front of him like a supplicant, remains impassive, not returning the greeting.

The door to the courtroom opens and another court official beckons the prison guard to bring his charge inside. The two trudge forward into the arena of legal processing, an atmosphere humming with the whispers of the gallery and the anticipation of the waiting world. Brian George takes his seat in the sentencing dock, leaning forward and resting his hands on the small shelf before him, upon which a Bible lies. The prison guard retreats to the door, where he will remain standing until that point when the judge informs him to take away the sorry specimen of a man whom he has condemned to a life of captivity. Two court officials enter from a side door, followed by the judge, who appears from an elevated position. His gowns are red, shining in the glare of the light. All stand.

The judge moves papers and objects on his desk, shuffling them into an order to his liking. Then, having kept the assembled group on their feet for a time determined by him alone, he orders all to sit. A cacophony of scraping chairs, coughs and creaking pews is met with disapproval by the judge, who scowls, despite having heard this every day for decades. He is a man who requires order to be delivered as silently as possible.

'For those about to …' he commences in his deep lugubrious tones, but appears to lose interest after the opening few words, so that final words of this hymnal to the condemned are lost in a mumble of unheard confusion. In any case, it has been said and heard on so many occasions that it no longer holds meaning.

'We are here today to pass sentence on a man who has been found guilty of the most heinous of crimes,' he continues, now with clearer diction, casting his eyes down on Brian George, former lawyer, who feels a dryness in his mouth and a tightness in his throat in response to the actuality of the moment. 'Crimes,' the judge repeats, then coughs to clear his throat, eyes still on the former self-styled procurator. Brian George, a man now stripped on any formal title, experiences a spinning feeling in his head and, despite how hard he tries, he can no longer understand the words of the man in his high chair, clad in ancient robes, beneath a shield bearing images of creatures that have never set foot in the country or even the world, being mythical and supposedly symbolic. There can be no doubt that this old man has the full history of legal precedent behind him. Yet, his words are disjointed and certainly of no relevance to him, he now knows, as he is who now utterly rejects laws and tenets. Still, he strains to hear, but his mind tells him to block out the words. They will not come to pass, anyway. They will exit the larynx of the pompous man and from there fly away through the vaulted ceiling and up to the blue skies, empty of clouds. They are for the birds: those deceitful thrushes who are searching for a world to inhabit. Above the judge, now a blurred form of obscurity, a lightshade dangles. If the prisoner squints, he can refract the light into a line the colours of a rainbow, which expands and then rotates. This kaleidoscope is reminiscent of events experienced in a childhood which was not his. Perhaps it is an amalgam of all childhoods, all the rights and wrongs of growing up; events that shape a boy and then a man. The light expands further, then contracts into a single white light, burning the retina of anyone who looks too intensely upon its form. His senses shift in the blink of an eye, and he now hears a soft music, a lilting song delivered by the gentle voice of a mother or by a nurse upon whom he will suckle the milk of benevolence, rich and smooth in its humanity. The words of the song are hard to discern, but he considers them a cautionary tale.

Be careful what you ask for.

60

DI PRICE AND DS Hameed are not in court to hear the sentence delivered to Brian George, the man who conceived the idea for the killing of the scientist on Galahad Bridge several months ago now. They have done their duty in finding him and bringing him to court. The rest is out of their hands. They have moved on to other forensic enigmas and are already engaged in new cases, primarily working through the intricacies of a fraud operation that surprises the police officers in its audacity and scale.

Nevertheless, the circumstances of their most high-profile case linger in their thoughts, occupying much of their deliberations, like a concept too sullied to be addressed full-on, lingering in the long days of its reimagining. The city still reels from the aftershocks of the killing. Its population is disquieted, its undercurrent troubled. Only yesterday, a demonstration was held in the city to remember the loss of liberty caused by the death – or so it was pitched. As it turned out, the marching people were assembled with a jumble of gripes, a mixed bag of things to complain about. DI Price had avoided the streets on that day, being fatigued with the muddle of arguments that circled around themselves and landed on contradiction. His colleague, however, on a rare day off had been out, skirting the edges of the march from the bridge to the ancient castle. She had gone to do some shopping, not heeding the warnings of disruptions in the city centre, and had come across hordes of people gathering in the streets, shouting slogans and muttering about revolution.

'Makes little sense to me, Belinda,' says DI Price, hearing the account of the march from the younger police officer as they sit in the coffee room of the police station. 'An unhinged man with a chip on his shoulder gets an even more unhinged man to kill someone, and the whole world goes crazy. They've made a crisis out of a random event, turned the fantasy of a man into a conspiracy against …' He pauses, struggling to find a conclusion to his argument.

DS Hameed nods. 'I think if you asked most of those marching why they were doing it, they wouldn't have a clear answer. Some form of collective hysteria? Who knows?'

Fiona Banner, previously assigned to the bridge murder but now working in traffic control, enters the room and heads for the coffee machine. She acknowledges her former colleagues with a raised hand and a smile. Her eyes are dark, her skin pale yet waxy, reflecting the yellow sheen of the bare lightbulb.

'I saw you out on the streets, yesterday, Fiona,' says DS Hameed. 'Looked like a nasty crowd.'

'Tell me about it!' replies the constable, pressing a series of buttons on the coffee machine, which clunks into action, emitting a whining noise.

'We were just talking about all these demonstrations. Neither of us have much of a clue what they are about,' DS Hameed declares, looking at her colleague for confirmation of the fact.

'Search me!' replies Fiona Banner. She looks tired, giving the impression of one not in the mood for lengthy discussion about the whys and wherefores of the right to demonstrate. She takes her coffee, black and steaming, and heads to the door. 'Just hope they will settle down once the fellow is firmly behind bars,' she says before leaving the coffee room.

'I doubt they will,' says DI Price continuing the conversation despite the originator of the comment having left the room. 'They are not protesting against the man, as far as I can tell.'

He picks up this morning's newspaper, creased and badly folded on the coffee table. The headline refers to the protests: *THE PEOPLE TAKE TO THE STREETS*. Underneath is a picture of a man in dark glasses carrying a young child on his shoulders. The child holds a blue and white checked flag in one hand and an apple in the other. The flag design has become a symbol of the campaign to reclaim the streets from the fear that now engulfs them. The boy looks into the camera, half-smiling, as he should when having his photograph taken. He clearly understands little about the protest, his father deeming it necessary to bring him to the march to emphasise the sentiments he has expressed to the reporter and which are quoted in the accompanying text: *It is for him we are protesting, for his generation that we must walk the streets without fear, for the young who have the right to live their lives without the threat of violence.* The newspaper reports that further demonstrations are planned and that the campaign is gathering momentum, putting pressure on the government to act. It gives no precise strategy, and the demands of the protestors are far from explicit.

DI Price throws down the newspaper and rubs his eyes. He sighs deeply before drinking some more coffee.

'Further demonstrations are planned,' he says, repeating the lines from the paper.

'Like the boat demonstration?' she asks. She has grappled with the meaning of what was written on the banner before the boat exploded under Galahad Bridge, and has failed to comprehend why someone would stage such a stunt. *Brian George is innocent.* The two officers have not discussed it since; both are too incredulous to even contemplate its portent. The case has been given to another team to investigate. Brian George was clearly not innocent, and his involvement in the crime was proven beyond all reasonable doubt. Even the former lawyer himself capitulated towards the end of the trial and offered little resistance to the barrage of indictments. He was a broken man flailing in a sea of mists. It defies belief that there would be people willing to blow up a boat to claim his innocence. DS Hameed recalls what she said at the moment the photograph was shown to her at the time of the incident: *It makes no sense.*

The two detectives remain seated for some time, continuing

their coffee break for longer than they first intended. An air of fatigue has overcome their collective industry, the Brian George case having taken their psychological reserves to a low point. They possess an indolence towards their new fraud case: a flagrant misuse of the tax rules driven by stone-cold greed. It is hard to garner much interest in this most impersonal of crimes. Yet a crime is a crime. The police cannot discriminate between the myriad of excuses offered up. It is their job to bring the offender to the door of justice, wait at the door and let others determine the culpability and the penalty for the misdoing.

The court will consider, will level, will deliver the verdict in the full knowledge of variables, with the strong hand of moderation, with no top and no bottom, no beginning and no end, no hierarchies for the classes of criminal, who will each receive their time to be served, no questions asked, no special consideration. Some will be fortunate, others not. *A man is just the sum of his parts*, says the kind-hearted believer in prison reform who works the afternoon in the jailhouse school, teaching life skills for the time when their students will reintegrate into society. *We are all products of our having been pushed in directions uncharted and uncertain*, she says. We clamour for the recognition of our forefathers, yet rebel against their steadfastness. Progress comes in pushing the boundaries and straying over the lines. What is truly wrong is always wrought from some conviction; what the criminal act destroys is, in some small way, nurtured from the desire to create, to evolve, to immortalise.

And this can, by stealth and a series of circuitous arguments, lead to the concept that a man is innocent despite his crime. The public jury, making its mind up by snippets of information gleaned from the newspaper, the TV news and discussions in the bars and dining rooms of the land, plus an underlying desire for their prejudices to be fulfilled, come to their own decision on the most shocking of legal cases, and on a whole series of other matters.

Brian George is innocent.

61

JOHN CORN LIVED out the final days of his life in obscurity, sequestered from his people in a dark cave in the city's eastern forests, where wolves roamed and people rarely went. His teachings and his writings had all but vanished as commercialism became the new morality. His fall from grace had been as spectacular as it had been rapid, its reasons not understood by those closest to him. The despotic Hammond Scar had died in mysterious circumstances and the city was ruled by a new leader keen to practice more democratic ideals. The city breathed a little easier. A newfound freedom, coupled to the opportunities of novel wealth generation, put the populace at ease, needing fewer mitigations from the cruelty of their erstwhile existence.

John Corn was disillusioned anyway. He lamented the fickleness of his followers, who now chased the money-god in their attempts to pull themselves out of poverty, abandoning their beliefs. None but the most zealous could begrudge them that. These people had survived a generation of plague and oppression. Now the future looked brighter, and the city was opening up to the new world order with its promises of adventure and a life free of miserable servitude. Boats of a grandeur never before seen sailed down the river, flying flags of distant lands and smelling of exotic spices. New housing replaced the old slums, and river defences were constructed to prevent the misery of the winter floods that had become a regular occurrence since the farmers of the province had diverted the rivers to reclaim the marshlands at the foot of the mountains. The church bells rang once again, having fallen silent for the years of Hammond Scar. The Church's ministry was restored, and its elders were happy to welcome those who had settled for a new form of spirituality – one in which personal wealth was the bedrock, and giving alms to the poor took second stage. The monks who had been holed up, unseen in the monastery, were brought back into the fold, happy now to once again enter the city and preach to the people, who no longer died in plagues.

Some time after Corn's departure from the city, Jared Eden, the reclusive landowner who had made his money selling potions to the ailing masses, had also vanished, never to be seen again, leaving his mansion in the dark hills empty like a curious mausoleum to wealth. His servants had reported him missing to the city's authorities and had also reported that he had taken much of his laboratory equipment with him. None of them had any clue as to how he had been able to pack up the flasks, jars and dishes that he used in his lonely experiments. No one had seen a cart entering or leaving, and the sheer extent of his experimentation had meant that it would have required several large wagons to remove the items. Such was the suspicious nature of the man in his later years that he had employed a band of guards to watch over his property throughout the day and night. Yet, no one had seen his flight, nor any evidence of foul play. It was as if he had vanished into thin air, and with him the tools of manufacture of his potions. Few knew the recent subject of his work, but the circumstances of his leaving led many to concoct their own stories of what manner of witchcraft he was dallying with. A man had vanished overnight from a heavily guarded castle, taking with him the means to originate the essence of sorcery – this was the whispered talk in the hostelries and marketplaces of a city opening up, allowing itself to deal once again in tittle-tattle. Jared Eden's abode became deserted, and even the looters who patrolled the hinterlands of the valley and the western forests stayed away lest they be visited by the unholy creatures rumoured to be haunting the place.

Despite the prominence of both Jared Eden and John Corn in the city's life, a connection between the disappearance of the two men was barely considered. But there was indeed a connection between the two: the elixir of life. One had sought it, the other had viewed its concept with abhorrence. During his time as ruler, Hammond Scar, using any tactic possible to diminish the power and wealth of the bothersome apothecary, had exposed Eden's unnatural experiments in order to agitate his chief religious adviser. Corn's sensibilities had indeed been offended. He felt that Eden was engaged in activities contrary to morality. Life was sacrosanct, and man's tenure on Earth was not the decision of a mortal man. Corn had demanded a shutdown of Jared Eden's business dealings, even a confiscation of his wealth. Tighter regulations were brought in, new codes of conduct became entrenched in law. Yet, the diminishing power of government met the strength of Eden's money, causing stalemate. Jared Eden reinforced his private security and was able to do exactly as he pleased, safe in the knowledge that his pack of bloodthirsty henchmen were more vicious than Scar's, coupled to the understanding that any man can be bought out at a price.

So it came as a great surprise when Jared Eden vanished. He was at the height of his power and had long since beaten Corn's attempts to suppress him. He had seen the strange mystic go into exile, and had been allowed to practise more freely under the leadership of Scar's successor. His business was flourishing, and the city's trade was crucially dependent on him. Yet he became, in his final years, even more of a recluse. He never set foot outside his fortified mansion and was only seen by a few of his trusted staff. All this only added to the mystery of his disappearance.

By the time of Eden's vanishing, Corn was, for the most part, a forgotten man. It was more convenient for his erstwhile followers to resign him to history. Many regretted their dalliance with a new religion that they now viewed as unnatural, even ungodly. His name was rarely spoken. His life's work became hidden, like a stain on the wall covered up by drapes that were never pulled back – only to reappear in later times as the moral code for an obscure cult.

62

PARANOIA SEEPS INTO the collective tedium of a society desiring nothing more than to be shocked into thinking the worst of itself. The city is, after all, a gathering of disparate people thrown together and melded into a single form, breathing the fumes of lives held in high disdain; one which is destined to reach crisis point and then explode, casting the shrapnel of the consumer's debris, burning buildings filled with the cowering and the defeated, destroying the pretence of harmony. There is little surprise, therefore, that the act witnessed on the city's bridge all those long months ago has inflamed its people, who take to the streets and the waterways, chanting incantations derived from the doctrine of whatever tribe they follow, waving flags the colour of division, constructing banners that make little sense or mean everything, depending on the way the wind blows in each particular faction. The rumble of the malcontent as they stride down the street provides an ever-present accompaniment to daily living. The whisper of duplicity is never more than an eardrum away. The fetid air is filled with suspicion and the unwavering belief that forcing the moment to its destiny is the only course of action.

Many had thought, or perhaps hoped, that the culmination of the Brian George case – a guilty verdict and a lengthy prison sentence – would relegate the mistrust of the city's streets to the past. It is a time for cleansing, a time for reflecting on the folly of ideas that led to such a bloody outcome, or so the argument goes.

'Let us now heal,' says the city's mayor in a press conference delivered the evening of Brian George's verdict, designed to cool tensions amid riotous intentions. 'This is a time to remember, not to react. The man who orchestrated the crime is behind bars.'

The chief of police, flanked by the mayor and the city's MP, repeats these sentiments and says that this is no time for an uprising.

'Let the family of the murdered man have time to grieve.'

All three nod and speak as one, this triumvirate of the city's power. None expect anything other than disorder.

The chief of police then steps forward, positioning himself behind a wooden podium on which the coat of arms of the city's police force is displayed, to give the gathered journalists an update on their investigation into the boat bomber. 'Significant progress has been made,' he begins, using the tried and tested language of those meting out justice.

'What was the meaning of the banner erected on the boat prior to its destruction?' interrupts a young man in the front row, raising a hand but not waiting to be invited to talk. He refers to the banner which read *BRIAN GEORGE IS INNOCENT*, the image of which accompanied the headlines in every newspaper of the land and beyond.

The chief of police hesitates but considers it not in his remit to interpret the messages of those in the underbelly of society, so presses on with his disclosures. 'A foreign national has been detained and is believed to have been to orchestrator of the incident, which,' the chief of police is keen to emphasise, 'led to no casualties.'

He stops, uneasy at the rising level of chatter that has accompanied the interruption to his statement. He is not used to this sort of insubordination. He continues, sharpening the tenor of his voice just as a mother would to scold an unruly child. 'The foreign national is co-operating with the police officer in charge of the enquiry,' he says, almost shouts, his words being more or less drowned out in a cacophony of droning.

'What organisation does the suspect represent?' asks the same journalist, leaning forward on the edge of his seat.

The chief of police peers down from his lofty position, focusing on the journalist, who now jiggles on his seat like an excited schoolboy wishing to impress.

'I will answer some questions at the end,' he states firmly, returning to his prepared statement.

He rambles on for several more minutes, this time uninterrupted, but also unheard. The statement is bland, giving little away, but is broadly reassuring. 'We are not looking for anyone else in connection with the incident,' are his final words, designed not just to bring a finality to his statement but to suggest to anyone listening that further unrest is unnecessary. He steps back from the podium, inviting questions, then points to a journalist at the back of the room, deliberately ignoring the over-eager man in the front row.

'How many are being held in connection to the boat bombing? There was more than one person involved, wasn't there?' he asks. The chief of police strains to hear above the general murmuring in the room and asks for the question to be repeated.

'You say one man has been detained,' the journalist starts his question again, this time shouting, 'but witnesses reported several men. Are you not looking for others?'

The chief of police straightens his tie and coughs. 'As I said, we are not looking for anyone else in connection with the incident.'

The level of murmuring rises a notch, and the mayor steps forward and gestures to the crowd to keep the noise down.

The man in the front row now stands and bawls out his previous questions. 'What was the meaning of the banner on the boat? What group does the suspect represent?'

More shouting ensues. Repeated questions, screamed in some cases; finger-pointing; the thrust forward of recording devices, hoping to capture something of note above the din. The mayor becomes more animated in his attempts to subdue the gathered journalists. The chief of police fears the press conference, orchestrated to bring a sense of calm to the proceedings of the last few months, is now degenerating into an event similar to those seen on the streets. These men and women of the newspapers are an unforgiving audience. He dreads to think what they will print tomorrow: a headline implying chaos alongside his picture? *The city authorities are losing their grip*, they will say. *They can't even arrange a press conference without it descending into anarchy.*

The mayor finds a gavel on the lectern and bangs it three times, bringing a temporary quiet to the gathering.

'If we could have some decorum, ladies and gentlemen,' he urges. But this request serves the opposite function, and the noise returns to previous levels. The journalists start turning on each other, some berating colleagues for reducing the conference to this farce, others intent on having their questions aired, despite knowing that they will get no answers.

The chief of police, the city's mayor and the MP are ushered off the stage, retreating to an antechamber, from where the riotous crowd can still be heard behind the thin walls. The three men have, over the past few months, seen their city turn from a quiet centre of industry, a place known for its scholastic learning and its intriguing history, into a troubled cauldron of disquiet, a frenzy of argument and cynical counter-argument. But the fiasco they have just witnessed appears to be an escalation.

'I thought they were going to start throwing chairs,' says the MP, who is grey-faced and shaking. 'A pack of wild dogs would have more of a sense of dignity. What the hell's wrong with them?'

The chief of police is on his phone, calling up his subordinates to clear up this mess. 'Bring the heavies if necessary,' he repeats on several occasions.

The mayor sits down and cradles his head his in hands.

After a few moments, the shouting in the next room becomes quieter, only to be replaced by an approaching police siren, a comforting noise in the circumstances and one that makes the mayor sit to attention.

'What was the meaning of the banner?' he asks the chief of police, who has now ended his call and is pacing up and down the room. The chief of police stops instantly on hearing the question and looks confusedly at the mayor.

'What?'

'I mean, why would anyone think the man innocent? Why did someone feel the need to protest his innocence?' asks the mayor, in the manner of a small child who wishes to understand the curiosities of the world.

The chief of police shrugs. 'How should I know?' he says.

AN ENDING

ONE MAN WAKES from a night of terrible dreams. His face is ghastly white, moonlight reflecting off its surface; a light which travels both as a wave and as a particle, existing in different forms, just as the potential of history, which reiterates or does not exist at all. Winter trees sway in the gentle breeze, occasionally dislodging icicles which fall silently upon the blanketed earth. An owl hoots in the far distance where the icy river rises, and the mountain slopes roll down to the snow plains.

He throws on his shawl and stamps his feet to summon the circulation of blood. He wears remnants of shoes, battered and caked in dried mud, and the undergarments in which he has slept, indeed which he has not changed for weeks on end. He picks up his staff and his hat, ready to depart. There will be no breakfast this morning, the larder having been empty for several days. The seven-mile march will be accompanied by unending hunger, a raging ache in the pit of his unassuaged stomach. This will be the first time since last summer that he has made the journey, when vital supplies for the long winter had been hauled painstakingly across the ground. At his age and at this time of year, such an iteration will be a challenge, and the deprivations of his life will no doubt take their hold to impair his passage.

Outside, the air is cold and the wind is biting in its intensity. His feet sink slowly into the fresh fallen snow, immediately sending shivers up his legs and into his core as the poorly functioning shoes let in icy water. Hurriedly he moves on, placing his staff in the ground and stepping out with purpose. The moon is low in the sky and morning will break soon, but there will be enough time, he hopes, to make it to the agreed meeting point.

His journey, accompanied by the crack of ice and the crunch of snow underfoot, proceeds as well as he could have hoped, and before long a tinge of turquoise borders the dark shapes of the mountain range, highlighting its crags. The aching of cold in his feet is interspersed with sharp pains as jagged stones dig into his gnarled soles. He stumbles, and on three occasions falls to the ground, the strength in his legs failing him. One time he falls into the ditch by the side of the track, from which he is able, only by the most tortured of efforts, to extricate himself, bruised and soaked, returning to the path and his destiny. He is grateful that he has left the wolves behind him, deep in their forest lairs, unable to touch him now. They will not venture out this far, this close to the men who will, in due course, hunt them to their extinction.

It is now morning. The blueness of the sky has returned in patches, but the temperature remains low, and the traveller's cold is intensified by his sodden clothes, which freeze his skin and sap his journey's momentum. He plants the staff on the rough stone path and then notices, a few paces ahead, a large black beetle on the ground. Its size is such that it represents an obstacle to his passage. Indeed, he has never before seen an insect of this magnitude, not even in the deepest forests of his habitation, which are said to contain the most diabolical beings of creation. Uncertain whether it is alive or what threat it poses, he approaches and tentatively pokes it with his staff. It is unmoving, and he assumes it to be dead. He attempts to move it off the path, placing his staff between its body and the ground, struggling to pry it from the path and thus to flip it on its back, in which position, he reasons, it will be simpler to hit it with one forceful swipe into the ditch. But his levering of the beetle's body causes the supposedly dead creature to come to life, to cling to the ground more forcefully, drawing down its great hulk by means of contractions of its powerful legs. At the same time, the creature extends two prominent antennae from its dark black head, which flick and then gyrate, a response to the actions of an unwelcome predator that has disturbed its repose.

The traveller, alarmed by the beast, recoils and ponders whether he can skirt around it while remaining on the path. On either side of where the beetle rests there is a deep ditch filled with ice cold water, and no other way forward seems possible. He steps back and considers whether a retreat to the stone bridge he passed a few minutes before might reveal the source of a path across the field. But the time lost taking that route will undoubtedly lead him to be late for the meeting, even if the field were to be navigable, in itself unlikely given the recent rains.

Deadlocked, therefore, he stares upon the beast, which moves, or rather pulses, on the path, its antennae continuing to twitch, pointing in a multitude of directions, perhaps receiving information on its potential attacker, or merely warning. Its carapace shines, and the more he stares the more colours he perceives radiating from its surface. Blues and purples give way to reds and oranges, a reflection of the burgeoning sky, followed by yellows and finally a whiteness, dirty and stained like the trodden snow. And then, as though the scrutiny of the traveller has stirred the beast into life, it lifts its wing cases skywards and unfurls its wings, fluttering their lacy forms, expanding their size to twice its body length – mighty wings for the bulk of the beast. In an instant it is in the air, flying a short distance off the ground across the field and then higher into the cool air, its black form delineated against the white snow of the mountainsides in the cold-water valley. He hears a soft hum of wings beating in the air, a noise that becomes amplified as more beetles fly into view, crowding the morning air. Black spots, like floating stones, fill the sky, an army of arthropods.

The traveller ducks as several fly near to his head, winding and dodging in a chaotic frenzy. The air turbulence their wings create and their humming noises add menace, an uneasiness to the awakening day. In time, the swarming thins out as the creatures head eastwards, in the direction of the rising sun – a route dictated by the passage of the earth around its nurturing star in a journey it has taken for a time unimaginable and will take for an epoch undefined.

A single shaft of light now shines brightly through a break in the mountain's form, a pass favoured by animals that trek the hills and valleys in their daily fight for survival. The traveller's gaze is caught by the beam of light and he is temporarily blinded, his vision becoming white, contrasting deeply with the dank gloaming he has experienced thus far on his journey. He rubs his eyes, coaxing his dimming vision into action, beseeching them not to give up on him now, not at this time of his greatest need.

He looks around, squinting his eyes, which slowly regain their sight, and sees no more beetles. Their exit has been a swift occurrence; they have left no trace. He stands up tall, his aching back creaking as the vertebrae extend, and makes a sign to heaven, aware of the nature of supernatural signs. This will not be the last, he fears.

Light spills over the distant crags now, refracted with the hint of blue. There will be no red sky this morning, no warning, no portent from the heavenly hue which, according to an old saying, spells danger. The way is hard, the footsteps heavier now. His discomfort rises with each step forward, despite the warmth of the sun on his back, a gentle feeling like that of a caress after a long day of tribulation. His feet snag often on shards of unhewn rock, twisting the cartilage and the sinews of his old body, sending pains shooting up his legs and into his core, which is troubled yet stable, its ballast providing the impetus for motion, the hidden momentum.

He presses on, as he must, drawn by the duties of a man who has devoted his life to the quest upon which he is now embarked. He will meet the man and talk. And then what?

A raven flies up, a huge black form disturbed from its feeding on the deeply sown seeds of the earth. It caws as it flies, an admonition to its disturber, then circles three times above the path before coming to rest once again in the field. It pecks at the hard earth, uncertain of the malleability of this patch of soil, then rips at some ragged tufts of shrub before once again flying off, this time in the direction of the mountains, with the inadequate feast in its beak.

The man travels for hours more, latterly following the river, which will take him to his destination. A faint mist rises from the water, curling around the branches of the riverbank, coating the dead leaves in a fine dew, making them sparkle in the burgeoning sun. A family of otters are active in the early morning quiet, seeking fish and taking little notice of the traveller, whom they do not view as a threat. In time, the river receives another tributary, making it wider, more vigorous, and from here the city is seen for the first time in his journey with its distant silhouettes of houses and spires.

The traveller comes to a momentary halt. The prospect of his destination is now a reality, and although he has travelled this way many times before, he feels a sense of trepidation; fearful thoughts about what will happen this time. He recalls the occasion of travelling from the monastery to the city, so many years ago, when he was young and full of excitement and ambition. He had stood here on a warm summer's evening among the sheep and the cows that filled the fields of the fertile land. He recalls his profound attraction to the city, his unwavering belief that this was where he was destined to go, that this was the place where he would fulfil the desire that had planted a seed in his psyche; a seed that was as yet neither formed nor comprehensible. Now he views the city through different eyes, as only a man who has lived a life such as his can do.

He checks the sun rising to the east and knows he must hurry. There will be time for reflection and nostalgia at some other point in his journey.

*

ALL IS QUIET, all is calm. The bridge is empty, and the man who has travelled through the small hours treads its cobbles with a lightness he has not experienced for some time. He has not seen a soul since he entered the city, along the narrow streets and through the old stone gate, designed to repel undesirables but now accessed by anyone. The city accepts allcomers into its fold these days. It welcomes displaced refugees, promising to turn them into its citizens, upstanding and proud, diligent and industrious. Yet even they slumber now on this cold morning, which offers the prospect of blizzards and the likelihood of icy roads.

He stands in the centre of the bridge and looks up and down its span. Perhaps the man he is expecting is long since gone, or never intended to turn up. Or perhaps he is watching from a window, high up in one of the houses overlooking the river, working out his moment to appear, having seen that the traveller is alone, unarmed and unshielded. If that is the case, he is looking at a decrepit man, a man defeated, a man with little to lose, a man who will offer little resistance to whatever he has in mind. There can be little other interpretation of a soul at the end of its journey.

The traveller looks over the side of the bridge to the waters below, empty of traffic, flowing rapidly in black shadows and white peaks. Perhaps the man he has come to meet lurks beneath the bridge on the riverbank, unseen in the dark recesses frequented by vagrants. The man has a habit of staying out of sight, of not revealing himself. He is a man of the city who has a prominence in its workings yet is unseen: a hidden orchestrator, a conductor of men who is not apparent. He has built up his wealth from the shadows, locking himself in his vast estate on the edge of town, from where he conducts his fiendish work.

The traveller stamps his feet and rubs his hands together, turning friction to a heat, a paltry warmth which dissipates as soon as it is generated. He aches with cold and knows he cannot stay outside for much longer, while at the same time he understands that he has nowhere else to go. He has travelled so far, in such conditions, and for what? He was foolish to think the man for whom he waits will keep his word. Theirs is a relationship of distrust, of resentment, so why would the olive branch of the meeting be anything other than a ruse, a further part of the wicked man's game? He considers turning round and walking back but knows he does not have the strength to do so. He must seek shelter in the city. Despite his alienation from the place someone will offer him a bed for the night, out of charity towards an old man, if nothing else.

Yet, for now he waits, expecting nothing. He wishes only a conclusion to his journey in whatever form has been determined for him. A man for whom a sense of destiny is engrained has the time to wait. He possesses the patience of angels, the fortitude of one who awaits his end with a gratefulness for merely existing. The scriptures hold the key to all future lives, so he believes, and thus his own fate and the fate of every living being has already been written, from the moment the heavens were created and the sullied earth placed at its heart.

And fate now dictates that a man will walk upon the bridge and approach the traveller. He will talk to him and question his purpose. *Such an early time to be about*, he will say, *at this time of the year*. He will look the man up and down, reflect on his thin, ragged garments, most unsuitable for the season, and think that an old man should not be out on the streets like this. Perhaps he is confused? Perhaps he needs some help to find his way home? And the traveller will ask the man, who is young and wears a uniform the nature of which he cannot fathom: *Do you know who I am?* The young man will look again at the detail of his face, the crags and scars of a life lived in fury, and will think his question forms part of the spectrum of his confusion. Perhaps a delusion of grandeur? He will try once more to assist the old man, who stares down the river with a wistfulness he imagines relates to a lost memory, but he will come to the conclusion that the man has nowhere else to go. He will leave, thinking he has done as much as he can. Perhaps he will walk this way a little later to ensure the man has had a safe passage. *Poor soul*, he will whisper as he trudges off, horrified at the prospect of his own ageing.

And then (with fate returning to the present moment, in the blink of an eye, as it intermingles the expectation of better prospects with the predictability of disappointment), another man appears. He, however, is aware of the identity of the old man on the bridge, who is the one he has been expecting, the one for whom he has waited in the shadows on this cold morning, the one who is the subject of a mission decreed by fantasy and formulated in the depths of depravity by the man who now reveals himself.

He walks forward, a slow pace, deliberate in its solemnity, even portentous.

The traveller senses that this is the man with whom he will convene and watches him approach with an awkward gait caused by a weakness of his left leg, which he swings in an exaggerated circumduction. *A sorry sight*, thinks the traveller, but a common one, lameness being so prevalent in these times, a consequence of the harshness of living conditions and the virulence of disease that has afflicted the whole population in one way or another.

The approaching man wears a dark hat, peaked and with a shiny buckle at the front, in the style of a medicine man. In his hand he carries a staff, guiding his dysfunctional leg to safe ground.

The traveller waits the few moments of the man's tortuous journey on the unkind cobbles. *Of course the expected one will not appear*, he thinks, *he has sent a minion to do his bidding; his dirty work*. He is surprised, nonetheless, at the man who has been sent. He would have expected one more agile, more robust – not this paralysed old man in his curious garb. This is no show of strength, no threat, no repudiation. What is to become of the two of them? There will be no fight, neither party having the faculties for bellicosity. He now wonders how this will be resolved, despite having resigned himself to his fate from the moment of entering the city.

The old man stops a few paces from the traveller and straightens his bent spine, lifting his head to meet the gaze of the man he has come to meet. On the face of it, this is a meeting of two old men, both broken, both aged beyond the years of life expectancy, both living on borrowed time.

'John Corn?' says the old man with the staff to the traveller, in a voice so quiet in carries the risk of being blown down the river, unheard.

John Corn nods and considers extending a hand, a sign of his willingness to listen. But then he remembers himself and the burden of history that has fashioned this enmity. He remains rigid in his stance, offering nothing more than his presence.

'Thank you for coming. I was not sure whether you would make the journey,' says the old man, his voice stronger now, clearly audible. He removes his hat to reveal wispy white hair, tied at the back with a bow of red silk. With a shake of his head, the silk falls to the ground and his hair is freed of its constraints, flowing down around his ears and the nape of his coat.

John Corn studies the face of the old man, which is pock-marked, wrinkled, lined in unusual ways even for these times, when pestilence must carve its mark on each one who has reached adulthood. He estimates the man to be at least eighty, which, despite his decrepitude, is, nonetheless, an achievement in times such as these. His eyes remain bright, however, even in the morning dimness, and possess an intensity of gaze – a fixed, passionate quality, even an imploring one – so much so that John Corn feels the urge to ask him what it is he seeks, what the question is in his mind that is reflected through the dark pupils, large and expanding.

'I have asked you here today to explain – perhaps to form a truce,' continues the old man. 'You have taken against my works, and now I will lay bare what has occurred in all its macabre detail. You have been vindicated, John Corn. Your prophecies and your preachings have proved correct, and you have beaten me. I sought the ultimate medicine – the apothecary's holy grail – and my punishment is this broken body that stands before you.'

John Corn, remaining uncertain of the identity of the man before him, looks further on the face of the old man, attempting to light a spark of recognition for the battered physiognomy. Maybe the nose possesses the same slant, or the angle of his jaw is similar. *It is not him*, he thinks. *It can't be him.*

'Do you recognise me? We have met over the years, but not for some time. Perhaps a year or two has passed. And in that time I have been confined to my laboratories, devising experiments to reverse my current predicament. Latterly, I have locked myself away because of a deep sense of shame. The Almighty has punished me, and I now accept my penance.'

'Jared Eden?' asks John Corn, unbelieving.

A cool breeze blows and, for the first time this auspicious morning, a boat makes its way down the river, a brazier burning on its deck, lighting the way in the blackness of the water.

The two men are suspended in time, each one trapped in the discomfort of all that has passed between them. A disbelief binds them. The certainty that what has been disclosed is forbidden reduces the moment to silence. And out of this silence, each man hears in the recesses of his mind the distant music of angelic trumpeters, who play a tune composed at the inception of time, one which heralds the judgement of the age in which the two men exist and have shaped to effect such a conclusion.

And the sky darkens, and the clouds gather, and then, as is decreed, a great storm breaks, lightning flashing in the eastern hills, thunder resounding around the streets of the city, built in the plain at the bottom of the valley.

Jared Eden, straightening his form, becoming larger, more diabolical in his anatomy, continues to speak, his voice expanding to fill the recesses of the skies, which lash down rain. 'This is my body, which has insulted the might of the Almighty and which now bears the marks of his wrath, one which contains a broken and tortured soul, punished as it should be, tormented for an eternity. This is my elixir.'

And in that moment, now reduced to a speck containing all the moments of the dark ages of human existence, with time and space having become as one, John Corn comprehends the dilemma of his life thus far and, wanting nothing more from an existence forged in misery and destined to end in this moment, casts himself off the bridge into the black waters below.

The boat man, sitting by the brazier under his hastily erected shelter and warming his hands, hears a ghastly scream and then a splash but does not turn around. He steers his boat further downstream to a place of safety, in the deluge of rain, the worst storm in living memory.

Acknowledgements

Thanks to Karen Atkinson for editorial services and advice.

Thanks to Charles Wilkins for proofreading.

Typesetting by Book Polishers.

Cover design by Creative Covers.

Printed in Great Britain
by Amazon

24212846R00159